Nikos and Erika

Nikos and Erika

The Healing Power of True Love

Love Is All There Is

Sameer Zahr

To order additional copies of this book, contact:
Xlibris
1-888-795-4274
www.Xlibris.com
Orders@Xlibris.com
787288

I dedicate this book to my friend George Hatzis in Greece

PROLOGUE

NIKOS WAS IN bed, sleeping. Erika, who suddenly sat up in bed, feeling awkward and confused, awakened him. The room was dark except for a small night-light. Nikos looked at her lovely but pale face and asked her if there was anything wrong. There was no reply. He looked at her in silence and saw the mesmerizing profile of her adorable face, which seemed frozen by a dream. Erika had been undergoing therapy treatments the past four months, targeted to cure the damage to her liver. She had lost a lot of weight but remained strong. Nikos watched her for ten seconds, wondering if she would speak.

Then he hugged her and asked, "What is it, my love? A bad dream?"

Erika looked at him with her wide-open eyes and softly uttered, "I don't know . . . The dream was a bit weird in the beginning but then shifted to a peaceful ending. It was like two dreams in one."

"Please try to explain what you saw. What do you remember?" Nikos asked.

"At first, um . . . I saw a gigantic object jumping out of my abdomen and running away at lightning speed. Then all of a sudden, I saw two white angels with wings hovering over my head with peaceful smiles on their faces. The whole dream lasted a few seconds. Then I jumped and sat up as you saw me. Sorry to wake you."

"Hey, no problem. This is definitely an interesting pair of dreams. It is like a transformation from a state of fear to a state of love. The subconscious mind works in mysterious ways. We'll find out what it means and how it will be manifested for sure. Without any doubt, dreams are indicative of something that you repeatedly thought about or wanted. It could be something that occurred in the past or something that might still occur in the future. We'll get it interpreted one way or the other. Anyhow, we have an appointment in a few hours for your therapy in the hospital. Try to get some rest, and we'll see what happens," Nikos said.

CHAPTER 1

NIKOS BESTIDIS WAS a tall, handsome, and well-built man in his late twenties. He was a young professor of philosophy at New York University. Born in Athens, Greece, he was the son of a well-established shipping tycoon. He came to New York to study philosophy at NYU at the age of eighteen. His parents owned a nice two-bedroom apartment on Fifth Avenue overlooking Central Park. Nikos lived in that apartment during his college education and for many years that followed.

Nikos was a brilliant student, and his main interest initially was to study ancient Greek philosophy. He was naturally influenced by the culture of his country and its famous philosophers. Before Nikos moved to New York, he had studied the subject while in high school. It was generally offered to all Greek students, particularly about the three main philosophers, Socrates, Plato, and Aristotle. He wanted to dig deeper into their teachings and to understand why they continued to have great influence on modern Western philosophy.

Before Nikos left Athens, his father, Yanni, had asked him, "Son, are you sure you don't want to stay in Athens and learn our shipping business? You know you have a secure job here in our company, which you and your brother can take over one day."

"No, Father, I am only interested in studying philosophy, and I hope I can teach it one day," Nikos answered.

"Why can't you study philosophy here? This is the birthplace of the three greatest ancient Greek philosophers."

"I know. I really want to go to NYU, where I am already accepted, and I also want to have a different life experience on my own. I feel very protected here and a bit, um, spoiled, living a lavish life. I believe it is time for me move on. I am very grateful for the abundant and affluent life I've had here, but please understand my desire and trust me." Nikos beseeched his father to approve his move.

"You know you would be breaking your mother's heart, and your brother and sister will miss you as well. I will agree to let you go provided you promise to visit us at least three times a year and you try to spend your summer vacations with us as well," Yanni said, approving his son's request.

"It's a deal. I'll try my best, and thank you very much, Father."

Nikos was happy he was on a new mission to experience a different life on his own. There was one more request his father had insisted upon. His mother, Irene, was to accompany him on his trip to help him get adequately installed in the apartment, to open a bank account for his monthly allowance, and to show him how to procure his needs from nearby stores and the like. The plan was for her to spend about a week before he started his higher education.

On the flight over to JFK Airport in New York, Nikos and his mother enjoyed a one-on-one conversation, which they rarely had before. They were comfortably seated in the business-class section when Irene turned toward him and asked, "Hey, Nikos, how do you feel now that you are on your way to independence?"

"I feel OK with it, Mom. I am actually looking forward to living alone in the big city," Nikos answered assuredly.

"Aren't you going to miss the family and friends you grew up with?" Irene curiously asked her courageous son.

"No, not really. I felt that I was living in a cocoon of luxury, protection, and shallow interactions with other people. Um, I want to find out who I really am. I have no fear of the future on my own, and I am grateful for the love and financial support you and my father are giving me," Nikos answered confidently.

They paused for a few minutes while the flight attendant served them their meals and wine. Irene lifted her glass and wished him success in his new adventure. The conversation continued during the meal, and Irene asked Nikos, "How do you visualize spending your time, my dear?"

Nikos moved around in his seat, not sure how to answer, and then said, "I have no specific plan or schedule, Mother. I will be spontaneous and flexible to start with. I know I will major in philosophy, and that focus should help me slowly understand better life and the human mind. My studies will take priority over my social life."

Irene appreciated his answer and continued to seek more clarification. "But why philosophy, not business or medicine or law or engineering, for instance?"

"I don't know exactly why. Ever since the age of fourteen, I have been delving into the works of our Greek philosophers, and I became very impressed by the logic of their philosophies. What I find interesting is the contrast between, um, the wealth of their teachings and the lack of it, as we see in the current condition of our country. It is as if we learned nothing from our great ancestors," Nikos said with some frustration in his expression.

"So you think you can eventually help and get our country out of its misery?" Irene said facetiously.

"No, Mother, I have no such ideas. You must be joking. I have no interest in politics. I am curious to find out why the great Greek minds that introduced democracy to the Western world did not work well in our country nowadays. It prospered and worked very well in the United States and Western Europe. I find this to be quite condescending to our Greek heritage," Nikos said passionately.

There was a long pause after this last statement by Nikos. Then the two of them decided to rest and close their eyes before landing.

The plane landed on time at JFK Airport, and a car was booked to take them to their apartment on Fifth Avenue and East Sixty-Second Street. The doorman helped them out with the luggage to their apartment on the twenty-fifth floor.

Irene spent eight days in New York setting up her son comfortably. During her stay, she accompanied him to buy some winter clothes. His size had changed; he was now six feet tall, slim, and athletic looking. His dark-brown hair crowned his tanned, harmonious, yet masculine face, highlighting his piercing brown eyes, small, sharp nose, and full lips. He completed his registration at the university, and that experience of being with so many different young people excited him.

His mother warned him to watch out for beautiful girls who would be chasing him. Irene herself bought some designer clothes and shoes from the well-known boutiques on Madison Avenue. She looked quite elegant with her well-kept shape, though she was in her late forties. She also had brown eyes and brown hair, crowning a naturally beautiful face. She walked tall and gracefully with a display of pride, showing off her height of five feet and seven inches. Nikos enjoyed and appreciated his mother's presence with him and wished her a pleasant flight back to Athens.

The young man had the spacious apartment all to himself. He spent quite some time looking out at Central Park from the large windows of the living room. His thoughts and daydreams took him far into the future, and he cherished the opportunity to experiment with his life on his own. He also enjoyed browsing through the vast collection of books on Greek mythology that his father had placed on the shelves of the big room.

The first month alone, Nikos was still feeling his way around the city and the university campus. He was shy, and he abstained from seeking friends from either gender. He discovered that being alone without family and friends was not such a bad idea. He managed well to amuse himself, listening to music, reading, and occasionally watching news on the television. He went jogging in Central Park four or five times a week to stay in good shape.

He was seen a few times by his classmates eating his lunch alone in the cafeteria with a book in his hand. A couple of them tried to approach him to talk, only to see him smile back without replying or any reciprocal gesture on his part. He was quickly judged as a loner, and they respectfully left him alone.

Nikos noticed the questionable attitude manifested by some of his classmates, and he wondered if there was anything he could do change it. He was keen to continue with his inner search, and his priority was to learn more about who he was. His teachers noticed his uninterrupted class attendance and his attention to his homework. He excelled in his exams and was eager to take as many elective courses in philosophy and psychology as possible. He also enjoyed living in the big city without being bothered or harassed by others. He even appreciated the short subway ride from home to his college.

As he had promised his father earlier, Nikos went to be with his family for the Christmas and New Year's holidays. He quickly found out the difference in his daily life, and he preferred his New York choice better. He was bored during his eight-day visit to Athens. He was annoyed by the shallow questions thrown at him by his extended family members. He had no interest in going out or seeing his old friends again. His parents wondered if he was OK, and he reassured them that he was, only eager to go back to school. He could not wait to catch his flight back, and as he had promised his father, he would return for the Easter holidays.

*   *   *

During the second semester, Nikos, who had just turned nineteen, found himself in a class seated next to a beautiful girl about his age. Despite his previous routine not to socialize with any of his classmates, he became curious to get to know this particular young lady.

She noticed he was shy, so she took the initiative once after class and asked him, "Hey, we have been in this class for ten days now, and we don't even greet each other. This is not good. My name is Erika Sverenson, and I am from Sweden."

She offered him her hand, and after shaking hands, he quietly said, "Um, I am sorry . . . My name is Nikos, and I am from Greece."

"Oh, I see. What brings you here? I love Greece. It has amazing, beautiful islands."

"Well, I decided to study philosophy at NYU, so here I am."

"That is interesting! You forgot that Greece is ahead of all countries when it comes to the greatest philosophers in history."

"No, not at all. I don't deny that. I just wanted to have a new experience away from home," Nikos said reluctantly.

"What kind of experience, if you don't mind me asking?"

Nikos looked at her more closely and took a few seconds before he responded. He found Erika to be very beautiful and quite inquisitive. He felt comfortable being with her and said, "I grew up in a privileged home, somewhat spoiled by my father, who is big in the shipping business, and my mother, who believes that I am still a child. I wanted to experiment with a different life on my own and, um, discontinue being part of a protected environment. That is why I am here," Nikos replied, hoping she would stop being so curious.

Erika looked at him and smiled and said, "I am here because my father is the ambassador of Sweden to the United Nations. I love New York, and I love my parents. I enjoy very much living with them. I am their only child, and we have a lot of fun together."

"That sounds great, and I am happy for you. By the way, you have a beautiful name, Erika," Nikos said.

"Yes, in Swedish, it means 'ruling forever,' so watch out! Any meaning to your name, Nikos?"

"In Greek, it means 'people's victory,' derived from Saint Nicholas, the protector of children."

Erika liked Nikos and asked him if he was free to have coffee with her in the cafeteria. He said yes as his next class was in fifty minutes. They walked out from the classroom together, and Nikos thought she must be around five feet and nine inches and had an amazing body. She was a typical Swedish blonde with spotless white skin and enticing green eyes crowned by her arched eyebrows and sweeping eyelashes. Her sunrise-gold hair flowed over her shoulders. Her dainty nose and honey-sweet lips revealed her angel-white teeth. With her sculpted body and height, she could easily be a model if she chose to. He had not seen such beauty before and felt lucky he was a couple of inches taller than her.

Nikos controlled himself to remain cool and not show his excitement from being with Erika. She, on the other hand, had a happy-go-lucky flair and seemed to be quite outgoing. They sat down at a quiet table with their coffee mugs and smiled at each other for a while. Erika then bluntly asked Nikos if he had a girlfriend.

Nikos twisted uncomfortably in his chair and said, "No . . ."

Erika responded, "Uh-huh. How can a handsome young man like you not have a girlfriend?"

"Um, I've been focusing on my studies."

"Come on now, give me a break. Are you being truthful with me?"

"I have no reason to be otherwise," Nikos answered.

"How come you don't ask me if I have a boyfriend?" Erika asked facetiously.

"It's not my style to poke into other people's personal lives."

"Aren't you being sweet? Go ahead, ask me."

"Well, do you?"

"No, not at the moment."

"I see. What happened?" Nikos asked.

"So now you want to know! That's good, you are interested all of a sudden." Erika giggled while saying that.

"You asked me first, and I told you the truth. I had none in Athens, and I have none in New York. You don't have to tell me anything. We just met and are trying to get to know each other. That's all," Nikos responded emphatically while Erika started laughing loudly. He then asked her, "What's wrong? Did I say anything that offended you? Or am I, um, simply funny?" Nikos was curious to know.

"I like you, Nikos Bes . . . what?"

"Bestidis."

"Yeah, Bestidis! Meaning 'the best there is,' correct?" she asked.

Nikos started laughing when he heard that and said, "You . . . you're very funny indeed."

"Wow! At least I made you laugh."

They kept talking for the next thirty minutes, telling each other stories about their past lives and their future hopes. They laughed, and Nikos felt more relaxed around her. Unlike a few short relationships he had had before in Greece, this one seemed quite different, and he hoped it could develop into some real friendship. They checked each other's class schedules and found that they were taking two out of five courses together. They parted as friends and promised to have another coffee together soon.

* * *

When Nikos went back home, he sat down at his desk in the living room and decided to start a journal.

I had an interesting experience today. After practically four months of private solitude, I finally broke my silence and got to know a very interesting student from Sweden. She was not only very beautiful and sexy looking but also smart and funny. What should I make of such an encounter? Will a potential friendship with Erika deter me from my focus on myself and my studies, or is it part of getting to know myself better through the eyes of another?

I don't know how this relationship will evolve. All I know is to remain true to myself and not allow anyone to steer me away me from my path toward self-realization and inner joy. I will tread these new waters slowly and hope for the best.

Nikos had a hard time sleeping that night. He could not take Erika's image out of his mind. He also knew he would not be seeing her again for two more days. They did not exchange phone numbers or email addresses. He did not even remember her family name until he had checked out the name of her father online, the ambassador Sven Sverenson.

They smiled when they saw each other in class again. Erika looked dazzling, wearing tight jeans and a light-green cashmere sweater. Nikos appeared timid next to her and wondered if she was trying to impress the rest of the men in the class, or was it all to please him? It was best not to guess. She was who she was, and no one could change that.

As expected, they talked together after class and were under the radar of many other jealous young men who wished to be in Nikos's place. They proceeded to have coffee together. Her tight jeans showed her firm buttocks, which impressed many viewers walking behind her.

"So how were your last forty-eight hours? Did you survive without me?" Erika put on her funny hat from the start.

"Are you always forthright like that?" Nikos said after getting a small electric shock from her words.

"Why not? I might as well tell you that you were in my mind. Should I, um, deny myself that feeling?" Erika said defensively.

"Wow, I am flattered. I don't know what to say."

"Just say the truth, Nikos. Express how you felt the past two days and how you feel now," Erika said philosophically.

"Um, I don't know how to respond to that unless you are pulling my leg. The truth is, um, yes, I did think about you," Nikos replied.

"In what sense, my friend? Did you miss me, or you just dreamed about me?" Erika asked jokingly.

"I don't know if I should laugh or cry. We just met, and now you are talking to me as if we are old lovers." Nikos wanted a clarification.

"Come on, Nikos, can't you tell we are lovers already? The writing is on the wall, cutie! Don't deny yourself the pleasure of loving me!"

Erika said that without intending to shock Nikos, but the poor guy was shocked regardless. For her, it was a given that all men should immediately love her. He remained silent for more than a minute with his thoughts racing all around before he heard her laughing, which unsettled him even further.

He said, "Erika, I . . . I can't tell if you're serious or not. I am not used to such outright statements. I hope you are not playing with my nerves. I am a very sensitive person, and I don't take such words lightly. Please clarify your position."

"What position? That we are already lovers? That does not need any clarification. You and I know we are. It is our destiny, you silly man," Erika said with a serious look on her face.

Nikos thought for a few seconds and then asked her, "Don't you think it is a bit presumptuous to assume that any man you meet should, uh . . . immediately fall in love with you? I find this to be a conceited assumption on your part. You are very beautiful and sexy, but is that the only criteria to love someone? I personally want to also love the inner beauty of a girl. I hardly know you. Can you take it a bit easy on me?" Nikos felt relieved to have expressed himself truthfully in this regard, and he was not concerned about her reaction to his words.

Erika laughed and said, "Bravo, Nikos, the truth finally comes out, I love that! I was pulling your leg to check you out. I admire your cautious stance and self-esteem. I like your sensitive demeanor also."

Nikos was not sure if Erika was truthful in what she said or if she merely was trying to appease him and cool him down. She sensed his struggle and wanted to change the subject.

She asked him, "Why don't we go out together, um, for dinner this weekend?"

"Now that's a good idea. Let's do that. I'll give you my mobile number, and we can text each other about the time and place. Is that OK with you?" Nikos said with a smile gracing his face.

"It sounds great. Where do you live, by the way? You want a restaurant near you?"

"I live on Fifth Avenue in the low sixties. It is my parents' apartment, and they let me use it," Nikos said.

"You must be kidding me! We are neighbors! My father was given a town house in the low seventies, also on Fifth Avenue. What a coincidence," Erika said with a surprised look on her face.

"Wow, that's great! We can eat at a nearby Italian restaurant on Madison. How about tomorrow, Friday night?" Nikos asked.

"Fantastic! Give me your address on Fifth, and I will stop by to see you before we go to the restaurant. How about that?" Erika asked.

"No problem. Here is my exact address. So you will pick me up then, a role reversal, say, around six thirty, and we can have a glass of wine at my place and then go out around seven. OK?"

*   *   *

The concierge in the building called Nikos at six thirty and told him that Ms. Erika was there to see him. Nikos told him to let her come up. Nikos was waiting for the elevator to arrive. And when Erika came out, Nikos said, "Wow," upon seeing her.

She walked toward him dressed in a miniskirt and high heels. Luckily, she was wearing a nice winter coat on top, though she had left it unbuttoned. He had expected her to look more conservative. He greeted her with a peck on the cheek without saying another word. They walked into the living room, and she took her coat off. She noticed that he was nervous. She complimented him on the beauty of the apartment, hoping to break his silence. He did not respond.

Then she said, "You seem to be quite shocked, seeing me look like this. Does it bother you?"

"Um, a bit, yeah."

"You'll get used to it after a while," she said while she circled around for him to see her all around without her coat.

"What can I say? You look amazing, and I'm not so sure I can handle it."

"Why not, you silly man? Just enjoy it!" she said in a giggly manner.

"Well, I guess I am not as liberated as you are, and what is it with those high heels? You are taller than me now."

"Yup, that's the look, my man!"

"OK, how about a glass of wine?"

"You don't have anything stronger?" Erika asked.

"I am sorry. I don't. I am not a drinker anyhow," Nikos said defensively.

He proceeded to open a good bottle of wine from the stock available in the apartment and looked at her from the corner of his eye, noticing her long legs as she sat on the sofa in a seductive position. He had never experienced such a situation before and realized how naive he must have been. He walked back with two glasses of wine in his hands and offered her one. Then he sat next to her on the sofa. They cheered and clinked their glasses before taking a sip.

Erika sensed that Nikos was not comfortable, and to make him feel more relaxed, she asked him, "Why do you like philosophy so much?"

Nikos was relieved to hear that as he did not want to focus only on her astounding looks. He confidently said, "Ah, you know I am Greek. And I am sure you know about the famous Greek philosophers that, um, existed more than four hundred years before

Christ, starting with Socrates. I studied his teachings, which were written by Plato and other students, and I loved it all."

"You're so lucky! Because I am new to all this, you can be my private tutor on this subject, right?"

"Well, don't get so excited. I am not sure I can be a good teacher like them," Nikos responded.

"Oh, come on, Nikos! You know you can. Tell me in a few words what the most essential teaching of Socrates is," she said.

Nikos quickly responded, "It was his unique method, which emphasized the fact that humans learn through the use of reasoning and logic—that is, through debate—until a solution is found for any problem discussed."

"Wow, you're good, my friend! Tell me more."

"Um, perhaps later. Can we go to eat now? I'm getting hungry, and the restaurant is a couple of blocks away."

They finished their drinks and walked to the Italian restaurant nearby. Nikos was elegantly dressed and had a nice cashmere coat to keep him warm. He looked very handsome.

They sat at a quiet table and placed their orders. Erika asked Nikos to continue his deliberation on Greek philosophy. Nikos found her request intriguing as he thought she was more interested in fun and light conversation. He first explained the meaning of the word and said, "The origin of the word in Greek, *philia*, means 'to love,' and *sophia*, 'wisdom,' so there you have it. To love wisdom."

"Wow, I understand why at that time, it was like a religion to them," Erika said to impress Nikos.

"Yes, you're right. Greeks worshipped many gods for centuries before Christ. Philosophers were highly respected. Anyhow, you will be studying this in college. Tell me more about you."

"What do you want to know?" Erika asked.

"Well, where did you grow up, and what do you like to do in your life?"

"I grew up in Stockholm. I was not a very good student. My father moved around as a diplomat since I was twelve. I am nineteen now and have been in New York for about six months now. I don't know what I want to do in life yet. I am still a freshman in college, as you know. I like to have fun and have someone in my life, to be in love all the time," Erika answered with a cute smile gracing her.

"Interesting. Do you believe we should all have someone to love all the time in our daily lives?" Nikos wondered.

"Absolutely! Love is my religion," Erika replied emphatically.

"Opa!"

"What does that mean?"

"Well, it is just an expression of surprise or admiration."

"Then what does love mean to you, Master Nikos?"

"Hmm, I like my new title. There are eight different types of love, by the way, so which one is it that you worship?"

"Can you name them to me please?" Erika wanted to be amused.

"OK, here we go, and listen carefully. *Eros* or erotic love. The first kind of love is eros, which is named after the Greek god of love and fertility. *Philia* or affectionate love. *Storge* or familial love. *Ludus* or playful love. *Mania* or obsessive love. *Pragma* or enduring love. *Philautia* or self-love. And *agape* or selfless love. So pick and choose your favorite."

"Wow, and you know them all by heart. You must be a love expert then." Erika was surprised and impressed at the same time.

Nikos wrote them down on a piece of paper to give her and said, "Go ahead pick one."

Erika looked at the paper and smiled. She took a minute to think and then said, "My goodness, if I were to choose only one, I would choose *eros*."

"I thought so. That's honest and reflects your true self," Nikos commented.

"How about you?" she asked him joyfully.

"*Agape* is my favorite. It is the most spiritual type of love. You give love and expect nothing in return. That's why it's called selfless love," Nikos added.

"Gee . . . we're so different. Can you be more than one type?"

"Of course, but there is always a favorite, which represents one's real choice," Nikos answered.

"So I am selfish, and you are not," Erika said in a complaining tone.

"No, no, you don't look at it that way. You are more into the physical aspect of love. You enjoy touching and being touched. It is tangible, and you can feel it and see it. There is nothing wrong with that as long as it does not develop into a *mania* type of love, which is obsessive and then becomes negative." Nikos enjoyed philosophizing.

"Mamma Mia! Can I be your student and just learn from you without going to college? I am ready to move in with you and sit by your feet," Erika said and laughed her heart out. Nikos joined her laughter when he heard that too.

"I am going to keep that paper and think about love some more. I am having so much fun with you, Professor!"

They both went silent for a while, just looking at each other with soft smiles. Before dessert was served, Erika moved her hand closer to his and held it softly. Nikos did not know how to react but kept his hand attached to hers.

Then the silence was broken when Erika said, "I like you, Nikos."

Nikos blushed and couldn't muster enough strength to respond in kind. He simply replied, "That's very sweet of you, Erika."

"Sweet . . . Is that all you can say? Dessert is sweet. Do you like me?"

"Erika, don't get so excited. We just met, and *of course*, I like you. Why else are we here?"

"That's better. You know I belong to the *eros* kind of love, so you need to get used to that if you want us to be friends in the future," Erika said bluntly.

Nikos remained silent while the dessert was being served. Then he said, "Erika, I am new to this. I appreciate how you manifest your feelings in such a warm way. I . . . I am shy and timid still. My friends in school may think I am gay and enjoy hiding in the closet. They're totally wrong. I know I am straight, and I just prefer to spend my time, um, thinking and reading rather than going out with girls. Perhaps you had a different experience, which is fine. It takes me more time to adapt to a new situation. I hope you understand."

"I understand . . . as long as you don't remain rigid. I love to hug and kiss the men I like," Erika said without any hesitation.

Nikos was mesmerized by her forthright admission of the *eros* type of love that she lived by. His distant thoughts were interrupted when he heard say, "I thought maybe we could go dancing tonight, but I don't think you are ready to do that kind of stuff yet . . . Am I right?"

"You're right. I am sorry. It is too much too soon for me. Let me digest the pleasure of being with you this evening, and maybe I will be more willing soon," Nikos said sincerely.

Erika did not say a word and had a sober look on her face.

They kept an amicable tone, and Nikos walked her home after their dessert. It was a pretty silent walk, and Nikos did not even hold her hand. She must have thought that he was gay as she had never experienced such cold behavior from all the other men she went out with. She lived in a nice town house on Seventy-First Street, off Fifth Avenue. He gave her a peck on one cheek and thanked her for a nice evening.

Then Erika told him, "Please call me tomorrow."

CHAPTER 2

NIKOS WALKED BACK home that night, reflecting on his first outing in New York since he had arrived five months ago. He thought about Erika, whose character he found rather intriguing. She was very beautiful, outgoing, and liberated, which was so different from his character.

He struggled with the fact that they were somewhat at odds as it pertained to establishing a new relationship. Nikos preferred to take his time and evaluate his vibrations before taking any action, whereas Erika preferred to jump right into a new relationship and openly express her physical desire if she liked the man she was with. It could be a cultural difference between them, he thought. He was from a conservative upbringing, and she was from a more open and liberal one.

Before Nikos went to sleep, he stayed out in the living room, looking out at the nighttime lights of the city and the park. His thoughts expanded quietly into the dark horizon and beyond. He faced his fears and tried to address them to ensure the integrity of his intentions. He sat at his desk and pulled out his journal and wrote.

> *I was in the company of a great-looking and sexy woman tonight who would not have minded to sleep with me. Why did I chicken out and not take advantage of such an opportunity? Many other men my age would have jumped at such*

an occasion. So what am I afraid of? Falling in love or a long-term commitment or a distraction from my academic goals? What if Erika is only interested in mere physical pleasure and cares less about the complicated ideas that I imagine? Am I too premature to take on such opportunities more easily? Perhaps I can learn from her to relax for a change. Maybe she's the one who can help loosen me up a bit to overcome my naivete.

Nikos went to bed pondering these thoughts and asked himself if he should try to see her again during the weekend.

*　　*　　*

He woke up on Saturday morning, itching to give Erika a call. He thought that it would not be fair for him to shove aside a potential relationship that could alter his old and conservative outlook on his life. He convinced himself to act like a man without past fears and take the bull by the horns. Around midmorning, he felt courageous and dialed Erika's cell phone. She answered, and he greeted her.

"Hi, it's me. I hope you had a restful sleep. Do you know how to ice-skate?"

Erika responded to his weird question with a good laugh and said, "Good morning to you too. Did you have fancy dreams about us all night? To answer your question, of course, I ice-skate. I was one of the best hockey players in high school. Why do you ask?"

"Will you, um, teach me?" Nikos asked in a timid tone.

"Wow, that's easy, big guy!"

"OK, thanks. I keep looking at the skating rink outside my window, and it inspired me to check if we can ice-skate together. I think it can be a lot of fun, so how about we meet there around eleven and give it a try?" Nikos felt good asking her.

Erika paused for two seconds and said, "Fine, let's do it. I'm sure we can rent skates there. See ya!"

Nikos was happy she had accepted to see him and maybe teach him a new sport. He put on his jeans, a warm sweater, and a scarf and was eagerly waiting for her to arrive.

Erika arrived five minutes late, and they were both smiling when they greeted each other. They rented the skates and proceeded to the rink. Nikos felt nervous and had to hold her hand before he could take his first step. Erika assured him it was easy and told him to relax. He asked her to go first and show him how. The rink was crowded with skaters of all ages as it was a beautiful and warm, sunny day in the park.

Nikos could not believe his eyes when he saw her whisk her way through, turning right, left, and backward as if she were taking an easy stroll on the street. Many other skaters slowed down to watch her graceful moves, and she was applauded when she came back and stopped next to Nikos. He was dumbfounded, his mouth open, looking at her in wonder.

When he relaxed his lower jaw after a few seconds, he said, "Wow, I am so impressed. Will you teach me? I can give you free philosophy lessons in return."

Erika smiled, took his hand, and said, "Come with me, and we'll go slow. Just feel your moves and don't look down. Keep your head up and enjoy."

Nikos skated on, staying close to the railing. Then he developed enough courage to move away, closer to the middle. He fell a few times and laughed and then stood up to do better after each fall. They laughed, and Nikos enjoyed a few hugs from Erika whenever he felt he was about to fall.

After thirty minutes, Nikos was able to skate for a few feet unsupported, and that encouraged him to go for more. They stopped before noon and sat at the bench to rest and take their skates off. Nikos smiled and looked at Erika.

"I've never had so much fun. Thank you." And he kissed her on her cheek.

"I'm happy you enjoyed it, and this is something we can do together anytime you feel like it."

"Goodness, you're so good, and no wonder you are in such good shape," Nikos cheerfully told her.

"It's been a while since I skated, but it's like walking. You don't lose it."

"Thanks again. May I buy you lunch at Cipriani? They make great pasta," Nikos asked.

"Great, let's go. I've never been there. I hear it's good."

"It's like my own kitchen, one block away from me, and I eat there a lot."

Seven minutes later, they walked in, and the restaurant manager greeted Nikos and offered him the same table he always sat at by the window.

Erika was impressed and asked him, "Do you come here alone?"

"Um, yes."

"What a pity . . . You enjoy being alone?" Erika asked him bluntly.

"I don't know yet. I am trying to find out."

"What are you, a monk? Why not live in the Himalayas? You can meditate all day and eat noodles once a week and never talk to anyone. Besides, you can find out more easily about yourself as a loner. How about that?" Erika said facetiously.

"Erika, please, take it easy on me."

"Tell me, Nikos, did you have a girlfriend in Greece, and do you miss her now?" Erika asked, curious.

"No, I didn't. I just had several acquaintances, both boys and girls, but never a relationship with any. My parents found this to be strange and hoped it would be different for me here in New York," Nikos replied.

"Herregud!"

"What did you say?"

"I said, 'oh my god' in Swedish. You mean to tell me you've never had a love affair with or a crush on another girl before? How old are you, eleven?"

"Um, Erika, please don't insult me. The truth is that I . . . I did have a crush on one a year ago, but it never developed into a relationship. I don't know why, and I'm not gay. She was beautiful and sexy and, um, even willing to sleep with me, but I chickened out."

Erika could not believe her ears and sarcastically said, "Wow, she and I can be good friends, and we belong to the same club. I don't know if I should pity her or me. No, perhaps we should both pity you, jerk!"

"OK, OK, now why don't you tell me about you, dear goddess of love?" Nikos was getting agitated and responded sarcastically.

"For your information, dear Greek philosopher, I have had several love affairs since I was fourteen. None of them lasted more than a few months. I even had an affair here with an American guy last semester before I met you. I have no fear of loving men I like, and I have no qualms or demands about the longevity of each affair. One day, one week, one month? I always move on without any hard feelings. I actually walk away from situations that become heavy and demanding. I am too young to have long-term commitments. I just want to have fun. Call me a slut if you like. I don't care. I am proud of who I am, and I know what I want. It is that simple, OK?"

Erika was adamant about her status in this regard and was oblivious as to whether Nikos would understand her. She believed in the power of truth and did not intend to hurt his feelings, only to shake him up a bit because she liked him. She liked his slim but strong body, brown hair, and handsome face with his sharp nose and piercing brown eyes. He had the perfect height, and she loved his two dimples when he smiled.

Nikos was astounded by her straight talk and self-confidence. He wished he could be as sure about himself as she was. He did not comment right away and used the time to have a few bites from his plate while thinking about what to say next. Erika kept looking at him and wondered what was going on in his confused mind.

She ate a few bites herself, and then she heard him calmly say, "I admire your strength and perseverance to abide by the knowledge of who you truly are."

"Nikos, isn't the essence of all the philosophers' teachings to abide by the truth? I know who I am, and perhaps it's time you know who you are."

Nikos heard her loud and clear and suggested they have coffee together in his apartment and listen to some music. Erika nodded.

A few minutes later, they were in his apartment. He asked her if she liked Greek music, and she said she was only familiar with Vangelis. He happened to have one of his CDs, and he put it on. He said he had an espresso machine, and she agreed to that too. He left her alone in the living room while he went to the kitchen. He was deeply excited about having her in his place and wanted her so badly. When he returned with the coffee, he found her standing by the window.

She turned back and said, "You have such a beautiful view from here!"

"Yup. I spend a lot of time where you're standing to think and daydream," Nikos happily responded.

"It's good to know you are a dreamer too. There is hope for you."

"Can you stop being sarcastic, please? What do you want from me?" Nikos demanded with a louder voice.

"I want to kiss you and hug you and make love to you. Are you blind, deaf, or what? Can't you tell that I like you and want you? Or should I wait and ask for an appointment first?"

Nikos was taken aback, and after a short pause, he felt a sudden rush and put the coffee cups on the coffee table. He walked straight toward her and started kissing and hugging her. He threw away all his fears and hidden reservations and followed his natural instinct of physical desire.

Erika was pleasantly surprised, and she immersed herself happily in his moves, which aroused her. She felt his strong muscular body and closed her eyes to devour the taste of his mouth and the overall pleasure she'd been waiting for.

They were both fired with passion, and within seconds, they undressed each other and felt the electricity of their naked bodies wired together. They could not control the rush of blood in their togetherness, and they made out for several minutes, enjoying the excitement of their intertwined bodies. Nikos did not have any protection and had to interrupt the making-out moves. Erika was so aroused and did not want him to stop. She whispered in his ear to continue as she had her protection on. They made love on the sofa, and Nikos ended up having a wild orgasm that he would remember for the rest of his life. It was his first lovemaking session ever. He fell in love.

It took them a few more minutes to wind down while they kept their naked bodies warmly connected. They later turned and looked at each other with big smiles on their faces.

Nikos could not help but tell her, "You are something else. I don't know which planet you come from, but . . . but this has been a magical first experience for me. Thank you."

"Please don't thank me. Thank yourself for finally seeing the light and discovering the joy of the moment with someone you care to be with," Erika said affectionately.

Nikos walked Erika to the main bathroom and asked her if she would like to have a bath in the large tub.

She nodded and said, "Only if you join me."

Again, this was a first for Nikos, and he thought, *Why not?* Nikos filled the tub with hot water and added the salts and bubble soap that his mother had left behind. They both stepped in. They admired each other's bodies and had a great time talking and laughing together while splashing water all over the floor.

Fifteen minutes later, Nikos stood up and put his robe on. He gave Erika one of his mother's bathrobes and went to the kitchen to make two fresh cups of coffee. While in the kitchen, Nikos was experiencing new warm vibrations that crept into his system and that he had never felt before, and he was very satisfied. He could not take the image of Erika's stunning body out of his mind. Her expertise in the act of lovemaking confirmed his earlier hunch that she was a "goddess of love."

He walked back into the master bedroom and found her lying down naked on top of the bed cover, and the robe that he gave her was thrown on the floor. The sight of her incredible body aroused him again. He begged her to have coffee first. She sat up and finished her coffee in three sips, encouraging him to do the same. Then they went at it again and had a second round of ecstasy.

They later woke up after taking a nap for about one hour. They showered and got dressed, wondering what to do next.

Nikos said, "If you're still up to spending more time with me, how about we go see a movie at six near the Plaza Hotel?"

"Fine with me. We can then order a pizza when we come back," Erika said.

"Deal! Let's do it."

"So tell me first. How do you feel now?" Erika asked curiously.

"Truly, there are no words that can describe how I feel now. What can I say? Amazed, shocked, loved, smitten, relieved, pleased, numb, I can go on and on to no end. You win," Nikos said, with short pauses between every word.

"You see! I hate to say, 'I told you so.' That's good! No more taboos."

"How about you, Erika? How does it feel to make love to an inexperienced debutant?"

"You're a virgin, and it felt heavenly!"

They enjoyed the rest of the weekend together and parted ways early Sunday afternoon. Nikos called his parents and told them how happy he was, living in New York. He spent the rest of his afternoon studying and reading more articles about Greek mythology.

Before going to bed, Nikos took his journal out to write his thoughts about the events of his weekend.

> *A drastic detour in the path of my normal daily life has occurred this weekend. It felt like a big storm had come and gone in the splash of a second. I turned into a practitioner of eros from being a creature of agape. I allowed the power of another type of love to rule over me. Erika was a great persuader, with her perseverant force, beauty, and passionate love. The storm tested my will and stopped the naivete of my previously structured and dull life. The wind this time came from the cold north, but instead, it was hot and exciting, contrary to what one would normally expect from that region.*
>
> *I felt like a new car had been broken in. It took me to a different road with flowers on both sides. A road decorated with warm feelings and exotic*

vibrations. This new introduction to this type of love swept away all the past fears and taboos that had crippled my early youth with warped perceptions. I was released from my previous imprisonment and the barriers of a stifling culture. I was flown over a warm and loving field of open-mindedness. I appreciate more who I am now, and I like myself more fully. I think I am in love already. Thank you, Erika, for teaching me how to be true to myself and enjoy the precious moment of love.

*　　*　　*

Nikos went to his classes on Monday. He looked forward to seeing Erika again in the afternoon class that they took together. He felt rejuvenated with new energy and desire to excel in both his studies and his new love life. They were happy to see each other again when they met.

The subject was Plato, a student of Socrates. Erika tried to focus on the explanation by the professor and was confused. She did not fully understand Plato's theory of forms, which was the tool the philosopher intended to use to solve ethical and worldly problems. She learned that Plato founded the Academy in Athens, the first higher-learning institution in the Western world. After the class, Erika asked Nikos to explain in simple words what the theory of forms was all about.

Nikos said, "Simply put, Plato split the world into two—the material realm and the mental realm. The first is subject to change, but the second is permanent. In other words, our perceived senses in the physical forms are subject to change, whereas our mental forms perceived through our mind remain unchanged."

"Aha! I understand it better now. Why can't you be my professor? It's less complicated and more fun."

"OK, I will read to you ancient Greek stories at bedtime to help you go to sleep," Nikos said jokingly.

"Why? Are they so boring, they would put me to sleep? I, uh, don't like that. I want to fall asleep in your arms sometimes. No philosophy in bed, please!" Erika said seriously.

"Now what would you like to do this evening?" Nikos asked, eager to know if she has free.

"I would like to go horsey-horsey on your back. Will you let me ride on your back when you're hopping on your four legs?" she asked.

"Of course, I will, my dear. Make sure you bring a saddle with you as I only have a whip," Nikos answered with a pretentious laugh.

"How romantic!"

"Now seriously, what would like to do?" Nikos asked again.

Erika put on her poker face, paused for a few seconds, and then said, "Honestly, I can't see you tonight. I . . . I have another engagement."

"Oops, with whom? Not with me but another? Um, perhaps I shouldn't ask," Nikos said, not knowing if she was serious or joking.

"Another. Why? Did you miss me already?" Erika responded with a smile.

"Uh-huh. Don't tease me, please. I take matters seriously, and I don't want to be taken for granted."

"What do you mean, Nikos?"

"For me, what we did this past weekend was very special and meaningful. It was *not* just passing time or having fun. It meant much more than that to me. You may look at it differently, and it is your prerogative to see it the way you want."

Nikos looked sad and disappointed because he now thought that Erika liked him for physical pleasure only. He thought she seemingly had no problem with changing partners as she saw fit.

Erika sensed that he was taking things too seriously, and from her experience, she was alerted that he could be falling in love with her. She was not ready for a new exclusive relationship with him. For her, falling in love was a big burden, and not all men understood that.

She interrupted his thoughts and said, "What is it, Nikos? Is it so hard for you to understand me?"

"I don't know. This is all new to me, and I may need some time to digest it all. You may like different flavors of ice cream in your parlor of *eros*. Perhaps I am cut from a different cloth, or someone who enjoys the same flavor all the time," Nikos said confidently.

Erika hesitated before she spoke. "I understand. Um . . . you may be right. Let's give it some time and see what happens."

"OK then. We all make conscious decisions in life. I know I like my one ice cream flavor, and I'm not eager to try another. It is your prerogative to choose your own, and I wish you the best of luck," Nikos responded with a cold smile.

"I hate to see us part ways like this. Neither one of us is judged right or wrong here. Let's try to keep in touch. I like your company and your love!"

"OK then. Have a nice evening, Erika. I have to go now."

Nikos left the scene, somewhat shaken, and he struggled to keep his head high and uphold his dignity. He walked nervously outside the campus toward the subway station and went directly home. He felt confused during the short subway ride. He could not think straight and kept looking at other people in the car, wondering what the heck was going on. He thought he had a loyal friend who loved him for who he was. And he felt quite disappointed it was not true. He was amazed to find out how some relationships could be so short-lived.

Was I not good enough for her? He doubted himself.

At home, he had some leftovers for dinner and had no interest even to do his homework. He decided it was best if he could jot down his feelings, so he opened his journal and wrote.

> *I ought to tear up the part I wrote yesterday and reconsider my thoughts regarding my relationship with Erika. She comes from a different world indeed. I am responsible for not understanding her clearly when she spoke about her desire to have sex with any man she liked. I thought that she might have said that to tease me or to lure me to commit myself to her. I allowed my ego to convince me that I was not the kind of man whom a woman could turn her back on so quickly. Apparently, I was wrong.*
>
> *I learned my lesson, and it is consoling to some degree that the relationship was in its early stage. Thus, my wound can be healed faster. I should be cool about this now and realize that some people have different behaviors and different criteria for*

their emotional and physical needs. I don't regret
having learned that not all people have the same
expectations from life. I will get over the hurt, and
I will continue to move on and abide by my own
beliefs.

Nikos felt much better after writing in his journal. He decided to focus on his homework while listening to some light classical music. He managed to sleep well despite some tossing and turning caused by the creepy stuff in his subconscious mind.

*   *   *

Several weeks went by, and the only exchange Nikos and Erika had was hi and bye in school. Nikos found another seat far from hers in the classroom. He planned to go to Athens for one week to celebrate Easter vacation with his family and some friends from high school. Erika stopped him after class one day and asked him how he was doing.

He looked at her for a second before he said, "I am fine. Thanks for asking. How about you?"

"I miss you, and, um, I am sorry if I offended you."

"No, it's all right. I am still grateful for the short time we had together and the lessons learned from that experience," Nikos said calmly.

"Any chance we can meet again and talk things over? I can't get you out of my mind and can't forgive myself for hurting your feelings," Erika asked.

"I don't know. I am quite busy and preparing to go to Athens for my Easter holidays," Nikos said nervously.

"Oh, I see. I wish you would take me with you. I would love to meet your family," Erika rushed to say, leaving Nikos somewhat shocked by her request.

He took a minute to think, looked away, and then looked back at her, straight in the eye, and said, "Do . . . do you not know when to stop? You may not have any respect for my feelings, but don't you normally think before you speak? You want to meet my family all of a sudden? What do I introduce you as? My girlfriend? Or no, wait, the one who slept with me one weekend and then dumped me?"

"Gee! You're still upset with me, aren't you? I see. Fine, forget about it. Can we at least have some coffee now before you run away?" Erika begged.

"OK, and for your info, I am not the kind who runs away. Ask yourself," Nikos said reluctantly.

They proceeded to have coffee in the cafeteria, but Nikos was still feeling tense being with her again.

She was quite carefree and said, "Look, we can still be friends, no? I know you may not love me anymore, but I . . . I still have feelings for you."

"Huh. It's easy for you to say. I don't know if I can really trust you again. A friend's trust has to be earned first. You dumped me cold handed, and that still did not . . . I mean, did not sit well with me," Nikos told her fearlessly.

"I did not intend to dump you or hurt you. I thought you were mature and strong enough to understand my, um, stupid and uncontrolled behavior when it comes to relationships."

"I hear you, and I understand that's your preferred choice, but again, it does not jibe well with me or my principles. We differ in this regard. You did not even wait and stay with me for a few months as you had allegedly managed with others before me. So please, I deserve some respect," Nikos insisted.

"Fine, will you give me another chance? I like you a lot. You may be able to help change my stupid behavior," she asked again.

"Why? You ran out of bed partners already?" Nikos said aggressively.

"OK . . . I'll see you around."

Erika felt insulted, and she got up from her chair and left abruptly. Nikos remained seated and did not react or try to stop her sudden exit. He felt he might have been too aggressive and wished he could apologize.

He left after a few minutes to unwind and regroup his thoughts. On his way home, he wondered how different he and Erika were. How could he change her character and her lifestyle without her own willingness to do so? He realized that unless she changed her thoughts, she could not change her life. Erika thought it was OK to change relationships whimsically, the reason why she became oblivious and inconsiderate to the reactions of the men involved.

Since that weekend with Erika, Nikos had spent all his time at home alone. Though he was used to being alone, Erika introduced him to a new taste of life. Being alone was not the most admirable thing to have anymore. He missed the company of people and hers in particular. He had always had company when he lived with his family in Athens. He did not make any efforts to befriend new people since he had broken up with Erika, not even to befriend young men his age. He began to analyze his own character and whether he had become antisocial. He kept himself busy, studying while looking forward to his trip to Athens.

Before the week ended, he saw Erika from a distance in college, walking with another young student her age. He heard them talk and laugh. Erika did not see him, and he quickly changed directions to avoid seeing her more closely. He expected her to be regularly in the company of men, and it was evident she was not the type who tolerated staying alone as he did. Nevertheless, Nikos could not deny that he felt jealous. This scene prompted him to consider looking for new friends. Perhaps this could help him keep Erika out of his mind.

Nikos started preparing for his visit to his family in Athens and went out to buy them some gifts to keep up with the tradition. His mother had also asked him to pick up a dress she had ordered from Valentino on Fifth Avenue. She told him to ask for Tatiana Smirova, the salesperson in charge. Nikos went to the store and asked for her.

When she showed up, he was taken aback, admiring her beauty and graceful, sexy walk. He introduced himself and shook her hand. Tatiana, a blonde about twenty-one years old, was about five feet and seven inches, slender, and blessed with a beautiful face, highlighted by her big green eyes, cute nose, and puffy heart-shaped lips. She smiled at Nikos and kept eyeing him with admiration. Nikos felt her vibrations and responded in kind.

Tatiana took her time to prepare the packing of the dress and started a conversation with Nikos, curious to know if he was available. She happened to be single and ready to meet new friends. She told him she was originally from Russia and had been in New York for the past two years. Nikos told her that he was taking the dress to his mother in Athens, where he planned to go in a few days for the Easter holidays. Tatiana said she loved the time she spent in Greece three years ago. Without further ado, Nikos was courageous enough to slip her his mobile number while processing the payment order. He asked her to call him in two weeks after he returned from his trip.

Much to his surprise, she said, "Why can't I call you this evening after work?"

Nikos wondered about her aggressive, outgoing style and said, "Fine with me. I'll wait for your call."

Nikos left the store, wondering if this was another person like Erika, though she was not as stunning as Erika. He decided that it would not hurt to find out. It was worth a shot.

At 7:10 p.m., his cell phone rang, and it was Tatiana, who said, "Hi, it's me, Tatiana. Free to talk?"

"Yes. Hi."

"I was thinking if you're free for a soft drink, unless you, um, you have something else to do," she courageously said.

"No, I'm free. How about the bar at the Pierre?" Nikos answered.

"Good. I can be there in ten minutes," Tatiana was excited to say.

"OK, I'll see you in ten."

Nikos went down to meet her. The Pierre Hotel was in the next block. He arrived two minutes before she did and sat at a nice table, waiting for her. She walked in wearing jeans and a top that revealed her beautiful shape. He liked that casual look more than the store attire she had been wearing. She appeared relaxed and comfortable to be with Nikos. That helped put him at ease as he was normally tense in similar situations.

They exchanged talks about how they ended up being in New York. She was proud to say how she had managed to convince her store in Moscow to arrange for the transfer to the Big Apple.

Halfway through their cocktails, Nikos asked her, "How come a beautiful girl like you is not in a relationship?"

"I was, but it ended two months ago, and I am over it now. Actually, I ended it because he, Oleg Moltov, became quite obsessive and extremely jealous," Tatiana said.

"Um, I'm sorry to hear that."

"Oh, don't be. I am so relieved he's out of my life. It was a torture and a big disappointment after a whole year of trying to make it work."

"Does he try to reconnect with you?" Nikos plainly asked.

"No. Thank god because he is not around anymore. He's a Russian diplomat who had to move back to Moscow. I don't see him or hear from him anymore. Tell me about you." Tatiana was eager to learn about his status.

"I am here in New York to study, and no, I am not in any relationship."

Nikos did not find it necessary to talk about his one-weekend relationship with Erika. Upon hearing him say he was free, Tatiana's face lit up as if a glowing light was crowning her head. She assumed that she and Nikos were about the same age, and she found him to be a very handsome and polite young man. He told her that he was studying philosophy, a subject he really loved.

She did not show any interest in his studies and asked him, "How long will you be gone in Greece?"

"One week. And I leave this coming Saturday," Nikos said.

They talked for another forty minutes, and Nikos had to apologize for not inviting her to dinner as he had to finish his homework for an exam tomorrow. Nevertheless, he expressed how grateful he was to have met her and that he would be very interested to see her again after his return from his trip.

She appreciated his honesty and told him she understood and would be looking forward to receiving his call when he returned. He promised to call, and they parted, feeling good about each other. Nikos gave her a goodbye kiss on her cheek after walking her out to the entrance door and turned right toward his building.

Nikos was pleased he had met Tatiana, an interesting young lady who was not aggressive, pushing herself on him as he had experienced with Erika. She was beautiful but without seductive attempts in her behavior. They established a mutual respect, and he appreciated that. It was evident that not all people were the same.

He remained cautious and reluctant to make any suggestions that he might regret afterward. He did not mind if Tatiana thought he was aloof or not ready to dig deeper in the relationship. He could always prove her wrong afterward.

CHAPTER 3

T HE FLIGHT TO Athens was uneventful, and the plane landed on schedule. Nikos was happy to see his family again. His mother, Irene, thanked him for bringing over the dress. She asked him about Tatiana, whom she had briefly met while shopping during her previous visit to New York. Nikos told his mother they had a soft drink together and agreed to meet again after his return.

She looked at him in wonder and said, "Uh-huh. I thought she was in a relationship. That's what she told me then."

"She broke up with her partner because she found him 'obsessive' and the jealous type. Besides, he went back to Moscow, and, ah . . . they don't communicate anymore," Nikos explained.

"A drink, hmm? Did you like her?" Irene asked, curious.

"She seems to be a nice woman. It was easy to like her. It's too early to see if anything can develop out of it," Nikos said in a carefree tone.

"Was she, um, the only girl you met during all that time?" Irene asked because she knew her son was the bashful type.

"Mom, I met another lady in my class, and after one weekend together, we broke up. Why are you so curious to know, Mom? I am in New York to focus on my studies, not to indulge in serious relationships now, OK?" Nikos said, trying to halt her inquisitive nature.

"That's great, but it wouldn't hurt to have some company after school and especially on weekends," Irene emphasized.

"OK, Mom, I hear you and will see how it goes with Tatiana after I return. Can we join the rest of the family now?"

Nikos moved with his mother to see the rest of the family in the living room. He waited for his father to come home shortly. He sat with his elder brother, and his younger sister was roaming around. His elder brother, Pavlo, was being groomed by his father to eventually take over the shipping business. He asked Nikos whether he was determined to continue his studies instead of joining the family business.

Nikos reassured Pavlo, "I am committed to become a philosophy professor. That's my dream, and that's what I want. I have no interest in the business world or shipping, which I am sure you like."

"OK, fine. Do you have any friends, by the way?" Pavlo asked.

"I'm working on it. Too busy studying."

"Working on it? What are you, a recluse? You live in New York, not in a jungle in Africa. Why are you closing the door on your social life? Why don't you instead become a monk or a priest? Come on! You're a man, so live like a man, have girlfriends and see guys to have fun with." Pavlo scolded Nikos and kept shaking his head, knowing that his brother, though very handsome and charming, was a shy person who preferred to live alone, reading philosophy books.

Nikos did not appreciate his brother's remarks and answered back, "Listen, Pavlo, you live your life, and I live mine. You nurture your social life as you please."

"You bet I do. I have many girlfriends, and I frequently see my male friends," Pavlo proudly said.

Nikos laughed quietly and thought to himself how Pavlo lived like a male Erika. They both enjoyed hopping from one partner to the next.

Pavlo asked him, "Why are you laughing? What's so funny?"

"Nothing. You remind me of someone I met who thinks and lives like you, except that she's a woman," Nikos said sarcastically with mild laughter.

"A woman? Now that's interesting! Tell me more. Tell me."

"Come on, Pavlo, it's private," Nikos stealthily said.

"Nikos, don't tease me now. There are no secrets between us. A while ago, you said you have no friends, and now you say 'it's private.' I am your elder brother, so tell me, what's going on?" Pavlo insisted on hearing the full story.

"It's really not that important. I met a beautiful girl I liked, my age, in one of my classes. She said she liked me too, and we spent one passionate weekend together. Then, um, she turned to be only interested in having physical pleasure with men she liked. She had no interest in long-term relationships. So like you, she prefers to hop from one man to another. That's why I laughed."

Nikos thought that what he had said was enough to get his brother off his back, but no, he wouldn't stop. Pavlo guessed that the girl had dumped him, so he kept hammering for more.

"Uh-huh. You loved her, didn't you? And you were hurt, weren't you? I am right, no?" Pavlo said, feeling victorious in his assumptions.

"Let's stop this conversation, Pavlo. I regret that I even started it with my laughter. All I meant is that the two of you would get along real well together because you have similar desires for your social life."

As soon as Nikos finished saying that, he was saved by the bell and stood up to greet his father, who had just walked in.

The next day was Easter Sunday in Greece according to their Julian calendar. The celebration tradition included, among other things, red-dyed eggs (red to symbolize the blood of Jesus) and roasted lamb. It is well known in the Greek Orthodox religion that Easter is the most important holiday as it commemorates the resurrection of Christ.

The family was into neither the midnight church service nor the candle-lighting traditions though. They mainly enjoyed the social aspect of Easter. It brought the extended family and friends together to eat, drink, and have fun. Nikos was not particularly interested in this tradition but had to appease the wishes of his parents and be present with them.

After a few days with his family and seeing some old friends, Nikos was eager to fly back to New York. He truly started enjoying being alone, away from the noise and the crowded atmosphere of home living. He also was curious to meet Tatiana again. She had left a good impression on him, with her balanced and soft demeanor.

He spent a little time with his father, who was always busy working, and avoided as much as possible having continued talks with his curious brother, Pavlo. In fact, Pavlo showed up with two different girls in the same week, and Nikos found this quite bizarre. He had another small session with his mother, Irene, during which she reminded him to get to know Tatiana better. She asked Nikos about his summer plans once he was finished with the second semester, which was about a month away.

Nikos told her, "I don't know yet, Mom. I may take summer courses to graduate earlier or travel somewhere. I'll let you know."

"You're most welcome to come back here, of course. You can take the boat and sail around the islands. And you can invite a friend to join you too. How about that?"

"It may not be a bad idea. I'll let you know, of course. Thanks, and I hope you also come and visit. It's your place, after all."

Nikos liked his mother's loving character and keen desire to see him happy. The day before his return, he received an unexpected text message from Erika wishing him a good holiday with his family and saying that she missed him. She added that she'd been in bed the last several days, suffering from fatigue. Nikos wondered why she had sent him that message. It disturbed him, and being the compassionate man he was, he struggled and thought about answering her. He decided to think about it during his flight back to New York.

He also asked himself whether Erika was seeking his attention and sympathy with her alleged story of being sick, or was she really suffering from her illness? He had almost gotten over her after two months of solitude, and now she was knocking on his door again. She was quite an enigma to him. Would he be able to trust her again? Erika was a beautiful woman who was not in touch with her soul. He did not respond to her message, though he felt he should at least be polite and say something.

* * *

Nikos arrived at JFK Airport as scheduled. He was happy to be back in his comfortable home. It was early Saturday evening by the time he had settled down. He wondered if he should call Tatiana or answer Erika's message first. It was a new experience for him to decide whom to contact between two women.

He decided to send a short message to Erika first.

Just got back from Athens. I'm sorry you're not feeling well and wish you a speedy recovery. I hope you can make it to class on Monday. See you soon.

He felt better that he got it out of the way and proceeded to call Tatiana right away.

She answered, "Hello, this is Tatiana."

"Hi, it's me, Nikos. I just got back from Athens. How are you?"

"I'm fine. Thanks for calling. Did you have a good Easter with the family?"

"Yes, how about you? How did you celebrate Easter?"

"Nothing special. I spoke to my family and went to some friends' home, who also celebrate and serve Orthodox Easter treats, you know."

"What are you doing now? Are you free to meet? Maybe we can have dinner at Cipriani near me."

"I would love to. I was planning to go see a movie, but I prefer to see you."

"Nice! What time suits you?" Nikos asked.

"How about seven?" she said.

"Why don't you come and meet me first at my place, and then we'll go down to eat half an hour later?"

"That's sounds good. Give me your address."

Nikos gave her the address and had about an hour to get ready. He felt good vibes talking to Tatiana and looked forward to seeing her. Nikos was experiencing a different kind of chemistry with Tatiana compared to the one he had had with Erika.

The concierge rang him up at seven sharp and announced her. Nikos received her at the door with a hug and walked her into the living room.

He heard her say, "Wow! What a place, and what a view. You should see where I live. It's a dump compared to this."

"Well, I am grateful to my parents, who let me use it. They've had it for several years when my father had to spend much more time in the city before. How about something to drink?"

"Sure. Do you need any help?" she asked.

"No, thanks. It'll take me a minute. Relax and take a seat or watch the park."

They sat across from each other and chatted generally for several minutes about his time in Athens and her time in the city. Tatiana had a genuine smile on her face and expressed how happy she was to see Nikos again. Nikos loved looking at her amazing big green eyes and admired her choice of a lovely light-green knee-length spring dress.

Tatiana noticed his look and moved nervously in her chair. "Nikos, you are such a gentleman and a smart, good-looking man. How come you don't have a regular companion?"

"I'm more ready to consider now. I wanted to be alone for a while, focusing on myself. I wanted to find out what I really want from my life," Nikos calmly replied.

"I see. So you are more open to develop friends now, I believe?" Tatiana asked with a smile gracing her face.

"I guess I am, yes."

"Good! Do you see a potential for us becoming good friends?" she asked.

"*Yes*, why not? I am comfortable around you," Nikos replied.

"That sounds good. I look forward to that. I am easygoing and happy, no pressure or demands. I just go with the flow, and I am thankful for every moment I have."

"I appreciate what you said. That allows the universe to guide us in the direction we both want and at the right time," Nikos said.

Then they wrapped up their conversation and went down together to have dinner at Cipriani. Nikos was given his normal table, and he ordered a bottle of water. They left the choice of dishes to the chef, and they just relaxed, sipping their wine and continuing with the conversation that had started in the apartment.

Halfway through dinner, Tatiana asked Nikos, "Why do you study philosophy?"

"I've been fond of philosophy since the age of twelve. Particularly, I am fond of the great ancient Greek philosophers. Perhaps that is why I am a bit drawn back or bashful as some believe I have little tolerance for light-headed people or abnormal behavior. I believe in logic and a balanced life. I also shun people who show off or are pretentious. Otherwise, I am OK, and I'm open to develop new relationships."

"It's so good to hear you talk so calmly and philosophically about what you want out of your life. You must be very sensitive as well," Tatiana responded.

"Bravo! You know me well already. Unfortunately, to many, I am sensitive. That is why I have tendencies to be alone sometimes," Nikos said half-heartedly.

Tatiana responded, "Good to know. I am pretty easy when it comes to people. I tolerate many undesirable situations because of my work as a salesperson."

"Allow me to ask you. Um, you're beautiful, cheerful, and fun to be with. How come you haven't found the right partner yet since you broke up with your ex?" Nikos started digging.

"As I said earlier, it's been a couple of months only, and I took my time to regain my self-esteem. You met me at the right time, I guess, as I am fully over him now."

"I understand that, Tatiana, and let me tell you . . . you deserve better." Nikos wanted to cheer her up with encouraging words.

The food was being served in three courses during the conversation, and they both enjoyed the choices made by the chef. Nikos then suggested they go up to his place for coffee or more wine. Tatiana said she would love to.

Nikos put on some soft music in the background and offered her wine, apologizing as he had no other drinks. Tatiana looked so thrilled to be in his company and sat at the sofa, waiting for him to join her with the drinks. Nikos sat next to her and wondered if he should make out with her. He was hiding a sweet revenge for what Erika had done to him.

He developed enough courage and told her, "I find you very attractive, and I would like to hold your hand if that's OK with you."

Tatiana looked at him and smiled before she said, "Come here. Sit closer to me so I can also kiss you. I am very attracted to you. Can't you tell?"

"Wow, that's so good to hear. I've been looking forward to kissing you and hugging you too," Nikos said with a passionate tone.

Tatiana put her glass of wine on the coffee table and grabbed him by the hand and pulled him to sit close to her. They kissed and hugged for a few minutes, and the temperature between them was rising. Nikos paused and looked at her beautiful eyes and shook his head, smiling. His bashful side resurfaced, and Tatiana noticed his hesitation to continue making out.

She kissed him on the cheek and told him, "It's OK. No pressure if you want to stop here for now."

"No, my dear. It is just that I . . . I would like us to ease into the physical aspect of our new friendship."

Nikos hesitated before sharing these words. He reminded himself of what Erika had done to him. He was reluctant to build up his hopes only to find himself fallen again.

Tatiana read his mind and said, "Nikos, my dear, what are you afraid of? You're not a kid anymore, and I am not here to hurt you. If you want to slow down, it's fine with me. If you want to continue, I am here for you."

Nikos was not sure about what she said. He felt the difference in her character, and without further hesitation, he kissed her, and they started making out again. This time, the fire between them was too hot, and he suggested taking a shower together to cool off a bit. She nodded with excitement and started unbuttoning his shirt, signaling her readiness to go all the way.

Two naked bodies under the showerhead were enjoying the cascade of warm water while hugging and kissing. Instead of putting on bathrobes, they ran to bed wet and naked. Nikos whispered that he had no protection, and Tatiana said not to worry; she had been taking birth-control pills quite regularly. They consummated their first lovemaking session breathlessly. Then they went under the covers and kept hugging each other until they both fell asleep.

Nikos woke up around midnight and found her sound asleep and decided to leave her alone. He hugged her from the back and went back to sleep again. In the early hours of the morning, they woke up feeling aroused, and they made love again. Nikos thought to himself, *She's good, but she's not Erika.*

They stayed in bed together until eight, took a shower, and put on their robes to go to the kitchen for some coffee and toast. They were so happy hanging out together, and they started laughing at the jokes that Tatiana cracked. Nikos complimented her on her hidden talent and said he wished he had it in him to remember jokes.

Tatiana said she knew a joke about people like him who study all the time. She said, "A guy asked his friend, 'Hey, bro, send me good jokes.' His friend answered, 'Sorry, I have to study. Exams are coming.' The guy said, 'Good one! Send me more.'"

Nikos laughed and ran after her to grab her.

She said, "I have another one, but no running after me again! One guy sent a text message to his friend, asking, 'Hey, what are you doing?' His friend replied, 'Texting the most beautiful girl in the world.' The guy said, 'Oh! How cute!' His friend said, 'Yes, but she's not replying. That's why I am texting you.'" Tatiana then added, "So text me if you need a break from studying."

They sat down at the kitchen table, drinking their coffee, and ate some toast with jam. Nikos said, "You know what? These jokes between friends sadly remind me of how lonely I am sometimes. I am without male friends—any friend, actually—except you now, of course."

"Nikos, all you have to do is to open up, and believe me, a guy like you will attract many—I mean, *many*—friends from both genders. You are a rare breed, my friend. Go try it. I am not the jealous type. No, I'm kidding. Why don't you attract male friends first? I will try and fulfill the female part on behalf of all other jealous women out there."

Nikos could not help but laugh some more, and he told her, "Do you always joke like that? You're very funny!"

"Life is too short not to laugh."

"OK, now on a more serious subject, do you have any plans for the day?" Nikos asked.

"No, not really. How about you?"

"I am not repeating the joke you told me on studying, but I have to do some homework this afternoon, so I am free till, say, three? Meanwhile, we can go to the Met Museum. They have ancient Greek statues I can impress you with. What do you say?" Nikos said.

"I would love for you to teach me more about your culture."

"OK, let's do that, and we can have lunch at the Met as well."

And so it was. They enjoyed the rest of Sunday and agreed to keep in touch. Nikos went back home by 3:00 p.m. and dug into his books.

*   *   *

Back at NYU on Monday, Nikos caught up with the classes he had missed during his absence. Semester exams were scheduled in a couple of weeks, and he was fully prepared to do well again. In his afternoon class, he saw Erika, who did not look well. He waited till the end of the class and walked over to check on her.

She looked at him, gave him a sad smile, and said, "I see you're back, and you didn't call to check if I'm alive."

"Um, I'm sorry, but I sent you a text message wishing you well. Were you expecting more from me?" Nikos answered defensively.

"Why are you ignoring me?" Erika asked angrily.

"Oh! Wow. Take it easy, young lady! On what basis were you expecting me to keep in touch with you? Were you not the one who turned her back on me? You took me for granted and assumed I was available as a standby lover, correct?" Nikos vented out his angry feelings.

"I thought you were a forgiving person. Maybe I was wrong," she said.

"Now wait a minute! Forgive what? You really think you can step all over me and . . . and pretend nothing happened? Well, my dear, I am not your doormat. Try this game with all the other men you like. Oof . . . I am in a good place now, and I don't need to be treated like that again."

"Good place, huh? Are you seeing another woman?" she asked with a vicious smile on her face.

"I don't believe you are entitled to know. I never asked you whom you're going out with, and I—what, you're jealous now?" Nikos confidently said.

"Um . . . I still have feelings for you, my beloved professor," she answered.

Nikos was shocked. He paused for a while and then said, "Erika, you are confused. I truly believe you should consult a psychologist. You need help. I can't help you."

"Nikos, please, I promise to be loyal to you. I got sick of running around aimlessly, and I learned my lesson. I owe you a big apology."

"Erika, please hear me. I wish you well. Please take a break from all your physical activities and see a specialist for a couple of months. Find out how long you can tolerate living alone without meaningless sex. Um . . . just to realize what you really want from your life. Here, think about it, please, and I'll give you a friendly hug for now." Nikos finished his talk amicably, showed her that he cared about her, excused himself, and left.

Erika was sad and truly wanted to be with him again. She realized the mistake she had made by turning her back on him. She started seriously considering professional help and wondered whether it would best to go through that experience away from him, in Stockholm.

Nikos went home, had a phone chat with Tatiana, and agreed to see her again on Wednesday evening. He did not want to appear too eager by asking to see her every night. He also needed to focus on his studies. He appreciated the fact that Tatiana was not too demanding or pushy. They agreed to talk for a few minutes every evening to keep the momentum going.

After doing his homework, Nikos took out his journal and wrote.

I sense a new development evolving in my character since my return from Athens. I am now experiencing a new friendship with Tatiana, who seems to be a fun-loving companion. I admire her self-esteem and mature outlook on life. She's either a different breed or perhaps more in need of a companion herself.

Erika, on the other hand, continues to haunt me. She admitted her wrongdoing in abusing the start of our relationship. She's now apologizing and asking for another chance. I advised her to see a therapist and figure out how to have a more normal life. I suggested to her the need to analyze why she had the habit of having to have sex with a multitude of different men and why she was not able to stick to a continuous relationship with just one. I was willing to be that man. I loved her, but she disappointed me. I don't know if I can trust her again, even if she alleges to be cured after her therapy sessions that is, if she decides to do so. She may need to find out if she can get rid of her addiction to sex as such. I forgive her and wish her well.

Nikos saw Tatiana every couple of days, and they spent time together as good friends. Tatiana was a good tennis player, and they played on weekends. They also played chess at home a couple of times a week. Final exams for the second semester were taken, and Nikos excelled in all the courses as expected.

In one conversation, Tatiana reassured Nikos that she was a one-man woman, and he wondered why she had said that. They both agreed to take eight days off and go sailing in the Greek islands. Afterward, he would take two or three more summer courses at NYU. He did not hear again from Erika, which surprised him. Tatiana was very excited about the trip.

CHAPTER 4

BEFORE FLYING TO Athens, Nikos coordinated with his brother the availability of the family motorboat with the captain for one week. They spent the first two days in Athens visiting the family, who truly admired Tatiana as a new friend. Curious, Pavlo was particularly thrilled to see his younger brother with a beautiful girlfriend, and one late afternoon they had another one-on-one conversation while Tatiana and Irene were out shopping.

Pavlo sat next to him on the big terrace of the impressive house, overlooking the sea. It was built by their father on a small hill in the suburbs of Athens. Holding a drink in his hand, Pavlo said, "Wow! You have good taste in women, Nikos. This lady is hot. Where did you find her? In school?"

"Thank our mother for the introduction. I met her at Valentino when I went to pick a dress for Mom before the Easter holidays, and, uh, we got along well since then," Nikos briefly said.

"Interesting. Steady with one girl for more than two months, eh? I wish I could do that!" Pavlo said, smiling.

"Of course, you can, big macho man. I am sure you met some very nice girls before, but you chose not to stick to someone you really liked. You have to listen to your heart sometimes, not only follow the direction of your other head, between your legs," Nikos said compassionately.

"Opa! My philosopher brother is an adviser now!"

"I mean it, Pavlo. You're twenty-six now, and soon, you need to start a family. Our parents count on you for an heir to the throne after you're gone. Do you ever think about that? I'm out of the business line, and it's your sole responsibility now. Make Papa happy!"

"Easy on me, tiger. Don't worry, I will. Actually, there is one particular girl I met who comes to mind. I dropped her then because she wanted a serious relationship. I may call her again and focus on becoming a one-woman man. Um . . . just like my younger brother." Pavlo smiled and showed interest in what Nikos had told him. He seemed serious for a change.

Nikos was happy to chat with his brother for a while longer before the ladies came back. He briefed him on how Erika had tried to lure him back into her life again and how he had pushed her away to work on her inner self first. Pavlo advised him to keep his options open and asked him about his plans with Tatiana, and Nikos said he had none. His main focus was on his studies, and whoever was in his life had to understand that and accept it.

Pavlo confirmed the availability of both the boat and Captain George, who would take them to four or five Saronic Islands of the Cyclades that are close to the mainland. He said, "You decide together which islands to see first. The boat, as you know, is sixty feet long and has three staterooms, with a very comfortable master room. You don't need to jump from one hotel to another, only hop from one island to the next. You will have a great time!"

Pavlo looked very happy to see Nikos taking time to have some fun with a lovely girl. Nikos thanked him and gave him a big hug. They both said they were thankful to their father, who provided the whole family with such abundant luxury.

They all had dinner at home that evening, and the boat journey was scheduled to start the next day. His father, Yanni, welcomed Tatiana and wished her a good boat journey with Nikos to the beautiful islands. He asked her about her background and her education and told her how well she spoke the English language.

Then he said, "I am sure you noticed that we have a unique person in Nikos. I am proud of him. He chose to take a different route for his future. I mean academia instead our family business in shipping. Thank god I have Pavlo, who decided to stay with me and to help me in running our business."

"You're right, sir, in saying that Nikos is unique. I don't have a lot of experience with men, but he is unique in that he is polite, kind, and focused on what he wants from his life. I am happy he accepted me to be his friend. I love the moments we spend together, and I admire his dedication to be the best in his studies. Nikos is truly one of a kind. Allow me to thank you and Mrs. Bestidis for your warm hospitality and for accepting me as a guest in your home."

Nikos kept looking at her silently and thinking about what Erika was doing now.

* * *

The first stop of the boat was in nearby Kea. The island had a different look to its buildings from the rest of the island group. It was close to Athens, and it got busy during the summer. Kea boasted old history, quiet beaches, and small seaside villages. The couple spent the afternoon swimming in a bay on the other side of the island. They had an early dinner at a well-known seafood restaurant nearby, famous for its fish-soup delicacy.

After dinner and with plenty of daylight left, they continued sailing for another hour toward the island of Spetses. The island was known for its good-looking houses and its cobblestone streets. The people here played a big role in the Greek War of Independence. No cars were also allowed, and it had nice beaches a few kilometers away from the town. Nikos had been to Spetses before and asked the captain to berth the boat overnight in a quiet bay.

They lay down, watching the stars in the dark-blue sky above. Nikos told Tatiana how much he liked this island's culture and character. Tatiana felt so romantic.

She turned to look at Nikos with her teary eyes and said, "I don't know how to thank you for having me here with you. I've never been anywhere like this with a man whom I truly admire so much. Thank you and thank you again."

Nikos appreciated her sweet words and leaned over to kiss her on her tender lips and then said, "I'm happy we are together. I enjoy your company, and I cherish your good feelings of gratitude. It is the simple things in life that mean a lot to me. I admire your sincerity and honest demeanor. And I hope we can continue to be good friends in the future."

"Me too. If there is a will, there is a way. I promise to be loyal to you, to support you in all your decisions. I trust you and will give you the space you need to live your life as you see fit. I will make sure I don't do anything to suffocate our relationship and will allow ourselves time to breathe," Tatiana spoke affectionately.

"Wow, Tatiana, I should learn about the philosophy of life from you. I don't need to go to school anymore." Nikos giggled when he said that. He leaned over again and gave her a warm hug. He was not sure, however, if she could be falling in love with him or if she was just saying it conveniently.

Later on, they went to sleep in a very comfortable bed and felt the soft movement of the boat from side to side.

The next day, they sailed to Hydra. Another island in the Saronic Gulf, it kept its original character. No motor cars were allowed also. It had stunning old villas on the waterfront, little cafés and restaurants, and several museums. It was known for its secluded beaches as well. The boat arrived before noon and parked near the center of town. They walked along the pedestrian streets. Nikos had also been there before and took Tatiana to a nice tavern in town and had authentic Greek seafood and drank ouzo, which went well with it.

After lunch, they visited a few small museums that helped Tatiana understand the local culture. Around three in the afternoon, they went back to the boat and asked Captain George to take them to the secluded Bisti beach to swim. Nikos admired Tatiana's body and soft skin, which was tanning slightly already.

They had cocktails on the boat after resting for a short while in their stateroom. They waited until it was dark, and then Nikos suggested a light meal that night and preferred to watch the stars and go to bed early. They slept well in quiet Hydra and woke up early to continue sailing to ancient Delos, a special place in Greek mythology. The island was close to Mykonos, which Tatiana had already visited.

Nikos knew its ancient history well and wanted Tatiana to learn about it. On the way over there, Nikos told her, "According to Greek mythology, the twin gods Apollo and Artemis were born on this sacred island. The ancient town was a bustling commercial center as well as a shrine. The island still has ruins that include a vast terrace of marble lion statues. Delos was developed after the middle of the third century BC with twenty-eight huge columns that housed shops and workshops. You will find remains of the sanctuary of Apollo and his temple farther north. If you climb another five hundred feet, you get an amazing view of other islands nearby and see the monuments of Zeus and Athena and the temple of Hera. You see along the way remnants of a big theater and the houses of the old wealthy people. The most lavish house, in mosaic, was that of Dionysus, the wine god. The interesting thing about Delos is that it was a place of worship for many foreigners as well. It had sanctuaries of Syrian and Egyptian gods like Isis, built by traders who visited Delos by boat from the East Mediterranean."

"Wow, Nikos, you know so much about your ancient history. I am so impressed," Tatiana said after listening carefully to him.

"Well, Delos stands out because of the large number of gods it had. That is why it is called the sacred island. You will feel its energy when you are there. Actually, I felt its energy when I swam in its sea too."

When the boat arrived and docked near the ruins, Tatiana saw for herself what Nikos had explained on the way and was mesmerized by the explanations he had given her. He later invited her to join him for a swim. And after changing their clothes on the boat, they jumped in. Tatiana fully agreed with Nikos about the unique energy the water had.

Tatiana asked Nikos if they could spend the night close to the island to get as much energy from it as she could. Nikos agreed and said there was one more island he would like to show her, Hora (or Tinos), or at least the church of Panagia Evangelistria.

The next morning, the captain sailed the boat to Hora. Before the boat was anchored, Tatiana saw the varied landscape of the island between the mountains and the beaches. Nikos pointed out to her that the town was hidden behind one high mountain, and most homes had stone walls. He said the highlight of the island was the church, which was built in 1882 when a nun had found a lost icon of the Virgin Mary. The icon, which was supposed to have healing powers, attracted pilgrims to visit from all over the country and abroad. The icon, referred to as Our Lady of Tinos, became the patron saint of the Greek nation.

When they got close to the impressive church that was built in honor of the Virgin Mary, Tatiana read a small guidebook that Nikos had given her. She found the church fascinating, with hundreds of silver lamps hang from the ceiling, each dangling a votive offering: a ship, a cradle, a heart, a pair of lungs, and a chainsaw.

> The church, built of marble from the island's Panormos quarries, lies within a pleasant courtyard flanked by cool arcades. The complex has sweeping views all around and museums (with variable hours) that house collections of religious artifacts, icons, and secular art.

Nikos had already told Tatiana to wear respectful attire, as requested by the church. They spent about thirty minutes wandering around and looking at the various precious items. They walked around town for another hour and ate some gyro sandwiches before they returned to the boat. Nikos asked her if she would like to see another island before they returned. She hesitated for a few seconds and then told him she would like to stop in Mykonos that evening and go to the famous disco club by the sea.

Nikos knew what she was talking about. He had seen it from a distance a couple of years back. He remembered how the place was crowded with people dancing in their bathing suits to very loud music. He paused for ten seconds, looked at her, and smiled, and then he said OK.

Captain George knew exactly where to anchor the boat close to the disco club around ten at night. Tatiana took Nikos by his hand and ran ahead of him toward the dance floor. They stayed at the club till midnight, and Nikos had never had so much fun in public before. Nikos had not danced that much before, and they ran back to the boat giggling with laughter and soaking wet from sweat. They immediately took a shower together while laughing.

Before they went to bed, Tatiana asked Nikos, "Are you a magician? Because whenever I look at you, the rest of the world disappears."

That deserved another passionate hug and kiss, and they had a memorable, loving session before they crashed and fell asleep like logs. That was their last stop before heading back to Athens the next morning.

Nikos could not remember the last time he had so much fun, thanks to Tatiana, who had made it so special. He looked at her on the boat ride back and expressed how he felt. She was nicely tanned and wore nice shorts that showed her long well-shaped legs. He opened up and told her how much he appreciated their friendship.

Tatiana was on cloud nine, feeling pampered and appreciated by this young, intelligent, and considerate man. She was truly tempted to tell him that she loved him but decided it was premature as it could also interrupt his focus on his studies.

For the time being, she looked at him straight in the eye and said, "Nikos, I want you to know that you are my man. You can count on me to be there for you anytime. I hope our friendship can last for a long, long time."

"You are sweet and loving. I will try my utmost to nourish our friendship," Nikos responded politely.

They sat together on deck, inhaling the warm, fresh sea breeze while having coffee. A few hours later, they arrived, and they both thanked the captain before they disembarked. A car took them back home to spend the last two days with the family before returning to New York. Nikos had promised to take Tatiana to see the Acropolis and the new nearby museum the next day. Nikos's family was thrilled to see him so happy. The time came to say goodbye. They wished them both good luck and a happy future together. They exchanged hugs and kisses before the family car drove them to the airport.

*　　*　　*

The car from JFK dropped Nikos off first before continuing to Gramercy Park, where Tatiana had rented a small one-bedroom apartment. She did not take her cell phone with her on the trip. She then checked her phone and was shocked to find a host of messages from her ex-boyfriend, Oleg, who had been in town for the last five days, wondering where she was. The people at her work had told him she was away. He had asked her to call him and left her a room number of the hotel where he was staying.

Tatiana sat down to regroup from this shock. What should she do? Call him and face a troubling situation or not respond at all? He knew where she lived and where she worked. She decided to consult with Nikos for his opinion. She was shaking when she called him. She told him what had happened while still sobbing.

Nikos was taken aback hearing her story. He thought for a while and then said, "Look, Tatiana, I'm sorry, and I understand how shaken you are now. Unfortunately, he knows where you live and work. If he is still in town and calls you again, I think you should take his call and tell him the truth. If he insists on seeing you, do that but in a public place, not in your apartment. You cannot hide from him, but have no fear. He will not hurt you. He should understand that you moved on. If he becomes aggressive, then calmly call 911. Please keep me advised!"

He cooled her down some, and she felt she was not alone with him close by. "OK. I will do what you said. I will keep you posted, and I am sorry to bother you with this nonsense right after such an amazing trip together. Kisses and thanks!"

Two hours later, after she had unpacked and taken a shower, her phone rang; it was her ex, Oleg. He was calm but angry. He spoke in Russian, of course, and asked to see her.

She developed enough courage to answer, "Why do you want to see me, Oleg? We're not together anymore, and I am seeing someone else now, and I am moving on with my life!"

"But I still would like to see you. May I come over?" he asked.

"Look, I have an appointment later, but for old times' sake, I can meet you at the park here in thirty minutes. I cannot stay long, OK?"

"Why can't I see you at your place?" Oleg insisted.

"I told you I'm with someone else, so please have some respect."

"Fine, I'll see you in the park in half an hour," he answered angrily.

There were many people sitting around in the park when they met. Tatiana was nervous when she saw him and tried to hide it with a false smile.

They found a bench somewhat distant from the noise of kids running around, and after a minute or so, Tatiana asked Oleg, "What brings you to New York? I . . . I thought you are happily stationed in Moscow."

"I came to see you. After two months, I found out that, uh, I still love you and miss you. I didn't give you advance notice because I wanted to make it a pleasant surprise."

"I'm sorry to disappoint you, Oleg, but I am with someone else now, and, um, I cannot connect with you anymore," Tatiana said emphatically.

Oleg tightened up angrily, and after a few seconds, he blasted out, "You cannot do that. You are still my girl. If you turn your back on me, I swear I'll . . . I'll make sure you are deported from this country. I still have strong contacts with the immigration people, as you know!" Oleg found it hard to breathe.

"Don't threaten me. Feel free to do what you can. I don't live in a jungle here, and I am a legitimate resident of the United States. So it is in your best interest to leave me alone. I don't want to see you or hear from you ever again. If you try to do anything stupid or harass me, you better watch your back. Goodbye!" Tatiana said angrily and courageously.

She then stood up and walked out of the park and jumped in a taxi on the street. Oleg tried to get her attention by asking her not to leave, but she did not look back. She gave the driver Nikos's address. A minute later, she calmed down and called Nikos. When he answered her call, she started sobbing and stuttering in her attempt to talk. When she controlled herself, she told him what had happened and asked him if she could come over as she was not sure what Oleg might do. Nikos, the compassionate and loving man he was, quickly said, "Of course."

Tatiana kept looking behind to check if, by any chance, Oleg was following her in another taxi. Though she could not tell for sure, she hoped that he was not. Ten minutes later, she entered the building. The concierge had been alerted to her arrival in advance and immediately let her take the elevator. She told him in case another man walked in, asking about her, to make sure to say nothing and send him out the door.

Nikos was waiting for her when she came out of the elevator and hugged her warmly. He rubbed her back to stop her from sobbing and crying. He gave her a glass of wine to get the edge off her racing mind. He did not say much, and he let her unwind first.

After a while, she sat next to him and said, "I'm so sorry to . . . to put you through this! I didn't know where else to go. You are the only one I can trust and feel safe with. I was not expecting Oleg's visit at all. As I had told you before, I thought it was totally over between us. It is not that I like him or love him, yet now he alleges he still loves me and . . . and wants me back. I told him to get lost, and I am not afraid of his threats."

"You did right, Tatiana, to tell him that, and I don't think he can do anything about your legitimate work visa. He is just showing off and testing you to get you back. You see, people who are of the obsessive and jealous type are sick in the head. They are addicted to that sort of behavior, but they are not necessarily harmful. Let us see if he causes you any harm. We can easily engage the police to take care of that. Meanwhile, you're welcome to stay with me until he flies back," Nikos said compassionately.

Tatiana was touched. She turned to his side, hugged him, and said, "Thank you, dear Nikos, for your support. Tomorrow I will go to work and see if he bothers me there. I also need to go home and pack some stuff to bring here, if it's OK with you."

"No problem. I'll be home after six. It is getting late now, so I suggest we go to bed. Tomorrow is another day. I will hug you to make sure you sleep well," Nikos said with an encouraging smile.

"I would love that."

Tatiana went to work the next morning at nine and managed to change her clothes and into the store attire before the doors opened. She alerted the security man not to allow a man asking for her to come in but to notify her in case he insisted. Lo and behold, Oleg showed up at the store around ten o'clock. He asked to see her, but the security guard told him to please wait while he checked to see if she was available. The security guard informed the store manager to notify Tatiana while he remained near the door to watch Oleg. The manager came back and told Oleg that Tatiana was busy with a client and could not see him.

Oleg got angry and started accusing the manager. "Stop playing games with me. I'll wait here all day if I have to. Ask someone else to be with her client. I must see her now."

The manager would not tolerate such behavior and answered back angrily, saying, "First, you don't talk to me like this. Second, unless you are here to buy something, I suggest you leave us before we call the police."

Oleg was too stubborn and agitated. He replied, "Go ahead and call the police and explain to them what I am doing wrong. I am staying here."

The manager, Francine, thought for a few seconds before she answered, "You can wait outside. This is private property, and you are not welcome here. You are trespassing, and I ask you go outside right now."

Everyone in the store was looking around and wondering what was going on. The security guard told him to please step outside and had his hand on the button of the police pager if he didn't.

Oleg had no choice but to go outside. After a couple of minutes of being closely watched, his ego obliged him not to wait any longer, so he walked away. He felt rejected and revengeful. He went to a café nearby, ordered a cup of coffee, and dialed Tatiana's cell phone number.

There was no answer, and he left her a message in Russian. "I wanted to give you a last chance to come back with me to Moscow. I don't care whom you're seeing now, but I want you back. I fly back to Moscow this evening. If you don't call me back agreeing to my request, you will regret it, and you'll understand why soon. Good luck."

She, of course, did not call him back, and if he were to be believed, she was somewhat relieved that he was leaving New York the same day. She had no idea in which hotel he was staying for her to find out if he had checked out. She had deleted the number he left earlier. She called Nikos around six and briefed him on the event and the message. Nikos told her to wait for him in the store, and he would accompany her to her place to get some clothes and spend another night with him just in case Oleg decided not to leave.

Nikos walked over to the store located on Fifty-Fifth and Fifth Avenue and picked up Tatiana to go to her place in Gramercy Park. She lived on the second floor in a small old building with no security whatsoever. They walked up the stairs and were shocked to see her door lock broken and the door flung wide open. The small one-bedroom apartment was totally ransacked.

They saw sofa pillows on the floor, the coffee table upside down with broken legs, two dining chairs broken, the TV thrown on its side, and shelves emptied with books all over the place. The bedroom mattress was turned upside down, with blankets and covers bundled on the floor, and all drawers were emptied, their contents on the floor along with dresses and other stuff from the closet.

Nikos held Tatiana tight, asking her not to sob and cry. She kept her hand on her mouth while walking around to see what else had happened. Her small kitchen was similarly ransacked, with pots, pans, and broken plates thrown all around. She looked at Nikos, in awe of what she saw, and he told her not to touch anything. He took out his cell phone and took many photos of all the rooms in detail. He told her that she had to call the police to report the incident.

*   *   *

Tatiana did, and the police arrived after seven minutes. They also took photos and asked her to come with them to file a police report. Nikos stayed with her during her interrogation at the police department nearby. Tatiana gave the police Oleg's full name after telling them the story and showing them the Russian message he had left on her cell phone. She also showed them a photo of Oleg, which she luckily had saved in an album.

Tatiana did not know which hotel he had stayed in during his visit to New York, and the police checked with eight different hotels close by before they located a three-star hotel he had registered in on the west side of Thirty-Second Street. The police were told that he had checked out at one o'clock that same afternoon. They deduced that he might have taken the Aeroflot flight to Moscow at 5:00 p.m. Tatiana was told not to worry, and they would advise her if they could get hold of him in Moscow via the American embassy. They also told her that he would be on the wanted list of all the country borders, air, land, or sea. "That's in case he tries to come back."

Nikos then went with her to the apartment to salvage whatever she could. On the way, he bought a new lock for the door from a locksmith. Tatiana took whatever clothes she could find convenient for another short stay with Nikos and then put the apartment back in order. Nikos was very supportive and compassionate throughout the ordeal, and Tatiana was so grateful he was there by her side. Nikos took her back to his place and offered her a drink before they went back downstairs to have a calming dinner at Cipriani on the next block.

During dinner, Tatiana held Nikos's right arm across the table and said, "I don't know how I could have managed on my own, I am so grateful. You are truly god sent, and I can only reciprocate by being grateful and loyal to you. I'll do whatever you ask me to do."

"Oh, Tatiana, just be the person you are, sweet and loving. Have no fear of anything. The angels are protecting you as they protect all good souls. Don't thank me. You have also been sent to me," Nikos responded in kind.

Tatiana felt much better hearing his words, and the red wine helped as well. She continued to express her feelings of appreciation and said, "I know I am feeling vulnerable now because of what happened, but I want you to know you have already occupied a good place in my heart. I will not forget the good times we had together, even now that the situation is unexpectedly sullied with my past headaches."

"Don't worry about what happened. He knows now he has no claim over you anymore," Nikos said.

"I hope so, my dear. He can be more vengeful. We don't know what he might do next. He can be resourceful and annoying. I know his entry is blocked from coming back, but . . ."

"Tatiana, please take him out of your mind. As long as you don't plan to go to Moscow anytime soon, he is no more a threat to you. Relax," Nikos tried to reassure her.

"Sweetheart—do you mind me calling you that?" she said.

"Of course, you can. Go ahead. What did you want to say?"

"I hope he does not do anything to hurt my family. He knows where they live."

"I don't know what to say. You know him better than I do, and I hope he doesn't."

The two of them changed the subject and talked about the trip they had just had in Greece. Nikos told her he would forward to her the photos he had taken while they were together. They finished their dinner, feeling more relaxed, and walked back up to the apartment to have an early sleep after such an eventful day.

The rest of the week was spent without any further disturbance. Nikos gave Tatiana a hand in cleaning up and fixing the apartment the following few days. He bought for her a few items to replace those that were damaged and begged her to buy some clothes. She said she had cheaper access to clothes from Valentino because of the big discount.

Tatiana felt obliged to call her parents and tell them what had happened with Oleg. She warned them to be careful as he might be vengeful and do something to hurt them because his hands were tied in New York. Also, she begged them not to tell her elder brother, Vladimir, who might confront Oleg and start a war between them.

The following month passed without any disturbing messages or moves by Oleg, and his earlier threats to have her deported were muted. The only annoying part was that Tatiana felt she was being watched and followed after work on her way home or even the days she visited Nikos. After a week of observation and after consulting Nikos, she informed the police that she was being followed.

A detective in civilian clothes walked behind her one evening to see for himself, and indeed, she was being stalked. The police detective confronted the stalker, who then admitted that he was paid by a Russian guy to do so and to report Tatiana's evening moves. He said he was not a stalker but a hired private eye by a man called Oleg . . . something.

The police confiscated all the files and photos the private eye had in his possession just before he was supposed to dispatch them to Moscow. He signed a document stating he would stop this task. The police notified the CIA and asked them to contact their friends in Moscow to cooperate. The police in Moscow interrogated Oleg and instructed him to stop or go to jail. He finally got the message and stopped harassing Tatiana, even from far away.

*   *   *

Nikos and Tatiana had two months of calm and tranquility. They saw each other twice during the week and on weekends. They became close friends, and Tatiana enjoyed visiting Nikos and cooking for him. They had warm evenings at home, and Tatiana created a homey atmosphere for him, which he truly appreciated. He succeeded in using the three free evenings a week alone to focus on his studies. He was taking three courses during the summer period, and he excelled in all of them.

Around early September, Nikos received a text message from Erika asking after him and telling him that she had spent her summer in Stockholm. She said she was now back in New York to prepare for the new semester of her second year. She asked if they could meet again. She missed him, and he was always in her mind. Nikos was spending the evening alone that day, and the message confused him. He thought that Erika had forgotten him. His pulse went faster when he had read she still missed him.

In an inverted way, Nikos's ego was boosted by the fact that she was still trying to see him. He felt perhaps he possessed a certain magical charm that the other men she went out with did not have. *No*, he said to himself. *I should not think like that. I am satisfied with the fact that I have been experiencing self-esteem. Now two beautiful women seem to like me. Should I open the door to Erika again?*

However, as he was considerate, he decided to send Erika a reply to her message by email.

> *Hi, Erika. Glad to hear you spent your summer in Stockholm, and I'm sure you enjoyed yourself. I went for ten days to Greece with a new friend I met. I came back to take three summer courses. This way, I may finish the bachelor's degree one year earlier if I take three courses every summer. Otherwise, all is well, and hope to see you at NYU soon.*
>
> *Regards,*
> *Nikos*

CHAPTER 5

C LASSES FOR THE new scholastic year started in September, and Nikos took five courses: Philosophy of Science, Philosophy of Evolution, Cognitive Psychology, a history course about the Civil War in America, and another interesting course called Modern Spirituality. Nikos noticed that Erika was not in any of the courses he had chosen, and he wondered why. He was truly expecting to see her and became curious about why she was not in any of them. He enjoyed the Modern Spirituality course.

He noticed the presence of an interesting student, James Cordwell, who was taking two courses at NYU while attending a Christian seminary to obtain a doctorate degree in divinity. James happened to be sitting next to Nikos in the philosophy class on evolution. They were introduced to each other before the class started. James was a slender masculine-looking young man in his early twenties. He was of average height with a short dark beard that contrasted with his white skin. The two of them hit it off well, and Nikos noticed the continuous smile on his face. They were both keen to get to know each other better and agreed to go for coffee in the cafeteria after class. After sharing their background stories, they moved on to ask academic questions.

James said, "Wow, Nikos, what a story about your love for philosophy since the age of twelve! You must be a master of the great Greek philosophers then. Also, I find it interesting that you chose the course on evolution to find the 'logic' in its theories.

I took the course to decipher its contradiction to what the Bible teaches."

"You're right about the contrast in our different approaches to the same subject. This should allow us to have decent debates together as we move along with the course. I also saw you in Modern Spirituality. Perhaps you can tell me why you're taking the course here and not at the seminary. Don't they teach it there?" Nikos asked.

"Yes, they do. But I heard that the professor here is more open-minded than, um, the conservative old priest there," James explained.

"Good to know. This is also new to me. I grew up as a nonpracticing Greek Orthodox, and I could not muster enough desire to digest its routine rituals. Perhaps this course here can help me appreciate my religious beliefs differently," Nikos admitted.

"Perhaps. Yes, and this would be another topic to discuss together as well when we meet for coffee again," James responded.

The two new friends were happy they talked, and they looked forward to many more visits together in the days ahead.

*   *   *

Nikos did not see Erika around NYU for several days. He thought perhaps she was taking other courses at different hours. Besides, she had not answered his last email, which he found unusual. He was curious, and he checked with the registrar's office to see if she had even registered for her sophomore year. He was surprised to learn that she had not. He wondered why and left it at that. He was curious to know if she had followed his advice to see a therapist. He decided to send her another email message.

Ili, Erika. I did not receive a reply to my last message, and I have not seen you around at NYU for two weeks now. Is everything all right? I hope all is well, and I send you warm regards.

Nikos

Thirty minutes later, Nikos received the following email reply from Erika.

Hi, Nikos. Thank you for checking on me. I decided to go back to Stockholm and continue with my therapist as you suggested. I made it my priority. I am doing much better now, learning how to subdue my pretentious ego about my addictive bodily pleasures and focusing on looking for beauty within. I want to thank you for your therapy suggestion. That showed me how you cared about my well-being. I need two more months of inner search, and now, believe it or not, I'm living a life of abstinence for a change. I may or may not go back to NYU—still discussing with my parents. Thanks again, and I give you a big hug!

Erika

Nikos was pleased to read her message and by the fact that she was looking inwardly with the help of a therapist. He felt good that she had followed his advice. That altered the anger Nikos had toward her into a respectful appreciation that she was working on changing her lifestyle. He wished her well and hoped she would come back to New York. He became anxious to see the outcome of her therapy on her life. He wrote her back, expressing his gladness that she was taking care of herself, and hoped he could see her soon.

Tatiana came to spend the evening with Nikos after work as planned. She insisted on cooking something light for him and brought a nice bottle of the wine he liked and table candles to create a romantic atmosphere. Nikos appreciated her touch. While she was preparing dinner in the kitchen, Nikos noticed how Tatiana's main interest, apart from her job, was to satisfy his physical needs and comfort. He wondered why she had no keen interest in enriching her mind with intellectual food as well. He thought it might be worth addressing this observation with her during dinner.

At the nicely set table with two scented candles, Nikos thanked Tatiana and said, "Sweetheart, I appreciate your continued attention to create this wonderful atmosphere for us here. I have a question to ask you, if I may. How do you spend your evening time when you're alone at your place?"

"What do you mean? Do I cook for myself?" she asked.

"No, not that only but after you eat at home. What do you do the rest of the evening before, um, you go to bed?" Nikos politely asked.

"Not much. I do work around the apartment, read some magazines, watch some news, do some thinking about us, and wish you a good night," she answered with a smile.

"Do you have any interest in reading books?"

"Eh, rarely," Tatiana quickly replied.

SAMEER ZAHR

"Why is that?" Nikos asked curiously.

"I don't know. I just don't. Why do you ask? Do you think I should?"

"It's not my job to tell you what you should do or not do. I was just wondering if you have any urge to nourish your mind with added intellectual knowledge. That's all," Nikos told her with caution.

"I see. I guess we are different, you and me in this regard. I am not a lover of books like you are. I hope that does not disappoint you, Nikos," Tatiana said with a concerned look on her face.

"Let me tell you why I am bringing up this subject. You know that I enjoy your company and admire your loving attention toward me. Sometimes when we are done with dinner, I would like to have a discussion or a debate with you about something intellectual. That's me. Say you're reading a book, and you find something interesting to share or discuss with me. I would love that. I have no interest in TV news or magazines. For me, it's a waste of my time. I hope you understand why I ask."

"Um . . . I hear you, and you may have a point there. But please tell me honestly—do I bore you because I cannot match your intellectual faculties?" Tatiana sounded a bit irritated asking that.

"No, no, you don't bore me. But when you are here with me, sometimes I wish I could discuss with you what's going on in my classes and the new material I am studying, things like that." Nikos wanted to reassure her that he was not complaining.

"So what do you suggest I should do, my dear professor?" she asked more calmly.

"OK, let's assume you are interested in the fashion world. You are a good salesperson, right? How about, um, taking a couple of courses online that could enhance your progress in this field? You can even get a bachelor's degree online, as you may know. After a couple of years, you will be more qualified for a higher position or a new managerial job in a bigger place—that is, if you have the ambition to do so," Nikos explained.

"That's not a bad idea at all. Thank you. I'll look into it." Tatiana was thrilled to consider this new thought.

Nikos then continued to say, "By the way, I met an interesting young man who is taking two courses with me, Philosophy of Evolution and Modern Spirituality. His name is James Cordwell, and he is studying for his doctorate in divinity at the seminary. We hit it off well, and we meet for coffee after class to discuss and debate some issues."

"That's great news, my dear. You are starting to have male friends now."

"Yup!"

Nikos thanked her for a wonderful dinner. They cleaned the table and did the dishes together. They went to the living room with their glasses of wine to continue their conversation and relax before they went to bed.

*   *   *

The second time Nikos and James had coffee together, Nikos asked him, "Is the Christian leadership concerned by the increasing number of people in their various congregations who claim they are spiritual but not religious?"

"Personally, though they may not admit it publicly, I believe the answer is yes. I imagine this concern is being discussed at the highest levels. Why? Membership and attendance have been dropping in the last few decades, and that is of big concern if the trend continues to be downward in the future," James explained.

"Are they doing anything about it? Are they willing to compete with the greater appeal that modern spirituality has achieved?" Nikos asked.

"As you very well know, change is not easy. Local leaderships are too reluctant to effect any change without guidance from the top, be it the Vatican for the Catholics or the World Christian Council that represents other faiths. Some courageous church leaders are more creative and aware of what needs to be done, and they're doing it, but not the majority, who still abide by the old traditions and rituals."

"But in history, all it took was for one strong individual to stand up and bring about a change, be it in religion or politics or in the government. Martin Luther did it and succeeded. The church itself was divided between Catholics and Orthodox and so on. Why can't there be a new strong leader that would persuade the leadership to implement new spirituality methods in their own traditional practices?" Nikos wanted to know.

"Um . . . actually, though I am hardly recognized in any circle or church, I personally would like to be such a voice. Don't ask me how and when, but that is why I am studying modern spirituality and learning more about it—so I could write my eventual doctoral thesis along the lines you are talking about," James said bashfully.

"Great, James! You're my hero. Don't be bashful about it. You will succeed to bring about a change and a halt in the dropping membership of the church," Nikos stated encouragingly.

"You think so? That's very encouraging. Thanks."

The young men had to wrap up the conversation to attend other classes, and they agreed to have a follow-up discussion soon. They also wanted to discuss why evolution theories didn't jibe well among devout Christians.

Nikos called Tatiana in the early evening and asked her how she was doing. That day was for her to be alone, and the plan was for her to be with him the next day.

She was happy to receive his call and joyfully said, "I want to thank you for our last conversation, dear Nikos. It opened my eyes or rather woke me up mentally. You are right. I should do something more exciting and challenging. I am doing online research now to see where I could learn how to become a buyer and then apply for a job at a major clothing store like Bloomingdale's or Saks. What do you think?"

"That's great, Tatiana! I'm very happy to hear that. You'll be able to take business courses for a maximum period of two years, and you will be certified. You don't need a lot of help on the fashion end of it as you already have a lot of experience in this regard," Nikos said.

"Thank you. Not only will I rise up the ladder of success, but also, I hope you will be less bored with me," Tatiana said, partly to tease him.

Nikos paused for a few seconds before he said, "Come on, now don't take me so seriously. I'm glad it prompted you to do what you're doing now. I will leave you alone to continue with your research, and I'll go back to my studies. I'll see you tomorrow!"

"How sweet! I miss you, and good night."

*　　*　　*

SAMEER ZAHR

Another debate session was held between James and Nikos regarding evolution theories versus Christian beliefs. They both had heard lectures from the professor in which it was clear that what Charles Darwin had started with his book *On the Origin of Species* more than 160 years ago had turned many Christians into unbelievers. It had also established Darwin as the patron saint of modern atheism. The controversy between creations as described in the Bible and the theory of evolution involved an ongoing and recurring dispute about the origin of Earth, humanity, and other forms of life.

Nikos started the discussion, saying, "We now learned that since the mid-1800s, evolution by natural selection has been established as a scientific fact. Why is it that traditional Christians still reject this scientific fact?"

"If Christian leadership succumbs to the biological evolution of species on this planet, then you might as well kiss the Christian and perhaps other monolithic religions goodbye. This would also make the Bible meaningless. I don't think we can imagine such an acknowledgment by the church anytime soon," James answered, qualifying it as his own opinion.

"You don't think there can be a happy medium that can bring both sides closer together?"

"In fact, there are attempts to bridge the differences between these two schools of thought. Actually, Pope Francis has recently explained that God 'is not a magician' and that evolution in nature is not inconsistent with the notion of creation, and evolution requires the creation of beings that evolve. In other words, the pope is saying that evolution would not be denied as long as every evolving phase is acknowledged to be created by God," James explained.

"So do you think scientists and theologians would agree that the two concepts can be merged together?" Nikos asked while sipping his coffee.

"I understand that there are many books written by scientists and theologians agreeing that they see no conflict between their faith in God and the evidence for evolution. However, there continue to be some religious denominations that refuse to accept the occurrence of evolution. They believe in strictly literal interpretations of religious texts," James said.

"If I may add, I hear that quantum physics will further assist in explaining that there is no conflict between science and religion. Do you agree?" Nikos wondered.

"Perhaps it does. I am not very well versed in quantum physics. They say that the universe is always expanding and that new stars are born while others die. This cycle of birth and death resembles what we go through as humans. I think that we should agree that there should not be a conflict, and hopefully, this would slow down the departure of Christian believers from their houses of worship. What do you think?" James said.

"I grew up believing in logic, the heart of philosophical theories. I am nowadays expanding my thoughts via imagination, influenced by what Albert Einstein allegedly said—'Logic takes you from point A to point Z, but imagination takes you everywhere.' This is a quantum-physics manifestation of the expanding universe, and we expand with it too. Why? In essence, we are all part of the universe and interconnected as a form of energy, not separate matter. Hence, I do believe in the creator of the universe, God. I also believe in the theory of evolution, which is logical. They are not . . . I mean, not necessarily exclusive of each other. In brief, I am now leaning toward becoming a spiritual philosopher, and I will dig deeper into this new realm of thought," Nikos explained more clearly.

The two intellectual students enjoyed their session together, and Nikos suggested that perhaps they could enjoy a meal together soon.

*　　*　　*

Tatiana came over that evening and looked quite happy and excited. She hugged Nikos but could not wait to sit down to share her news. After a couple of minutes of calming down and a glass of water, she said, "I am so excited, and I can't thank you enough for encouraging me to pursue a more exciting future and life. I spent five hours last night researching online. I read several articles about what they call retail merchandising, another term for a buyer. Not to bore you with all the details, but I found out that I can get a certificate in this field in about one year. All I have to do is to take six to eight courses, mainly to understand the business end of it. They require a high-school degree and a minimum of two years' experience in the fashion-clothing business, which I have. Voilà!"

Tatiana, still excited, paused to take another sip of water while sitting at the edge of the sofa, facing Nikos, who was listening attentively with a big smile on his face. She took a breath and continued, "And I found the right school, which teaches these courses online and grants a certificate or diploma at the end of the year. So I applied and said I was ready to start immediately. I should hear back soon. What do you think?"

"Wow! You're quick, and I'm proud of you. It's great, and you will love it. It's right up your alley. Bravo!"

Tatiana then added that it was not very expensive and she could afford it from her savings. She asked him if he wanted her to cook some pasta or order a pizza.

Nikos said, "No, not tonight. We'll go out."

"Oh, I can't help it. I have to say it—I enjoy being with you! You're so good to me. I don't know if I could manage without you," Tatiana said with misty eyes.

"You're so sweet to say that, and I appreciate our relationship."

Nikos responded positively in general terms. It had been more than five months since they met, but he was not ready to commit himself to a relationship. Tatiana was not disappointed by his response. She remained faithful to her early promise not to be demanding. Besides, Nikos did not feel it was completely over with Erika. To lighten up the scene, Tatiana told Nikos a few silly jokes while walking to the restaurant.

"What did the patient with the broken leg say to their doctor? Hey, Doc, I have a crutch on you."

She paused to laugh and then continued with another. "Falling in love is like going deep into a river. It is easier to get in it than to get out of it."

She told another. "I don't know your name yet, but it must be Wi-Fi because I am feeling such a strong connection here."

And last, she said, "Can I borrow a kiss from you? I promise you that I will give it back."

SAMEER ZAHR

Nikos laughed loudly, noticing her hints of affection, and asked her, "Where do you get these jokes from?"

She answered, "Online. Where else?"

The rest of the evening went very well. During dinner, Tatiana shared her future expectations once she was qualified to work as a buyer in the big stores. Nikos told her that he wanted to introduce her to his new friend, James, who was going to be free for lunch on Saturday.

*   *   *

It was arranged for the three of them to meet for lunch on Saturday, and James was bashful meeting the beautiful Tatiana. She succeeded to loosen him up by telling him how much she admired his decision to be a spiritual leader.

He responded by saying, "I don't know how spiritual I'll be. Nikos and I talked about that, and I hope I can succeed to bring about a new tone of spirituality into my Christian environment. How about you, Tatiana? Any interest in spirituality?"

"Uh . . . I was born an Eastern Orthodox Christian, but I never really paid any attention to my religion. My parents did not take me to church or Sunday school, so I grew up in a secular world. My parents taught me to have good manners, not to lie, to be humble, and to live a happy life. So I don't know how to really practice spirituality," Tatiana said while Nikos was listening attentively.

Then James said, "If I may say, you do not study how to become spiritual. It is a mind-set and a desire that can be tuned. You have already practiced some spiritual attributes by following the advice of your parents on how to live your life. I assume that you believe in God as the creator of the universe, including you. If so, all you need to do is to learn how to connect with him via the Holy Spirit. Then in meditation, you will be guided accordingly. Nikos, am I saying it right?" James explained and passed the baton to Nikos to respond.

"Please continue. You're explaining it very well, James. If I may just add, we don't need to be present inside a building—call it a church or a temple—to connect with God. We can connect with him anytime and anywhere. That's being spiritual."

Tatiana looked at both these educated men and said, "Wow, what an honor to be in the company of two great minds and souls. I would be delighted to learn more from you, and I am so happy I met you, James. You should come over to Nikos's apartment one evening and try one of my pasta dishes," Tatiana said, looking for approval from Nikos.

Nikos said, "That's a good idea, Tatiana."

"Well! Thank you both, with pleasure."

The rest of the semester was productive, with Tatiana enjoying her new courses, Nikos studying his five courses diligently, and James appreciating his new friendship with them. Nikos continued his debates with James at least once a week, and they both helped each other in the areas they were better versed at. Nikos invited James twice to eat with them before the semester ended two months later.

Though James did not take any more courses at NYU during the following semester, he kept in touch with Nikos, and they advanced their friendship to a closer level.

*　*　*

It was quiet on the Swedish front, and Nikos had not heard from Erika for several months. He thought about her and wondered how she was benefiting from her therapy. Ironically and as if by telepathy, he received an email message from her that day.

Hi, Nikos.

I hope all is well at your end. I wanted to tell you that you are often on my mind. And again, I thank you for suggesting that I should take therapy sessions to control my addiction to uncontrolled sex and to handle my relationships with men altogether.

I am happy to report to you, dearest professor (I mean it), that I finished my therapy last week. The past six months have been enlightening, revealing, and very valuable. I learned how to control my appetite for sex, how not to rush into new relationships, and how to love myself by looking within.

So I passed the test, and now I am thinking about what do next in my life. I am learning how to meditate and connect with my higher self. I am reading self-help books. I am experiencing the joy of going within.

My parents suggest I go back to New York and continue at NYU. I don't know if I can do that, especially if you are tied up in another relationship, as you hinted in your last text message. Please take it as a compliment. You were the only one worthy of my love, and it's impossible to get you out of my mind. It was short but most meaningful because of your emotional sincerity and enjoyment beyond the physical part, which I did not appreciate at that time. While other men wouldn't care if I turned my back on them, you were furious and angry when I did it to you, and I love that about you. I am sorry if I hurt your feelings. I was so naive in understanding and appreciating your moral values.

I owe it to you for pushing me to do therapy. I am sure you are doing well at NYU, and I hope to hear from you when you get a chance.

Hugs and kisses,
Erika

Nikos was mesmerized to receive this good email message. He read it twice, trying to read between the lines and decipher her intentions. He felt confused. First, he did not expect that she would remember him as a loving person, and she repeated her apology about how she had mistreated him. He struggled for a while, and then he decided to sleep on it before he replied.

He would have loved to have a second opinion, but he knew no one to discuss it with except for his brother, Pavlo, which was not a good idea, and James. He decided to call James in the morning and confide in him. He certainly was not going to talk it over with Tatiana. She would not understand why he kept Erika's story a secret for so long. She trusted him with her Oleg story.

He called James the next morning, read him the email message, and explained to him the whole story. He asked him if he could advise him on what to do.

James responded, "Look, Nikos, first, you are asking an inexperienced man in this regard. Objectively speaking, it seems that this lady still has strong feelings for you. Why not? You are a good and handsome guy. Women can easily fall for that. She made you taste the pleasure of physical love in a unique way, not experienced by you before, right? That unique togetherness blew your mind away and put you off-kilter as a first-timer. Then you thought that you must be special and felt entitled to more of the same. So you innocently fell in love right away. But as you very well know, that's not necessarily true love. It was passionate love. The irony is you were the only one who felt it right there and then, while it took her much longer to feel and appreciate your love for her, so it made you angry. Now she senses that she may have lost you, and she regrets it. She now realizes that you are unique and you touched her heart."

"Yes, but, James you're telling me what I already know. Are you telling me to ignore her message, or should I answer back?" Nikos nervously asked.

"I can't tell you what to do. Listen to your heart and find out if you love her in a nonphysical way. Also take into consideration whether you are ready to damage what seemingly is a healthy relationship."

"Thanks. I'll think about it, and I will keep you advised."

Meanwhile, Nikos received a call from his brother, Pavlo, that Wednesday, telling him that he was coming to New York for a few days.

He cheerfully said, "I will come with my new girlfriend, Helena, with whom I have a serious relationship. I followed your advice, little brother, and it worked. How about that, huh, Nikos?"

"You're welcome to stay in the guest room, and I look forward to seeing you again. When do you arrive?" Nikos asked.

"This coming Saturday afternoon. I arranged for a car to pick us up. I can't wait to see you. You're still with Tatiana, right?"

"Yeah, yeah, of course."

"We'll see you soon!" Pavlo said and hung up.

Nikos was going to see Tatiana after her work that day, and he decided to send a reply to Erika beforehand. He prepared an email.

> *Hi, Erika.*
>
> *I received your sweet message, and I congratulate you on your finishing therapy. I am very happy that you now see the light in relationships more clearly. Please don't apologize again as the past is behind us, and I have forgiven myself for screaming angrily at you, and I am sorry it created a misunderstanding between us. It is good to move on and hope for a better life, as you're also doing now.*
>
> *I also would like to tell you that I am seeing a new lady friend now. Her name is Tatiana, and I met her a few months ago, and we hang out sometimes. She lives in Gramercy Park, and we see each other a couple of times a week. We share a friendly relationship, but I can't say I'm in love with her. I respect her, and I enjoy her company.*

She is not you, however. You come from another planet, my dear.

The second year in college is about to finish, and I hope you'll make the right decision as to what you want to do next. I hope to see you soon.

Warm regards,
Nikos

He read the message twice before he pressed Send. He felt better, telling her the truth about his situation. Tatiana showed up half an hour later, and they had a good time together as usual. She told Nikos how much she was enjoying her online courses, and he told her that Pavlo was coming that weekend with a new girlfriend.

Tatiana asked, "Do you know anything about her? Have you met her before?"

"Nope. He only said her name is Helena, and this one, he's serious about."

"Would you like me to arrange something for them when they come?" she asked, showing her desire to help out.

"No, sweetie, it's casual. Pavlo is quite independent, and he knows his way around New York. Thanks anyhow."

"OK, I'll just make sure the bed sheets are clean in the guest room and add extra clean towels in their bathroom."

"Thanks again. That's very nice of you, but no cooking at home, please. Let them go out alone, or we can eat out together. He's coming for a few days only."

"Whatever you say, boss. How about what he likes to drink? You only have wine," she remarked.

"Yes, you're right. We should buy a bottle of scotch and a bottle of vodka. Pavlo likes a good drink. We can buy them tomorrow from the liquor store nearby," Nikos said.

"I can pick them up on Friday on my way if you prefer," she cheerfully added.

"Fine. Thanks anyhow."

"I'll also bring some nice flowers to brighten up the place."

Nikos noticed that Tatiana was going out of her way to be considerate and helpful. After a light meal at home together, Nikos excused himself and pretended he had to read a book. He sat on a chair across from the sofa, where Tatiana was relaxing with a magazine, and he used the time to think for himself.

Why am I jittery all of a sudden? Is it the email exchange with Erika, or is it the efforts by Tatiana to show me that she loves me? If I had to choose one of the two, who would it be? I cannot make a choice at this stage in my life. I am dedicated to my studies, and a committed relationship could be distracting.

Do I take Tatiana for granted? Would I be OK if she decided to leave me? I prefer if we keep this relationship as it is now and not turn it into a long-term commitment. I prefer not to be alone all the time. I am flattered by her evident love for me, and I am sure it might not be easy to find another woman, except for special Erika, who is beautiful, sexy, loyal, and funny too. I hope that Tatiana will tolerate my cold response to her. With Tatiana around, I'm able to focus on my studies, but why do I miss erratic Erika sometimes?

When Nikos was finished with his thoughts, he closed the book, looked at Tatiana with a big smile, got off his chair, and moved to the sofa to sit next to her. They hugged and kissed before it was time to go to bed.

CHAPTER 6

PAVLO AND HELENA arrived Saturday afternoon, and the doorman notified Nikos of their arrival. Both Nikos and Tatiana waited for them at the main door and greeted them warmly with hugs and kisses. After drinking some water, the new couple excused themselves to take a shower. Before they came out again, Tatiana told Nikos that she liked Helena already. She was in her early twenties, a slim brunette with a beautiful face, big brown eyes, and a sharp nose. Helena was about five feet and seven inches and was working in the shipping business with her father, a ship owner. She was highly educated and spoke very good English.

They came out of their room thirty minutes later, looking fresh and well groomed. Outgoing Pavlo asked, "What do you have for a drink, guys?"

Nikos answered, "We have whiskey, vodka, and wine. What would you like?"

"Whiskey—whiskey at this hour, my man! How about you, Helena?"

"I'll have a glass of white wine—if you have it?"

"I'll join you, Helena," Tatiana said and asked Nikos, who was preparing the drink for his brother, if he cared for a glass of white wine too.

"I'm good, thanks," Nikos replied.

They remained standing in the living room for a while and enjoyed some canapés and mixed nuts with their drinks. The four of them sat down and continued their general chitchat. Tatiana spoke mostly to Helena, while Nikos caught up on the latest family news from Pavlo.

While the two men moved away from the sofas to refill their drinks, Pavlo asked Nikos in a low voice, "What do you think of Helena?"

Nikos gave him the "thumbs up" gesture.

Pavlo then asked him if all was OK with Tatiana, and Nikos nodded with a smile. He then whispered, "We'll talk later."

Around seven in the evening, Nikos suggested they all go to dinner at Cipriani, and Pavlo said yes right away. Nikos called the restaurant and reserved a table at seven thirty.

Meanwhile, Nikos asked Pavlo, "How long have you two been together?"

"Two and a half months now, right, Helena?"

She nodded and asked, looking at Tatiana, "How about you?"

"Um . . . about seven months, right, Nikos?" Tatiana answered.

Nikos said, "It feels like seven years. It's harmonious."

"Oh, how sweet of you to feel that way, my dear. It's so true," Tatiana said.

Helena could not help herself but told Tatiana anyway, "Goodness me! You have such beautiful green eyes."

"Thank you. Both my parents have similar eyes. So I'm lucky, I guess."

"How about we go to eat now?" Nikos said while patting Tatiana softly on the back.

As expected, the dinner was great, and they all enjoyed the good food prepared by the chef. They spoke, laughed at Tatiana's jokes, and drank two bottles of red wine before they went back up for a good night's rest. Sunday was a day of rest for Tatiana and Nikos. Pavlo chose to take Helena out to show her New York and its main tourist attractions. They even enjoyed dinner alone.

On Monday morning, Tatiana was the first to get up, shower, and get dressed to be at work by nine o'clock. Nikos took it easy because his first class was not until eleven. By the time he came out at nine thirty, he had found Pavlo in the kitchen preparing coffee. Helena was still taking it easy in bed.

"Kalimera!" Pavlo looked back at Nikos and greeted him.

"Good morning to you too," Nikos answered.

They sat together around the kitchen table and started drinking their coffee with happy smiles on their faces.

"So . . . what's new?" Pavlo asked.

"Erika sent me a message asking if we could get back together," Nikos replied.

"What? And?" Pavlo grinned and sat straight up at the table.

"I told her the truth—that I have a girlfriend."

"Good for you, Nikos. Try not to lose her. She's good."

"Her ex-boyfriend tried to get her back, and he ransacked her apartment when she said no," Nikos quietly said.

"Did she report him to the police?

"Yes, they took care of it. He is now persona non grata in the United States."

"Good! Do you love Tatiana?" Pavlo asked, curious.

"I'm not sure—"

"What do you mean?" Pavlo said before Nikos could finish the sentence.

"I feel that she maybe loves me, but I don't feel that way toward her."

"Why?" Pavlo looked irritated.

"I don't know. It's just too early for such a commitment. Besides, she's cool about it," Nikos said defensively.

"What? Are you nuts? Of course, she'll leave you if you don't show her affection. Soon, she could change her mind and look elsewhere. Trust me. I know women," Pavlo explained, pointing his fingers at his chest.

"What are you saying?" Nikos asked.

"What are you afraid of? That she'll bite you? Ask yourself first if you love her. If so, don't be afraid. You're almost twenty-one, and I can tell both of you are happy together. What more do you want?" Pavlo said emphatically to awaken his brother from his deep slumber.

"Fine, I don't know if I truly love her. I think I still have feelings for Erika."

"What?" Pavlo asked, though shocked.

"Yeah . . . she's always in my mind, and now she straightened out her act. Anyhow, how about you, 'love expert'?"

"I followed your advice. I got tired of running around and called Helena, whom I had met socially a few times before. Her father is a friend of Dad's. They're in the same business of owning cargo ships, and she's a very decent woman. We love each other, and we are not shy about it. We plan to be together for the long term," Pavlo said firmly and happily.

"Congratulations. I admire your change from your past lifestyle, and I admire your decision to focus on the one you love. She's wonderful, by the way. I like her, and good luck," Nikos said.

"Thanks. And good luck to you too, Erika lover," Pavlo said sarcastically and then stood up to go check on Helena.

SAMEER ZAHR

Nikos stayed in the kitchen for a few more minutes to regroup. He then went to their room and stood outside the door and said, "I'm leaving now, and I left you an extra key on the coffee table. Enjoy your day, and see you this evening!"

Pavlo heard him and opened the door, hugged him, and said, "I love you, man. Have a good day!"

*   *   *

Nikos met with James at a nearby café after his last class at four o'clock. They briefed each other on the latest. Nikos told him that his elder brother, Pavlo, was in town with his girlfriend. He also told James that he sent a truthful message to Erika, telling her that he was with Tatiana now and wished her well.

Nikos moved closer to talk to James and asked him, "James, I know you are a religious man seeking deeper spirituality in your life. How about your moral values while you are still a student? Do you believe premarital sex is, um, sinful?"

"Interesting question. As a friend, I tell you that I struggle with this. First, I have not yet decided whether I want to be ordained as a Catholic priest after my graduation. I may become a scholar instead, like many graduates choose to do. I personally believe that Catholic priests should be allowed to marry. Look around at the amazing number of sex abuse by many priests who are caught doing it. I think it's wrong that priests should not get married. All other Christian faiths allow marriage. Having said that, in my opinion, it is preferred *not* to have premarital sex not only for devout Catholics but also for everyone. But who am I to judge? I know that it is not practical advice as premarital sex has become the norm in most cases," James explained in more detail.

"I hear you, but is it sinful? Take my situation as an example."

"Again, I am not a judge of people's behavior. I also prefer not to use the word *sin*, though it is repeatedly mentioned in the New Testament. I prefer the term *oversight* because humans are not perfect. I believe in the concept of love in all its aspects—spiritual, social, or physical. God is love. It is more a question of when the physical part is to be engaged. Each one of us can be his own judge of its timing," James said.

"I appreciate your liberal observation in this regard. Were you ever in love with another woman before?" Nikos curiously asked.

"Yes, of course. I am twenty-two now, but I had a girlfriend until three years ago. I also had sex with her. She left me and broke my heart. I loved her deeply. Perhaps that is why subconsciously, I chose to study divinity," James responded.

"Have you gotten over her by now? Did you forgive her?" Nikos asked.

"Oh, yes to both questions. In a way, I am grateful to that experience. It taught me a lot about myself, and I am truly enjoying my current education. If I discover that I have an urge for physical love, I promise you, I will not become a priest. I have to be honest with myself," James replied in all sincerity.

"So you don't have such an urge now?"

"I don't, and I respect my abstinence."

On Monday, the day before Pavlo and Helena planned to return to Athens, Tatiana convinced Nikos before she went to work to let her cook her special pasta for them. She added that she would bring a good selection of French cheeses and baguettes plus two great bottles of red wine with her after work. She was so loving, almost begging him to agree, and he succumbed to her hospitable attitude.

Pavlo and Helena were back home around seven in the evening. They walked in, smelling a delicious scent coming from the kitchen. They knew that Tatiana was already cooking dinner and walked straight in to join her. Helena offered to help, but Tatiana insisted they go and rest and have a drink with Nikos in the living room.

Tatiana prepared a beautiful spread at the dining table with candles and some flowers. She used the special china and cutlery that Irene had bought long ago. Around quarter to eight, she walked out from the kitchen and announced that dinner was ready.

They all moved toward the dining room, and she heard them say, "Wow," one after the other. They started with her special pasta dish and salad on the side. The pasta was delicious, accentuated with the special red wine she had brought along.

They talked and laughed for an hour. Then Tatiana brought in the big cheese board with the bread, and they all dug in with pleasure. That took care of another hour of enjoyment. The surprise was the special tiramisu dessert she had ordered from Cipriani, which she served them with the coffee of their choice. The dinner party was finished around eleven. They all got up, thanking Tatiana for her great hospitality. The men moved to the living room for an after-dinner drink, while the ladies cleaned up the table and the dishes.

Before going to sleep, Nikos expressed his real appreciation of what Tatiana had done to create such a great dinner and atmosphere but had reservations about her.

Pavlo and Helena said goodbye the next morning, knowing they would not be seeing them when the car picked them up at 2:00 p.m. to take them to JFK Airport.

*   *   *

Exams for the second semester were within a week. Tatiana still had another seven months of studying online. Nikos told her that before the summer break, he would like them to go away on vacation for about ten days before he returned for his three summer courses. She could still do her homework online from anywhere. He gave her a choice between any of the countries in Western Europe or anywhere in the United States.

Tatiana thought for a while and said, "You know what I would really like? To visit other states in this great country. How about California? I hear it's beautiful."

"Good idea. It also crossed my mind. How about we fly to Los Angeles, spend a couple of days, rent a car, and drive the coastal highway all the way to San Francisco? I heard it's a beautiful drive."

"That sounds great!"

The exams were completed, and Nikos did extremely well. He registered for three more summer courses, which would bring his total credits to seventy-eight, leaving him with a balance of forty-two credits to reach the 120 required for his BA degree. He knew he could finish this balance of credits in two semesters next year, thus graduating with his bachelor's degree at the age of twenty-one.

Five days before the start of their vacation, Tatiana unexpectedly received an urgent text message from her mother in Moscow informing hcr that her father had a heart attack and was in the hospital. She immediately called her mother, who said that her father was in a coma and was being closely monitored in the intensive care unit. Tatiana was shocked to hear the news and happened to be at home with Nikos at that hour. She was trembling when she approached Nikos to tell him the story.

They sat together at the sofa, and she nervously said, "I should go see him, but honestly, I am afraid that Oleg would do something to detain me. I know how close he is with the immigration people at the airport, and he has many friends among secret-service agents. What would you do if you were in my place, sweetheart?"

"Tatiana, it's been more than five months since he was here last. The authorities in Moscow were also alerted to keep an eye on him. Besides, how would he know you're in Moscow? I wouldn't be afraid."

"Dear Nikos, you don't know this man. He's like a loose cannon. In Russia, people like him can easily go above the law and get away with it. He is a very vengeful person, and I bet you he's still watching me closely. Please tell me what to do . . . please!" Tatiana begged him, holding his hand.

Nikos stood up and started pacing back and forth in the big room in silence. After about a minute, he spoke. "We have to forget about the California trip now. If you can mc get a Russian visa, I'll go with you."

Tatiana could not believe what she had just heard. She jumped out of the sofa and ran to hug him, still sobbing. When she calmed down a bit, she said, "My dear, I know the consul, and he respects me. I can explain to him my story, and I am certain he'll grant you an entry visa within a couple of days instead of the normal two weeks. Let's go tomorrow morning and check it out."

"Fine. We'll go around nine. But tell me, is he still a good friend of Oleg's? If so, he will notify him, and that will blow everything apart," Nikos smartly said.

"Oh, he hates Oleg! Why do you think Oleg was sent back to Moscow? He was lobbying to replace the consul, and when he found out, he pushed Oleg away. Anyhow, I'll tell him to keep the news to himself."

"OK, you'll be the judge of that," Nikos said.

At the Russian consulate in New York, Tatiana was well received, and she managed to see the consul, Igor Piskov, right away. He was happy to see her after a long time, and he was aware that she was no longer together with Oleg, who used to work for him. She confided in him the reason why she would like Nikos to get an expedited entry visa: her father was in a coma in the hospital. She did not show any fear that Oleg might give her a hard time. She said that Nikos, her new boyfriend, had not been to Moscow before, and he would like to accompany her to also meet her family.

The consul, Mr. Piskov, thought for a few seconds and looked at Tatiana. He said he'd do it and that Nikos could come back to get the passport with the visa in forty-eight hours. Tatiana was very grateful to him and told him in Russian she would appreciate if he'd keep Nikos's visit confidential. He understood and agreed.

Nikos booked two business-class tickets to Moscow, departing from JFK in three days and returning a week later. Tatiana booked for them a room at a decent hotel near the hospital. She also called her mother to tell her about their arrival time after three days.

Tatiana stayed with Nikos during the waiting period before their departure. She called her mother every day to check on her father. He was still in a coma with no noticeable change in his condition.

*   *   *

Nikos got the visa, and the two of them boarded the plane on schedule. The flight was overnight, and Tatiana was nervous and could not sleep during the overnight flight. While having dinner on board, Nikos asked Tatiana to tell him more about her family and her upbringing. He also intended to deviate her attention from being nervous to a different subject.

Tatiana responded, "First, my father, Alexey, is fifty-six years old, and he has been in good health until the last couple of years, when his business started going downhill."

"Why? What was his career like?" asked Nikos.

"He's a mechanical engineer who worked in a steel factory for fifteen years and then started his own international steel-trading company sixteen years ago, mainly exporting steel products to Asian countries. His business was OK and his health too when I left Moscow three years ago. My mother, Tamara, lately had been telling me that he was under a lot of stress. He also smokes a lot, and he gained weight—"

"Sorry to interrupt you, but this explains why he had a heart attack, don't you think?" Nikos said.

"Most probably, yes. He also stopped working out, and he worried a lot about his falling business, according to my mother. You will see him. He used to be a very good-looking, strong man. They were married twenty-eight years ago, and I have an elder brother, Mikhail, twenty-six years old, who works with my father and is still single but has a girlfriend, Luda. He's also very handsome, tall, with green eyes like mine—"

"Tell me about your mother. How is she taking it now?" Nikos interrupted her again.

"My mom is a very strong woman, fifty-five, was born to a member of the communist party during the Soviet regime. She loved my father when they had met at the university and now has an executive position with a government agency. She's a gorgeous, tall, with dark-blonde hair and beautiful green eyes. She's added a few pounds the last ten years, but she carries it well. You'll like her because the two of you think alike. I mean, she only makes decisions that make sense and that are based on logic."

"Uh-huh. Good to know decisions that make sense. And how about you, smart girl? Did you do well in school?" Nikos asked.

"Eh, not bad. I'm not as smart as you are though. I spent a lot of my time playing tennis and daydreaming. I had a few boys running after me, but I had no interest except in one whom I had met on the tennis court. He disappeared after his graduation from high school. He's two years older than me. Other than that, I was a serious student, abiding by my mother's rules."

"How about work?"

"Well, after one year in college, I got bored and dropped out because I was offered a job at Valentino that later brought me to New York and to meet you, the great Nikos Bestidis."

After dinner, Nikos managed to rest for a couple of hours before the plane landed at ten in the morning at the Sheremetyevo International Airport in Moscow.

*　　*　　*

At the immigration passport-checking section, Tatiana went to the line for Russians citizens, while Nikos stood in the line for foreign visitors. They both made it through smoothly, and they hugged when they both cleared through, feeling more relaxed that the entry went without any hurdles. Tatiana was beside herself with joy.

They took a taxi straight to the hospital, the European Medical Center, in the center of the city. She texted her mother, saying they had arrived and were on their way to the hospital. Nikos suggested they drop their bags at the hotel first, which was close to the hospital anyhow. She agreed, and they both checked in at the Hotel Metropol Moscow and told the driver to take them there instead.

They went to their junior suite at the hotel, took a quick shower, changed their clothes, and took another taxi to the hospital. That was Nikos's first visit to Moscow, and he was impressed with the old historic buildings in the center. Ten minutes later, they were at the hospital and proceeded directly to the designated section and the ICU. They picked up a bouquet of flowers from the hotel shop to take with them.

Tatiana saw her mother from a distance in the hallway, sitting outside the ICU unit, and she ran toward her. They hugged with teary eyes. Tatiana looked through the glass window and saw her father in bed, hooked up to all kinds of tubes, and she cried. Nikos approached, and he was introduced to Tamara, the mother. She hugged him and thanked him for accompanying Tatiana. They all walked in quietly to the room where Alexey was. Tatiana leaned over and kissed his forehead and held his hand.

Tamara told her there were little signs of hope since yesterday as he had started moving his toes. His long rest for about a week now might have healed a part of the damage caused to his heart, but the doctors would not guarantee that he'd come out of the coma. The three of them stood silently for about ten minutes before they stepped out again to talk. The ladies spoke in Russian as Tamara's English was limited. Nikos did not mind, and he worked on the mobile phone to check his messages. One email message was from Erika in reply to his last more than three weeks ago.

> *Hi, Nikos.*
>
> *I apologize for the delay in answering your last message. I was in bed for a month treating another fatigue attack, and the doctor said it is a chronic hepatitis C virus caused by some earlier infection. Luckily, it's curable, and now I feel much better.*
>
> *I am happy to hear that you are with Tatiana, who seems to be a good girl. Is she Russian, by the way? Anyhow, I felt jealous because I can't get you out of my mind.*
>
> *I might come to visit my parents this summer when I feel strong enough again. I'll let you know. Perhaps we can see each other again. Can we still be friends at least?*
>
> *Stay well, and all the best,*
> *Erika*

Nikos scratched his head and looked around. He went to a water fountain nearby and quenched his thirst and wetted his mouth, which had dried up from reading Erika's message.

Tatiana looked at him and asked him, "Are you OK? Thirsty? What was that you just read? Did it disturb you?"

"Well, an old classmate of mine sent me a message saying that she suffered from hepatitis C and was now being treated. She's so young, and I never thought it could attack young people." Nikos composed himself before he could answer her with the truth. Then to change the subject, he added, "I'm getting hungry. Would you two like to go and grab a bite with me in the hospital cafeteria?"

Tatiana asked her mother in Russian, who said she preferred to stay near Alexey. Then Tatiana said, "Why don't you go back to the hotel and order room service? You may take a short rest in the room too. I am not hungry, and I will stay here with my mother for a couple of hours. I will take a taxi later and join you. Perhaps we can all have dinner together with my mother and my brother too?"

"OK, that sounds good. Besides, I don't feel so good in hospitals. They creep me out. Can you give me some rubles for the taxi? I don't have any."

"Of course. Here you are. I will text you before I leave here." Tatiana reached into her purse and pulled out a bunch of rubles and gave them to Nikos, who excused himself and said goodbye to Tamara.

*   *   *

Nikos went on his way to the hotel while Tatiana stayed with her mother, catching up on the latest gossip. She expressed how she appreciated Nikos and how grateful she was to have him in her life. Half an hour later, she froze in her seat when she saw a young man dressed like a doctor walking in the hallway toward where she was sitting. She was sure she knew him from ten feet away.

As he came closer and closer, she hollered at him and shouted, "Dmitri?"

He stopped walking and looked back, his eyes opened wide. "Tanyushka?" he said, using the nickname for Tatiana.

"Yes, it's me. Where have you been hiding the past seven years?"

"I am a doctor now. I finished my MD earlier this year, and I'm an intern at this hospital," Dmitri said in Russian.

"Wow! What a surprise to see you here. By the way, this is my mother, Tamara. Mom, this is Dmitri—I mean, Dr. Dmitri Romsakov, my friend from high school."

They shook hands, and her mother said, "Yeah, I remember. You used to talk about him a lot."

Then Dmitri was embarrassed and asked Tatiana, "What brings you here?"

Tatiana pointed to the room through the glass and said, "This is my father, Alexey. He had a . . . a heart attack a few days ago, and he's been in a coma. I arrived from New York this morning."

"Wow, may I go in and look at his chart?" he asked Tamara.

"Yes, of course."

The three of them walked into the room. Dmitri looked at Alexey's pale face and then at his chart at the end of his bed and started reading it silently. Then he said, "Sorry for this incident. But he's in the hands of very good doctors, including the head of the cardiology department. Let's hope for the best."

Then they stepped out. He looked at Tatiana and asked, "Did I hear you say New York?"

"Yes, I've lived and worked there for about three years now."

"Wow. I plan to be working at Mount Sinai Hospital in Manhattan. I start in less than three months for a year or two. I hope we can see each other in the big city."

"Sure. This is my mobile number, and please call me when you arrive. I'm so happy to see you again despite the current, um, circumstances," Tatiana nervously said.

"Great, and I'll give you my number here. That's if you have time to get together before you go back. Excuse me. I have to run to a meeting now. Great seeing you," Dmitri said and walked on. He looked back after a few steps and gave Tatiana a smile while shaking his head.

Tamara looked at Tatiana, who was frozen in her seat and looked absent in another world. She took Tatiana's arm and shook it, asking in Russian, and "is he the one you were head over heels in love with in high school?"

"Yes, Mom, who else? I tried for three years to find him to no avail. He just disappeared. I loved him so much during his senior year. I was sixteen, and he was eighteen, his last year in high school." Tatiana stuttered when she said it.

"How do you feel now that you found him?" her mother asked.

"How? My heart dropped when I saw him. He is, eh, the most handsome Russian man I ever met and the nicest. Not to forget the biggest love of my life," Tatiana said with misty eyes.

"So! What are you going to do? Call him? Or see him in New York? How about your friend, Nikos, who's been so good to you? Do you love Nikos?"

"Yes. Nikos is a wonderful young man, and I promised to be loyal to him. What do I do now?" Tatiana responded.

"Do you love him the same way you loved Dmitri?"

"I don't know, Mom. I am in a state of shock now. Ask me later."

Tatiana walked over to the water fountain for a drink just to be alone away from her mother's pestering questions. An hour later, she said she would go to the hotel and rest for a while. Perhaps they could have dinner together. She walked into the room again and stood by her father's bed for two minutes, kissed his forehead and his hand, and left.

She entered the room at the hotel and found Nikos sleeping. She snuck in next to him and hugged him. She was too uptight to fall asleep, so she seized the quiet opportunity to dig into her mind and think of what she should do next. His image in his doctor's attire remained so vivid in her mind.

She asked herself, *Assuming Dmitri is still available, should I try to reignite the love we had before? Would he still feel the same way he felt for me before when he used to be crazy about me? Why did he disappear six years ago without keeping in touch with me? Why? Did he care at all? I suffered from a broken heart for a long time after he was gone. Are men such a different species? Out of sight, out of mind? Or is it Dmitri only? Why did my heart jump again when I saw him? Did I love him so much more then, or did he lie to me when he told me how much he loved me? Was it destiny that brought us together again or just a coincidence?*

Should I tell Nikos that I met him and what he had meant to me a long time ago? How will he react when he hears me telling him the truth? Nikos has been so good to me, and I love him for who he is, but the truth is that it is a different feeling than the one I had toward Dmitri then. And maybe I still have it now.

Perhaps I should call him before I jump to any conclusions and find out his story first. Is he free or engaged or . . . married? But I did not see any wedding ring on his finger. Otherwise, I would torture myself for not asking him before he comes to New York. Should I also tell him in the same conversation that I am here with my boyfriend? Oof . . . So much is going on right now. My father too . . . I should not forget why I came to Moscow.

Finally, she managed to close her eyes for fifteen minutes, only to be awakened by Nikos, who turned from the other side of the bed.

"Hey, what time is it? When did you come in? How long have I been sleeping?" Nikos said when they both had opened their eyes.

"I came in half an hour ago, and it is now 5:00 p.m. I hope you rested well," Tatiana said with a low, soft voice, wishing she had slept a bit longer.

"Hmm . . . I'll go take a shower. It'll help wake me up."

When Nikos came out of the shower, he asked her what she'd like to do. She answered that maybe they would invite her mother and brother to dinner to change the atmosphere of the hospital. Nikos agreed, and they planned to meet at seven in the evening at a certain restaurant Tatiana knew already.

In the taxi on the way to the restaurant, Tatiana suggested to Nikos that he should take a private tour of Moscow, which could be arranged by the concierge at the hotel with a guide. He agreed to check it out. The taxi arrived on time at the well-known Savva restaurant in the center of Moscow.

Mikhail and Tamara were waiting for them, seated at the table. Tatiana introduced Nikos to her brother, and they all sat at a round table. Mikhail spoke good English, and Nikos felt comfortable talking to him. Nikos explained what he was studying and why his main interest was philosophy. Mikhail told him about his dad's business and how hard it was to manage in his absence.

The ladies spoke in Russian, and Nikos had no idea what they were talking about. He asked Mikhail if he had a lady in his life, and the answer was negative as he had recently broken up with his last girlfriend. Mikhail was a tall, handsome guy, twenty-six years old, with dark-green eyes and brownish-blond hair.

He asked Nikos how long he'd known Tatiana and if they had any future plans together. Nikos told him he was too young to make future plans, but he truly respected Tatiana and enjoyed seeing her a few times a week. Nikos found him somewhat nosy to ask such a question. The rest of the evening went well, and they all had a good time and enjoyed a very nice meal together.

Tamara was looking at Nikos from the corner of her eye and trying to size him up to figure out if he was the right person for Tatiana. Tamara was taken by Dmitri and became biased, favoring him in her mind.

On the way back to the hotel, Tatiana asked Nikos about Mikhail, and the answer was that he had found him to be preoccupied with his father and the issues at work; otherwise, he found him to be gentle and nice. They stopped at the concierge desk before going to their room, and Nikos arranged for a private tour to start at ten in the morning. Tatiana apologized as she could not join him and needed to be with her parents at the hospital.

*   *   *

When they got to the room, they undressed and put their robes on. They sat for a while in the living area before going to bed.

Tatiana asked Nikos about his impression of being in Moscow so far.

He said, "It is impressive from the little I saw. I am eager to find out more about it tomorrow. How about you? Um . . . how do you feel after seeing your dad?"

"It is very sad to see him like that, in bed with all the tubes trying to keep him alive. I hope he comes out of his coma while we're here so I can talk to him. My mother loves him dearly, and she would be very heartbroken if he does not pull through."

"Have faith and pray he'll wake up soon. I know you also love him a lot too. I am glad that you are feeling more relaxed now since Oleg was not in the scene at all to bother us," Nikos said.

"How about you? Are you still bothered by the email message your, um, lady friend sent you? Who was she anyhow?" Tatiana asked curiously. Nikos did not expect her to ask that question and thought she could be projecting.

"Bothered? No, we took a philosophy course together last year before I met you, and, um, I helped her understand Greek philosophy, and we became friends for a very short while," Nikos shrewdly answered.

"I see. Did she not take more classes with you after?"

"She's not in New York now. She went back home to Sweden last year. She lives there now. Her father was and may still be the Swedish ambassador to the UN. We exchange emails sometimes— as friends usually do. I told her about us anyhow."

"Uh-huh . . . that's interesting. Did you like her? Was she beautiful? Do you miss her?" Tatiana kept hammering Nikos with jealous questions. Perhaps she was projecting her won struggle.

"Tatiana, what's wrong with you? You heard what I said, no? And yes, she's very beautiful, but why are you so curious and feeling insecure all of a sudden? You know me. I don't live a lie."

"OK, OK, I am sorry. I don't know what hit me to ask you these silly questions. Come here. Let's hug and go to sleep. I'm tired. I didn't sleep on the plane, and I only closed my eyes for fifteen minutes this afternoon."

Nikos sensed that her questioning was a projection of something new she was hiding in her mind. He did not dwell on it and let it go.

They woke up around nine after a good night's rest. They ordered coffee and a light breakfast. Nikos got ready for his tour, and Tatiana prepared to go to the hospital again by taxi. On her way over, she asked herself why she had been so untrusting last night. She figured out how nervous she'd been since she saw Dmitri and was acting defensively. At any rate, she wanted to call him to find out first if he was a free man before building a fancy story in her head.

Nikos went on his private tour, and the guide explained that they would start with the Moscow Kremlin, the immense compound of churches, museums, and palaces, and then the Red Square to see the Kremlin office buildings, Saint Basil's Cathedral, and Lenin's Mausoleum. The guide said after a short break, they would continue to see the Bolshoi Theater, the iconic home of Russian ballet and opera. Afterward, they would stop for a light lunch at Gorky Central Park, known for its culture and leisure.

During a short lunch break, Nikos asked the guide for the afternoon program. The man said he planned to stop at GUM, an iconic and huge shopping mall with a glass roof, and then take him to a modern art gallery called Tretyakov, which featured a mixture of modern Russian and socialist-realism exhibits. The guide suggested that they finish the day with the gallery and perhaps continue with more monuments and attractions the next day.

*   *   *

Meanwhile, Tatiana was at the hospital with her mother, who had been there since eight in the morning. There was no change in her father's condition. An hour later, she asked her mother if she could use her mobile phone to call Dmitri as her American cell phone subscription did not allow calls from overseas. She excused herself to go for coffee while making the call. She sat down at a calm table in the cafeteria of the hospital with a coffee and dialed Dmitri's number. Luckily for her, he answered.

"Romsakov."

"Hi, Dmitri, this is Tatiana. How are you?"

"Tanyushka, hi. Thanks for calling. Where are you?

"I'm at the hospital. I came to see my father again."

"Oh, great. Are you free for lunch? We can have a bite here at the hospital cafeteria because I have to see some patients now."

"OK. What time?"

"At noon sharp. It's about an hour from now. Is that OK with you?"

"Sure. Um, I'll see you there."

Tatiana came back to where her mother was sitting with her coffee, which was slightly shaking in her hand. But she looked quite happy with a big smile on her face. He mother knew right away that she had spoken with Dmitri, and Tatiana nodded when she was asked and swiftly said, "I'm seeing him for lunch here at noon, Mother."

"Uh-huh. You look excited to see him."

"I am curious to know where he's at in his personal life. That's all."

"And what if he's available?" Tamara asked.

"We'll see. Um, one step at a time."

The doctor in charge interrupted their conversation and came to check on Alexey. And after a few minutes, he noticed some slight improvement in his nervous system and said, "It's a good sign," and left.

Both ladies smiled with a new hope. When it was time to go for her lunch appointment, Tatiana nervously excused herself and went to the cafeteria downstairs. She found Dmitri sitting at a table in one corner. He stood up and had two red roses in one hand. They greeted each other with a kiss on the cheeks. He handed her the roses, and she choked; she could not talk. They silently picked up some lunch and took their trays back to the same table. Tatiana still could not say a word.

Dmitri volunteered and said, "I'm so glad to see you again after such a long time. The flowers are to remind you of the love we had. Please tell me what you've been doing while I was studying to become a doctor."

Tatiana was still in awe of the energy that suddenly swept her off her feet. She then refocused her thoughts for an answer to give him.

"After high school, I spent one year in college, got bored, and left to work at Valentino here in Moscow. Three years later, I was transferred to Valentino in New York. I'm still with them while taking online courses to improve my career in the fashion field."

"You look more beautiful than ever. Wow. I am sorry I did not pursue our relationship. I went to St. Petersburg for my medical education."

"I see. We should have kept in touch. I was very angry you didn't, but hey, this is destiny," Tatiana said.

"Well, I'm sorry, but destiny also meant for us to meet again," Dmitri said with a smile.

"Why? You're not in a relationship now?" Tatiana asked.

"No, I've had a few short relationships off and on, you know, but my focus on my studies kept me away from commitment to any. How about you?"

"Like you, I had a few short silly relationships while in Moscow. Then I met a Russian man who was working at the consulate in New York, but I broke up with him after a while. He was the jealous, obsessive type. He came back to Moscow since then, and we're not in touch at all. However, I must tell you that, um, I have a Greek boyfriend now who agreed to come with me on this trip, to be on my side if my ex-boyfriend does anything silly. He is on a tour of Moscow as we speak. He has been very good to me, but he is a student studying philosophy at NYU, and he's a couple of years younger than me."

"Are you in love with him? I mean, are you committed to him?" Dmitri curiously asked.

"I love him for who he is, but we're not really 'in love.' Um, we don't live together. He's like you were, totally committed to his studies. He wants to become a professor of philosophy." Tatiana intended to be truthful.

"Listen, I'm happy for you. I would have liked for us to be together again, but I will not do anything to disturb your current relationship."

"Dmitri, I don't know what the future holds in store. Do you promise to contact me when you arrive in New York? I still have feelings for you, silly man. And I don't know where this present relationship is going. My friend's mind is not set on nurturing our relationship but on his studies. Please promise." Tatiana beseeched him not to disappear again.

"Fine, I promise to call you when I get there. I still have feelings for you too. I'll be working at Mount Sinai Hospital in New York soon, and this time, I will not disappear. I promise."

They exchanged their email addresses as well and agreed to keep in touch before they said goodbye with a big long hug, and then he took off. Back with her mother, walking slowly and trying to keep her balance, she told her mother that her lunch meeting with Dmitri had shaken her up. She showed her the roses he had brought with him, which they put in her father's room. Tamara was struggling to discuss their situation in more detail but decided to remain silent, surrendering her daughter's new situation to destiny.

CHAPTER 7

NIKOS AND TATIANA reconvened around 5:00 p.m. at the hotel. Tatiana was happy to hear how much Nikos had enjoyed the tour and said he arranged for the same guide tomorrow again.

He said, "What a city, and what a history! Moscow is really rich in culture and beautiful architecture. I am glad I came. How about you? And how's your father?"

"The doctor came and saw him. He told us he noticed some improved activity in his nervous system, and there's hope now."

"Good to hear! We have three more days here, and I hope you get a chance to talk to him before we leave."

"I hope so. Do you want to take it easy tonight and order room service later? Or if you want, we can check to see a Bolshoi ballet," Tatiana said.

"Eh . . . No, I am not in the mood for that out of respect to your father's condition also," Nikos said.

"Oh, that's sweet of you. We'll stay in then."

"How about you? You don't want to contact any of your old friends while you're here?" Nikos curiously asked.

"No, I don't feel like it. I saw an old high-school friend of mine at the hospital though. It's so funny. Hadn't seen him since I was sixteen. Suddenly, my mother and I saw him walking by, dressed as a doctor. We spoke to him. He's an intern now at the hospital.

He just finished his MD. He's two years older than me, but we used to play tennis together in school. What a coincidence."

"Interesting. How did you react when you saw him?" Nikos asked.

"We were surprised at first. We told him we were there to be with my father. He went in to see him but couldn't say anything after reading his chart. He said that my father was in safe hands with the best doctors around," Tatiana reported cautiously without further details, hiding her true feelings. She kept her past love relationship to herself. She did not tell Nikos she had lunch with Dmitri.

Nikos decided not to go further in the inquisition and left it at that. Tatiana was relieved though a bit tense and decided not to elaborate on the meeting she had had with Dmitri.

The next day was a repeat of the day before, with Nikos taking his tour of the city and Tatiana visiting her father together with her mother at the hospital. When they met again in the afternoon, Tatiana cheerfully told Nikos that her father opened his eyes for a short while, recognized her, and held her hand before he went back to deep sleep. The doctors hoped that by tomorrow, he might come out of the coma. Tamara decided to stay overnight with him and promised to text her if he woke up again. Nikos was glad to hear the news and agreed to go with Tatiana to try some traditional Russian food at a nearby restaurant for dinner. Mikhail could not join them as he also wanted to be with his mother at the hospital.

Nikos enjoyed the Russian food they ate but mostly enjoyed the caviar from the Caspian Sea with a shot of vodka as an appetizer. Right before dessert was ordered, Tamara texted Tatiana and wrote, "Dad woke up, and he talked." Tatiana texted her back, saying they'd be there soon. She told Nikos, and they both agreed to skip dessert and to go to the hospital right away.

When they entered the room, Tatiana immediately went to embrace her father with tears pouring down her cheeks, telling him how happy she was to see him again. His piercing eyes were teary, and he tightly held her hand. Then she shifted to English and introduced Nikos to her father. They smiled at each other. Tamara and Mikhail were so happy to see Alexey talking and smiling again. They stayed with him for half an hour and left to let him rest. Tatiana told her father she'd be back again in the morning.

*   *   *

The next morning, Tatiana returned to the hospital, and Nikos told her he would like to go to the Pushkin Museum and spend a few hours there. They agreed to meet again at the latest by 3:00 p.m.

While Tatiana was sitting with her mother outside the room, allowing Alexey to sleep a little, she received a Russian text message from Dmitri telling her how much he enjoyed seeing her again and, in case she was ever free again, to make sure she remembered him as he still cherished the good old memorable time they had together.

Tatiana showed the message to her mother, who right away said, "Hmm. He still has strong feelings for you. You're in trouble now."

"Mom, I can't turn my back on Nikos so easily. I have feelings for him too," Tatiana answered, not sure what she was saying.

Her mother looked at her with a questionable smile and said, "OK, time will tell. Are you going to answer him now?"

"Yes, I should. Um, what do you think I should say?"

"I don't know. Listen to your heart, my dear."

"Opa!" Tatiana responded.

"What's that?" Tamara asked.

"It's a word the Greeks use, um, when they don't know what to say."

"I see! You speak Greek now?" Tamara laughed.

Tatiana sat alone on a distant chair to prepare the reply to Dmitri's text message. She wrote back in Russian.

> *Thank you for your sweet message. I also enjoyed seeing you again very much. I always remember the good times we had together, though you broke my heart when you had disappeared on me. I welcome the opportunity of connecting with you again, and I hope you will keep in touch this time around.*
>
> *Kisses,*
> *Tanyushka*

Before pushing the Send button, she showed the text to her mother, who smiled and said nothing. Tatiana knew that her patriotic mother would prefer to see her married to a good Russian man like Dmitri. Tamara would not say it out loud out of respect to her daughter. But in her mind, Tamara would love to see Tatiana fall in love with Dmitri again. He was a rare find, and her daughter should not lose him. Besides, why stay in the United States? She would love for her to be back in Moscow and have many grandchildren to enjoy.

Tatiana read her mother's mind and said nothing either. What was ironic was that she now had a new conflict that she did not expect. She thought, *In a way, I am somewhat relieved that Nikos did not show me that he loved me. Did I really mean to tell him that I love him? Would it be different than the "I love you" I told Dmitri a hundred times before? Was my love to Dmitri a "true love" or just a crush of passion?* These thoughts tormented her. She prayed for some inner divine guidance.

Nikos sensed her confused state of mind when he saw her after his return from the museum. He had thought earlier that it was her father's condition that upset her. How come now she continued to be tense? They both had kept their secrets to themselves. She did not tell him that she had lunch with the man she had been madly in love with in high school, and he did not tell her about the woman he had had a big crush on either. In an awkward way, they were both not fully truthful to each other.

They had two more days in Moscow before their flight back to New York. Alexey, her father, was resting in his room and out of the ICU but still closely monitored. Tatiana spent the last day with him to cheer him up. They talked about the past, and she reassured him that she would remain closely in touch and visit them more frequently. Nikos spent the morning reviewing his summer studies on his laptop and joined Tatiana at the hospital in the afternoon to say goodbye to her parents.

*   *   *

They flew back home the next day, feeling satisfied with their visit. Nikos liked Moscow, and Tatiana was happy to see her family and to see her father back to life. Seeing Dmitri nevertheless was a double-edged sword, and the thought of him kept haunting her. Once the plane was flying at a cruising altitude, Nikos asked her why she was still uptight when her father was OK now.

Tatiana thought for a few seconds, turned toward him in her seat, looked him straight in the eye, and said, "I don't know. It felt strange to be in Moscow again. First, I was concerned about Oleg disturbing us, then I was concerned about my father's condition. But I truthfully tell you, the unexpected sight of my old high-school friend whom I had forgotten truly shook me up."

"How is that?" Nikos responded with concerned eyes.

"The truth is, um . . . I had a crush on him in high school. I was sixteen then, but I remembered how I was madly in love with him. Then he disappeared all of a sudden. I mean, he forgot about me as if I did not exist. I was heartbroken then, and instead of slapping him in the face when I saw him at the hospital, I . . . I felt happy to see him. Isn't that weird? Furthermore, we talked together for a while and as if he did not do anything wrong, and we acted as if we were still friends again. That, sweet Nikos, unsettled me and made me tense, as you rightfully noticed."

"Wow. I can imagine how you must have felt, and it must be tempting for you to reestablish your old relationship now. Right?" Nikos said sarcastically.

"He, Dmitri, also added to the intensity by saying he will be working at Mount Sinai Hospital in New York in three months as an intern and asked if he could contact me. I told him about us, but I also gave him my number, hoping we can all be friends. Was that wrong?" Tatiana said, wondering how Nikos would react.

"Um . . . it is what it is. We shall see what will happen. Don't think about it too much now. Focus on your work and finish your online courses. The universe will guide you to do what is right in due course," Nikos said coldly.

"You're right, and you're so cool about this. Others would have been suspicious and upset. I truly admire you for this attitude," Tatiana said, feeling somewhat relieved.

They both were quiet for a while, looking through the magazines and pretending the conversation they just had never existed. What Tatiana did not realize were the racing thoughts in Nikos's quick mind. He read between the lines and did not foresee a continued relationship for them in the near future. He then pulled out his laptop and kept himself busy, reviewing his courses, as he had no appetite to discuss the issue with Tatiana any longer.

The conversation between them during the rest of the flight was very light and covered with artificial smiles. The car service picked them up after they had landed at JFK Airport and dropped Tatiana at her place first. Tatiana thanked him for the trip, and they agreed to meet tomorrow evening. Nikos called James two hours after his return home. He told him about his trip, Tatiana's father, and the incident about her seeing her ex-lover from high school.

James sensed that Nikos was disturbed about that story, so he then asked him, "Are you upset that she saw him and they talked?"

"It's not that, James. We all meet people from the past. That's not the issue. I saw how tense she became after the fact. She admitted that she was in love with him."

"Many kids have crushes of some kind in high school. Don't make such a big deal out of it. Relax."

"You don't understand. The guy has an MD, and he's coming to New York, Mount Sinai, for his internship in a couple of months. She also gave him her number and agreed to keep in touch."

"So what do you want me to say, Nikos? That she might reconnect with him and rekindle their relationship? Everything is possible. So what? It's not the end of the world for you, is it? We do not control other people's lives, do we? Hang in there and see what happens." James tried to keep him focused.

"We'll see. It's just that I got used to having her around, you know. It's a light relationship, and it allows me to focus on my studies. I would hate to see it end." Nikos reacted selfishly.

"That's life, Nikos. Don't worry, good-looking guy. There will be others. That's if you can't live alone anymore."

"You said it. I used to enjoy being alone, but I changed since I had met Erika and now Tatiana. I like to share my life with another woman. It's more fun and natural, I find." Nikos admitted his true feelings.

"Who knows? Your lovely Erika might resurface in your life again. Would you consider her if she's willing to live with you?" James asked curiously.

Nikos scratched his head and wondered. "I didn't think about that, to tell you the truth. I might though. It is easier if at first, she lives at her parents' place nearby. Anyhow, it may be just a dream. We'll see what happens with Tatiana first. One at a time."

"OK, tiger, I have to run. Keep in touch—and welcome back!"

*   *   *

Nikos hung up with James and poured himself a glass of wine to unwind. He knew that Tatiana would call him later to wish him a good night. He took his journal and decided to write down his thoughts after spending an eventful week.

Just got back from Moscow, an interesting city rich in culture and beautiful old buildings but with awful traffic jams. I went there with Tatiana to check on her father, who had a heart attack and was in a coma, though he eventually came out of it. I also met her mother and brother. Tatiana saw unexpectedly an old boyfriend from high school and was taken by the incident, which shook her up. She admitted that they were madly in love at that young age. Her friend, an MD, plans to come to NYC as an intern, and he has her number. They agreed to stay in touch.

I am preparing myself to cope with an eventual fading relationship at the expense of her newly resurfaced flame of love. In any event and regardless of the outcome of what might happen, I am grateful to her being with me the last seven months. Tatiana is a good woman and deserves to have a happy life.

As I told James on the phone today, I may have to get used to living alone again, unless Erika reappears out of the blue. She says she is cured from her sex addiction and has become very selective with whom she would share her life with. She said she enjoyed a period of abstinence and said that she still has me in her mind as her favorite. That's flattering, coming from her, a true sex symbol and a super ice-skater.

I admit, I miss her company sometimes. I can't put my finger on the reason why. I might send her a message later to see how she's doing.

Nikos poured his thoughts out on paper and went to bed right after the call from Tatiana wishing him a good night's rest.

*   *   *

Summer courses began two days later, and Nikos was looking forward to increasing his knowledge in the fields of philosophy and spirituality. One of the two courses in philosophy was to explain what true reality was—to explore how philosophers and physicists, from Plato to Einstein and many others, had attempted to explain the nature of the world and of reality. The course was called Reality X. The course summary interested Nikos.

How much can we know of the physical world? Can we know everything? Or are there fundamental limits to how much we can explain? If there are limits, to what extent can we explain the nature of physical reality? Reality X investigates the limits of knowledge and what we can and cannot know of the world and ourselves.

The spirituality course was even more interesting. He had discussed it with James beforehand, and they had both chosen to take it together. It was called Connecting with Spirit, a "personal training program that combines private healing sessions with classroom training in meditation, personal development, and spiritual understanding. The purpose is to enrich your life through the love and wisdom of spirit." This course was only offered in the summer and was open to anyone, not only students at NYU. Students still added four credits to their overall program.

Tatiana came over around six thirty in the evening and brought with her food to cook. She told Nikos they'd been eating out a lot lately, and she wanted to make a meatloaf for dinner. He didn't mind and thanked her for it. She had three more months to finish her online courses and was looking forward to approaching the other big department stores for a job as a buyer. She had prepared a résumé and brought it with her for Nikos to edit and approve. Nikos read it while she was in the kitchen. He corrected a few sentences and words and offered to retype it for her.

During dinner, he told her about his summer courses and how he was looking forward to the spiritual course in particular. He told her she could take it as well; it was open to all. She said she couldn't as the hours interfered with her work schedule.

She asked him, "Excuse my ignorance—what is spirituality anyhow?'

Nikos explained the difference between spirituality and religion. He referred to the course he had taken with James earlier, but he underlined this new course as "an exercise that teaches individuals how to establish a personal relationship with God or spirit by learning how to meditate and develop personally and spiritually."

"Do we need that kind of learning?" Tatiana asked.

"You don't have to. It depends on what individuals seek. It is a personal healing process that helps cleanse the soul," Nikos said.

"I don't understand. Is that necessary to become a better person?" she asked.

"As I said, it's a personal choice. Some may need it, and some don't," he answered.

"You want to learn how to meditate and heal yourself?" Tatiana asked in wonder.

"Yes, why not? I would like to connect with the nonphysical source of all energy, which, to me, is the universal truth—or God, if you like," Nikos stated.

"Wow. A philosopher and a guru. What a combination," she uttered to herself.

"That's right. Each to his own, my dear. I personally would love to know who I am and what my purpose is for being on this planet. I choose my studies to take me in this direction. That's all."

"I congratulate you—and may all your dreams come true!"

Nikos thanked her for a delicious dinner and wondered if she would ever become spiritual. He spent an hour reading before they went to bed, still feeling the jet lag from the trip.

They continued to keep secret what they both were hiding from each other. It was the weekly email exchange that Tatiana had with Dmitri and the one Nikos had with Erika. The relationship between Tatiana and Nikos cooled off on its own. They were preoccupied with the secretive email exchange they each had.

* * *

Ironically, both Erika and Dmitri said that they would be coming to New York before the end of the summer. Erika had decided to continue her courses at NYU and Dmitri to start his internship at Mount Sinai Hospital. Neither Nikos nor Tatiana revealed the arrival information to each other up until about a week before the event occurred.

Tatiana, seated at the sofa one evening, was the first to inform Nikos. "I forgot to tell you. Dmitri contacted me and asked if I could help him find a studio to live in near the hospital. I found him one a few blocks away on the West Side, close to his work on Fifty-Ninth Street and Tenth Avenue."

"That's nice of you. When is he arriving?"

"A week from today, actually."

"That's good. It helps to have a friend in town to help out. Is it furnished?"

"No, he asked me to do that for him—basically a bed, a chair, and a small desk. Are you OK with this?"

"Dear Tatiana, I admire your willingness to help him. He's lucky to have you here. It is not easy for strangers, the first time in the city. Besides, he's an old friend, so why not?" Nikos said, preparing himself to tell her about Erika's return to the city in two weeks.

"I appreciate your understanding, Nikos. I will look tomorrow for furniture that can be delivered right away and have it sent to his new place. He also asked if I could see him when he arrives. I did not answer him as I wanted to see how you felt about it first."

"That's considerate of you, Tatiana. Of course, you should feel free to see him. You want to do that, no?" Nikos responded inquisitively.

"I would like to, and perhaps we should arrange to meet him together soon."

"I appreciate that, but it would be awkward in the beginning, don't you think? I believe you should meet him at the airport and take him to his place. You have the keys, and he would be happy to see you," Nikos said, hinting that it was OK. He had expected such scenes a long time ago when he first learned about Dmitri. Besides, he himself was looking forward to seeing Erika again.

Tit for tat, he thought.

"Oh, Nikos, you are so sweet and a true gentleman! Thank you."

"Hey, don't thank me. This is destiny. We have to be prepared that new changes might occur in our relationship. We go with the flow, as you once said. Why resist it? Get to know your friend again and see if there is any fire between you two still. It is what it is, my dear. Find out," Nikos said.

"Wow! What do you mean? Do you foresee our own relationship ending now? I realize it has cooled off some since the trip, but don't you think we can revive it? Let's not assume anything else now."

"I am not assuming anything. Like I said, we go with the flow. If the fire between us is being extinguished for any reason, we cannot force its revival, can we? No matter what happens, my dear, I am extremely grateful to have had a good time together. We had great fun, and I will never forget your sweet love. So it will always be a win-win situation," Nikos said calmly.

Tatiana moved around in her seat and said, "It's sad to hear you say that. Please let's not rush and assume that it's over between us. Please! I can't visualize us apart. You have been the best, most loving person I know. Let us try to rekindle our feelings for each other . . . please?"

"Sweetheart, it's OK. The worst-case scenario is that we can always be friends regardless."

"It's getting late. How about we go to bed and take an early rest tonight?" Tatiana asked warmly to change the discussion.

"It's all right. You go ahead and sleep. I have some work to finish before I go to bed. Sleep well," Nikos replied with the intent to be alone for a while. The appetite for romance had disappeared. He could sense that Tatiana was still deeply involved with Dmitri.

Left alone in the living room, he thought that he had no right to be angry with Tatiana as he was not that innocent himself either. He kept from her the frequent email exchange he had been having with Erika lately. He was instrumental in encouraging her to come back to New York and to continue taking courses at NYU. Neither one of them was shy to disguise how they continued to feel toward each other. Nikos became quite certain that he'd meet a new Erika judging from her detailed description of how she had spent her days, which started with a thirty-minute meditation. That hope helped him cope with the fading relationship with Tatiana.

The rest of the week was short and lacked the usual romance that existed between them. The warmth between them slowly evaporated, but they continued to be respectful to each other.

*   *   *

The day before Dmitri's arrival, Tatiana was at her place. She called Nikos to tell him that she was going to meet Dmitri at the airport and bring him home. She said she might be late and not to wait for her. Nikos politely said he understood and wished her a good night.

Summer courses were winding down in a couple of days, and Nikos focused on preparing for the final exams. He had enjoyed the course on personal spirituality that he took with James. He confided in James the recent changes taking place between him and Tatiana. He also kept James abreast with the emails he exchanged with

Erika, which had gradually become more romantic and hopeful. In fact, he was not reluctant to tell Erika that his relationship with Tatiana was fading away and why.

Nikos finished his exams for two courses the day Dmitri had arrived from Moscow. He was elated to see Tatiana waving at him when he came out. He was casually dressed in jeans and a blue sweater. He looked awesome compared to the doctor attire he had worn when she met him. She waved at him with a big smile gracing her face. She also was casually dressed and looked dazzling. They embraced, and Dmitri did not hesitate to kiss her on the mouth.

They took a taxi to the new place Tatiana had rented and furnished for him. He unloaded his two pieces of luggage, and she showed him the way to his apartment on the twentieth floor of a new building. It was a very large room, neatly spread with a queen-size bed, a dinette, a relaxing sofa for two, and a small desk with a chair.

Dmitri loved it, and he thanked her profusely with a big hug. He tried to undress her and make love to her, but Tatiana told him to take it easy as she had not yet officially broken up with Nikos. Dmitri controlled himself and understood. They shifted their attention to a beautiful and long conversation expressing how it was meant for them to be back together, and this time, it would be forever. They held each other and kissed to let out some steam, but they both abstained from going any further. Tatiana told him that she planned to tell Nikos the next day that it was over between them and to move her stuff out of his apartment.

She took Dmitri out on a walk in Central Park to have some fresh air and to have something to eat thereafter. While sitting on a bench in the park, she sent a text message, asking Nikos when they could meet to talk. He answered her to come tomorrow around six; by then, he would be done with his last final exam.

Tatiana knew that Nikos already knew what they would be talking about and felt free to spend the rest of the evening with Dmitri. They were back in his place drinking some wine and talking till almost midnight. Dmitri fell asleep around that time, and Tatiana helped him go to sleep and excused herself, assuring him she would be back the next day. His work at the hospital did not start till the following Monday anyhow.

Tatiana showed up on time to see Nikos. He had arrived at the apartment a few minutes earlier. They had a friendly hug, and he offered her a glass of wine, which she welcomed to get the edge off her nervous feelings.

After a short while, he started by asking her, "How is everything now? Did he arrive on time?"

"Yes, he did. We took a taxi to his new place and then went for a walk in the park, had something to eat, and then he went to bed early, tired from the jet lag," Tatiana answered.

"Uh-huh, you said you wanted to talk. The floor is yours."

"OK, I'll get straight to the point, and I know you know what I am about to say. Um, my feelings have . . . have shifted to Dmitri. This was confirmed also when we saw each other again yesterday. I just wanted you to know that I did not go to bed with him out of respect to you and for us to talk about it first," Tatiana nervously said.

"Mm-hmm. How considerate of you," Nikos said with a smile.

"Listen, Nikos, I can't thank you enough for our good time together and what you did for me. I am eternally grateful for your loving manners and support. I'm sorry if I . . . I hurt your feelings, but the truth is I cannot live with a lie anymore. You know I loved you in my own way, but the truth is I want to be with Dmitri now," Tatiana said with misty eyes.

"I fully understand. I expected that, and don't worry about me. I had the greatest time with you too. I appreciate your honest expression of your feelings, and I wish you two the best. Let me know if there is anything else I can do for you. Do you need help to move your few things out?" Nikos said lovingly.

"No. Not really. I'll put the few things left in a bag and leave. Promise me you'll be OK and try to be my friend if possible. I may call you to see how you're doing," she said.

"Come here and give me a big hug. I'm sure I'll miss you. I have James as a friend, and my old classmate from Sweden is coming back soon to continue her studies, so I'll manage, but I'll miss you," Nikos said and prompted Tatiana to cry.

"I'll miss you too . . ." Tatiana said while still sobbing.

Nikos sat quietly in the living room after Tatiana had left and began reflecting on the evolution of events and the changes that were taking place. The first thing that came to his mind was to write in his journal.

> *One door closes, and another one opens. We truly live in a mysterious world. An old chapter has been closed, and a new one is about to open soon. It has been good all along. I cannot complain. It was quite an experience with Tatiana. I learned that there are good women out there who can be loyal and faithful. She was also truthful when she saw a*

change coming. She respected me as much as I did. I wish her the best, and I am quite grateful for her time with me.

Within five days, I expect to see Erika, who is preparing to come back to school at NYU, to her parents, but as she also said in her last message, she's coming back mainly to be with me. She said, "You would be impressed by the new person I've become." I am now looking forward to meeting the new Erika and getting to know her better during the remaining ten summer days before school starts again.

Nikos felt good writing the above in his journal and decided to call James to see if he was free for dinner at eight at Cipriani. James said yes, and they both met at the restaurant on time. They enjoyed their time, talking about the course they took together and how it encouraged them to practice meditation now that they discovered its true meaning. Nikos was feeling better when he went to bed that night. Before he went to sleep, he wrote a few words to tell Erika that Tatiana was gone, and he looked forward to seeing her.

CHAPTER 8

IN THE BEGINNING of September, Erika arrived at JFK from Stockholm. Her father had arranged for a car to pick her up. She landed around three o'clock that afternoon.

She used her old American phone and called Nikos from the car. "Hi. I'm back, tiger! I can't wait to see you. Are you home now? My mom and dad are not home yet. I'll ask the driver to take my suitcases home and give them to the maid, and he will drop me off to see you first. I'm dying to see you, OK?"

"I'm here. Will I recognize you? It's been almost ten months."

"Maybe not. I look different now—you'll see! I'll be there in fifteen minutes, sweetie!"

When she walked out of the elevator, Nikos could not believe his eyes. She truly looked stunning; she wore jeans and a white top over her gorgeous body. But what he saw for the first time was a light radiating from her face. He opened his arms and ran to the middle of the hallway to give her a big hug. They stood there, hugging for ten seconds, and then they looked at each other, giggling with big smiles. They walked in and closed the door, and they kissed and hugged again. They sat down next to each other on the sofa, holding hands, finding it difficult to start a conversation, feeling choked by the excitement of being together again. They sat there for a while, just looking at each other, shaking their heads, not believing they were together.

After they settled down a few minutes later, Nikos offered her a glass of wine and said, "I swear, you look different! There is so much inner energy radiating from you. What did you do?"

"Nothing physical. I'll tell you why you see me differently now. I am also wearing my invisible inner beauty, which I manifest on the outside as well," Erika said eloquently.

"Yes! Yes and, again, yes. That's what it is. Wow! And hallelujah! I'll drink to that." Nikos raised his glass and clinked it happily with Erika's. Then he continued, "I am beyond thrilled to hear you say that, and I see its reflection on your beautiful face. How lucky am I to be in the presence of a true angel! Congratulations, and a million times congrats!"

"You're so sweet. Let me hug you again. I can't believe we're together now. I missed you so, so, so much. You are the only man I can say I truly loved, in and out. I'm so sorry I was away for so long, but it was necessary. I'm a much better person now. I know who I am and what I want from my life. I love myself now, and I know I want you, Nikos!"

"I'm so happy for you, and I see it all over your aura. You emanate pure love now, and I should always carry buckets with me to collect the cascades of your overflowing surplus. I can't wait to hear your evolutionary stories. I want to be inspired, and I am all yours too!" Nikos cheerfully told Erika.

"By the way, I registered already to take four courses this semester starting in a few days. One of them is about modern spirituality, which you told me you took. I have also chosen a philosophy course. Anyhow, it's good to be back in school. Gee! You are one year away from your BA, and I am still a sophomore.

Is that fair?" Erika said jokingly and put her hands on her hips to act out her happy complaint.

Nikos laughed and said, "You and I will be students for life. I will be finished with my masters the same time you finish your bachelor's degree. Don't worry."

"Oops, I need to go home now. My mother will be there soon. I promised to have dinner with them tonight. If I'm not too sleepy, I'll come back or call you to wish you a good sleep. Or no, let's be patient to see each other tomorrow. Will you walk me home?" Erika asked.

"Of course, my dear. Please rest well tonight and stay with them. I'm sure your parents missed you too. I am available tomorrow all day. Call me after you wake up—not before eight though," Nikos demanded.

"Yes, boss! Let's go now!"

He walked her home, holding hands and giggling with joy for them being together.

There was a joy of rekindled love on the other side as well. Tatiana and Dmitri were celebrating their renewed love for each other. They met every evening after work and slept together in his place because of his schedule to be at the hospital by eight every morning. Their love was more mature and meaningful now. She mothered him with her love and affection, and he welcomed it with appreciation.

Tatiana had sent out her résumés to the big department stores in the city, mainly the four big ones: Saks, Bloomingdale's, Macy's, and Bergdorf Goodman. Saks and Macy's wrote her back, asking for an interview. She was excited and had to explain to Dmitri how much that meant to her. He shook his head, not understanding the difference of one from the other. He was a doctor after all, not a fashion enthusiast.

She went for her first interview with Saks early in the week and was told they'd get back to her soon. Saks Fifth Avenue found her résumé interesting, and they were looking for a Russian-speaking employee to handle an increasing number of Russian clients. They offered her a job as an assistant buyer. Her salary was 50 percent higher than what Valentino had paid her. She took it going to the interview with Macy's and was very happy to be making more money. Dmitri was paid very little as an intern, and her participation to cover part of his expenses was timely.

Out of courtesy to Nikos, who had inspired her to upgrade her career, she sent him a text message sharing with him the good news and thanking him for helping her toward this achievement. Nikos was glad to hear about it and answered extending his congratulations, also wishing her future success and a happy life.

⁜   ⁜   ⁜

At eight o'clock the next morning, Erika called Nikos and told him she was bringing coffee and croissants from a bakery on her way over, and she'd be there before nine. Nikos got excited, took a warm shower, got dressed, and eagerly waited for her.

She arrived at ten to nine, smiling and skip-dancing in the hallway, happy to see Nikos. He approached her and took the package from her hand before she spilled the coffee with her moves. They hugged and walked inside, giggling together. She had four croissants in the bag, two plain and two almond, which Nikos liked. They sat at the sofa in front of the coffee table and slowly ate all four of them. She told him she woke up at six because of the time difference. She also said that she had a very good time with her parents, who had kept her awake till eleven at night.

"*Min kärlek*, tell me . . . how did you finish it with Tatiana?"

"Sorry, what did you say, um . . . karl . . . what?"

"Oops, *min kärlek* means 'my love' in Swedish. I'm sorry, but you might as well learn that. It sounds good, no?" Erika said.

"Well, to answer your question, it ended amicably. We were both civil and polite, understanding the reasons why it ended. I had expected it since the trip to Moscow, so I was prepared. And she had changed as well since she met her old flame, Dmitri. So it was a win-win situation. The universe timed it so well as it also coincided with your return, so it all worked well. The relationship was good while it lasted, but we were not in love. It was convenient for both of us as good companions. She's madly in love with her doctor friend now again, and they are living together. I am happy for her. She's a good woman and deserves to be loved," Nikos said sincerely.

"You're so sweet and so mature given how young you are. I can fully understand why she loved you in her own way. Any woman would love you. You are a rare breed, sir! Now it is my turn to love you if that is OK."

"I'm so lucky, Erika. I don't want to be loved by anyone else, believe me. Having you in my life is sheer abundance and more. I am blessed," Nikos said confidently.

"Tell me about you and James. How often do you see each other?"

"We used to see each other more often when we took a couple of courses together. Now once or twice a week—it depends on our schedules. He's my confidant, and I like his mind. He has a big heart and will make a great spiritual leader, I'm sure."

"How wonderful. I'd like to meet him," Erika said.

"You will. He knows our story. He always told me, 'Listen to your heart' whenever I asked for his advice. I did listen to my heart as I expressed how I felt in the last several emails I had sent you. I am eager to hear about your transformation," Nikos said.

"Well, thanks to you, Nikos, and after feeling guilty for the way I treated you, I decided to take your advice and have therapy. Actually, it was psychoanalysis—much more intense! I thought I would be done in two months, but no, I needed more, so I ended up doing it twice a week, two hours each session, for six months. What a long process it was! I shoveled out so much crap that I didn't know I had, and slowly but surely, I began to understand what was going on. I started feeling lighter and lighter inside of me, and I learned how to go within and connect with my higher self, to meditate with guidance from guided meditations by Oprah and Deepak Chopra. And then a new me came to the surface, a person whose soul had been cleansed and whose mind had been rewired with good thoughts and happy feelings. There, you have it—all in a nutshell."

"Wow, *min kärlek*!" Nikos repeated what he had learned. "I am beyond words. I better keep my mouth shut for a while to digest this great story of personal revision and transformation. You are a true spiritual being now," Nikos said joyfully and leaned over to hug her and kiss her.

"Again, you started it, Nikos. The angels sent you to me, to help me become a better person. I thank you for your guidance and your sincere love," Erika said while holding his hand with both her hands.

They felt the fire getting reignited between them again, and they gently kissed each other passionately. They could not resist the increasing warmth between them, which directed them to the master bedroom. They spent a whole hour having fun, starting with a warm bath, jokes, and laughs and then hugs and kisses like two fresh virgins meeting and mating for the first time in their lives. It was a new beginning.

They got dressed and decided to take a walk in Central Park. They passed by the ice-skating rink and remembered the fun they had had the first time. Erika offered to continue teaching him to ice-skate during weekends, and Nikos welcomed that. He again and again expressed how thrilled he was to have her back in his life, and she responded equally. He asked her about her health and why the fatigue attacks hit her twice in the last nine months.

She said, "The first time was from stupidly running around, um, in a meaningless marathon of physical pursuits. The second time was in the middle of my therapy while trying to get rid of my anxiety attacks. I feel much better now, and I hope with my new state of being and my positive outlook on life, this thing won't happen again."

"Did you have to take any medication to stay strong?" Nikos asked.

"I did for a while. I also took antidepressant pills and stuff, but since I regained my inner strength, my outer strength was automatically regained too," Erika happily said.

"Wow, Erika, I love the new spiritual person you have become. When you take the course on spirituality, you will understand it better. I also would recommend you to take the one course James and I took. It teaches how to have a personal relationship with the source of all energy or God. As you said earlier, you feel much lighter inwardly."

"Good. I look forward to that. Any plans for the Christmas and New Year's holidays? It is the end of the semester and our winter recess," Erika eagerly asked.

"I promised my family to spend it with them in Athens. I would love for you to join me. What do you say?"

"Oh, I need to clear it with my parents. They somehow assumed I would be with them. I'll see. Maybe they wouldn't mind. I told them how much I love you. Do you care for some lunch? I'm getting hungry again."

"Let's walk back to my favorite place, Cipriani. We can eat some pasta."

On the way to the restaurant, Nikos asked Erika about how she had managed the period of abstinence she referred to in one of her emails.

She looked at him with proud eyes and with a firm smile she said, "You may not believe it—I abstained from having any physical contact with any man for a period of seven months. I, the old horny Erika, succeeded to shut the door completely for two hundred and twelve days, and I am proud of it. You see, I saved all my energy for you. My reservoir is full of love in my heart and energy in my body for you, only for you, my dear."

"Mamma Madonna! What a revision of sorts. What a transformation of character. I am so impressed, you can't imagine. I am so proud of your inner strength that helped you conquer any withdrawals you went through. I love you. I adore you. And I admire you."

"Wow! I'm so flattered. Let's skip lunch and go upstairs. I can't wait. I want you so much now."

"Me too. But take it easy. You need to nourish your body first."

They had an enjoyable lunch and then went back up to the apartment and made love. They took an afternoon nap, which helped shake out Erika's jet lag.

*　　*　　*

When they woke up, Nikos asked Erika if she would care to go to a concert at Lincoln Center as the new season had just started. Erika said she would love to. Nikos checked the schedule online and learned that *Rigoletto* by Verdi was playing at the Met and Rachmaninoff's Piano Concerto no. 2 at Avery Fisher Hall.

When he mentioned this to Erika, she immediately said, "Rachmaninoff, please. I love that concerto. I cry when I listen to the second movement. You will too, I bet you that. Please find us tickets and find out who is the concert pianist."

"I know already, it is Anna Fedorova, the famous young Ukrainian pianist."

"Yes, yes. I heard her play this concerto before on YouTube. She's excellent. Please find us tickets. I can go home and change quickly and come back."

Nikos called and found two tickets in the tenth row of the orchestra section, and he booked them. The concert was at eight, and Erika had two more hours to get ready. She got up from bed, took a quick shower, put her clothes on, and ran out. Nikos told her to be back by 7:15 p.m. at the latest as he needed to pick up the tickets first.

Erika looked gorgeous in a long red silk gown, and Nikos looked very handsome in a dark suit with a red tie. They jumped in a taxi and went to Lincoln Center. He picked up the tickets, and they walked into the impressive hall, holding hands. The first half was the Symphony in C Minor by Edvard Grieg, a Norwegian composer and pianist known for his romantic music. Nikos always thought he resembled Albert Einstein with his hairstyle and face. The thirty-five-minute piece was very well executed, and the audience was eagerly awaiting the piano concerto after the intermission.

Nikos offered Erika a glass of champagne during the intermission, and then they returned to their seats two minutes before the loud applause that began when Anna Fedorova walked in toward the great Steinway piano on stage. She bowed before she sat down, and a minute later, she started. There was great silence, and she played extremely well as Erika had said earlier.

The second movement hit the emotional nerves of many in the audience. Erika held Nikos's hand tightly throughout the piece, and her misty eyes explained the beauty of the soft piano melody of the second movement. Nikos noticed and agreed fully with her sensitive reaction to the romantic melody delivered passionately by Fedorova.

Erika was truly on cloud nine when the concert was over. She thanked Nikos profusely as she had always desired to hear this concerto live. In the taxi going back, Nikos asked her if she cared to go somewhere else.

She looked at him and said, "Only in your arms. I just want to digest this beautiful evening and cherish the good feelings I have now."

"Fine with me," Nikos responded, and they went straight back to his place.

They spent the rest of the evening remembering the beautiful melodies of the concerto, talked for a while, and, an hour later, went to bed for a peaceful and memorable night.

The new semester was starting the following Monday of the second week of September, and the remaining couple of days before then were spent together. Nikos agreed with Erika that he needed at least two nights alone during the week to focus on his studies, and Erika was quite OK with that.

Perhaps later, I can persuade him to study together, she thought.

Nevertheless, they would be seeing each other at NYU as well, and they would be in touch on a daily basis. They agreed to take the subway together to go to NYU every morning. If their schedules allowed, they could also take the subway back in the afternoon. They had lunch together at the cafeteria every day. Nikos asked James to come one day and join them.

*   *   *

James came on Tuesday and met Erika for the first time. He felt he knew her already from all the talk Nikos had shared with him about her. James looked at her and said to himself, *What a beauty.*

Erika started the conversation. "James, I feel I know you already. Nikos spoke highly of you!"

"Don't believe a word he said. He gave me a big headache during your absence. Glad you're back to take some of the burden off me," James said jokingly. He enjoyed the laughter from Erika but not the questionable look on Nikos's face.

Nikos looked at him and said, "Thank you very much, 'Father' James. Are all my sins forgiven now?" They all laughed.

Erika then added, "I can see why the two of you are close. You enjoy picking on each other, right?"

"No, joking aside, we truly cherish our good friendship. It's been insightful and beneficial. I help straighten him out, and he teaches me philosophy," James said while still in the mood for jokes.

Nikos burst out in laughter and told Erika, "You see! Now he wants to take all the credit for bringing us back together. We owe him a big gift, don't we? I wish you had bought him a red necktie from the duty-free shop."

With a happy atmosphere like that, the introduction was superb, and the three of them got along very well. They talked about the concert, and Erika confessed how much she had missed Nikos and how happy she was to be back in NYC, mainly because of him.

James then asked Nikos, "How many courses are you taking this semester?"

"Five for a total of twenty-two credits. I have a balance of twenty credits, which I'll take in the second semester, and I'm done. Opa!" Nikos said joyfully.

"So you'll have your BA at the age of twenty-one. Bravo!" James stated.

"How about me? I want to finish early too, Nikos!" Erika jealously said.

"No problem. Take summer courses as I did."

"No. No, forget it. I want to enjoy my summer vacations with you."

James interrupted their loving exchange and said, "OK, you lovebirds. Erika, tell me about your spiritual experience."

Erika spent five minutes telling him about the process of transformation she had gone through. And she proudly admitted she was no more the crazy sex maniac she used to be. Then she concluded by saying how different and cleaner her inner life had become.

"I can see that, Erika. I've never met you before, but I see your inner beauty accentuating your outer beauty, and that is a double blessing," James said.

"Thank you, and I am very grateful. It keeps me humble."

The lunch hour passed quickly, and they all went in different directions, appreciating the time they had together.

*　　*　　*

One afternoon Nikos left NYU early at 4:00 p.m. Erika had a class at 5:00 p.m. They agreed to speak by phone when she was finished. It was his evening alone to study. On his way to the subway, he was curious to see how Tatiana was doing, so he stopped by her store on Fifth and saw her for a few minutes. He congratulated her on the new job that would start next month and asked her if she was well with her new life.

She said, "First, I want to thank you, Nikos, for stopping by and checking on me. You are a true gentleman. I am fine. Dmitri and I are doing well together. He works hard and late but seems to be enjoying his career. I would have liked for us to spend more time together, but you know how medical doctors are unpredictable with their time. How about you? Is everything OK?" Tatiana asked.

"Fine, fine. Erika is back to school, and we see each other often. She's changed a lot and now is more humble and spiritual than she used to be, so we're OK. I'm glad about your promotion and your new life. Stay well."

Nikos gave her a friendly hug and left. He was happy that there was no bitterness felt by either party from that relationship.

Erika called him at six thirty that same evening and told him that her parents were OK if she went with him to Greece for the holidays. Nikos was happy to hear that and said he would take care of the details. He spent the rest of the evening immersed in his studies for the heavy five-course program he had chosen.

Nikos and Erika spent the following months before the year-end holidays in harmony. They respected the privacy required by each other and loved each other as two mature adults. All previous apprehensions that Nikos had suffered from and all unstable behavior that Erika had lived by were gone. A healthy and stable relationship was established, and it flourished daily with hope for a greater future together.

They ice-skated together on weekends, and Nikos remained faithful to his jogging at least three times a week. He even succeeded to encourage Erika to go jogging with him twice a week at a slower pace. She even walked when she got tired. They just enjoyed doing things together to stay in good shape.

Nikos had already notified his family about the change in his social partners, and they were eager to meet Erika during the holidays. Nikos booked the tickets from December 22 until January 3 the following year. Erika was extremely happy to join him and meet his family. Erika asked Nikos if she needed to take fancy clothing with her. He said mainly casual, but one or two formal dresses might be needed. She told him she only had the fancy gown she had worn at the concert; all the rest were casual, mainly jeans and tops. Nikos offered to take her shopping for a couple of dressy outfits. She said her mother could do it. He said no; he wanted his taste in choosing to prevail.

The Saturday before their flight, they went together to some nice boutiques on Madison, and they chose three pieces: two knee-length solid-color dresses and one nice off-white pantsuit that he also liked on her. She looked amazing in all three outfits. And on the way back home, she chose two pairs of shoes: flats and low heels. Nikos had told her to try not to look taller than him. He also told her there was no need for swimming suits as the weather was still cold in December. Erika asked him how much he had paid so that she could ask her father for the money, but Nikos said to consider them as a holiday gift. Erika felt spoiled and thanked him for his generosity.

Two large suitcases were packed, and the car to the airport picked up Erika first. They arrived at JFK ninety minutes before takeoff.

* * *

They had an enjoyable trip to Athens, and Erika appreciated the business-class seats that helped her sleep for a few hours on the way over.

Nikos was excited to have her with him. He watched her asleep, flat in her tiny bed, and she looked like an angel. *What a difference a day makes.* He reflected on how she was before and who she had

SAMEER ZAHR

become now. He was tickled by the peaceful sight of her and then managed to sleep for two hours himself.

The plane landed in Athens's Eleftherios Airport around eleven in the morning, and the family car and driver was waiting for them. The drive was less than thirty minutes to his parents' villa in Vouliagmeni, on a hill by the sea.

Irene, Nikos's mother, was waiting for them at the main door. She was also very eager to meet the beautiful Erika, whom she had heard about. When she saw her come out of the car, she said to herself silently, *Oh my god! What a beauty.*

Irene hugged her son, who then introduced her to Erika. The two ladies hugged and kissed on the cheeks. Irene held Erika's hand, looked at her, and told Nikos, "Where have you been hiding this beautiful angel?"

Nikos immediately told Erika, "You see. I told you. You look like an angel. Now you believe it?"

Erika was embarrassed and flattered. She said nothing and followed them up the short stairs to the majestic house and its impressive lobby. She kept telling Nikos, "Wow . . . wow." Irene showed them their room upstairs, and Erika jumped on Nikos and threw him on the bed.

She said, "Why didn't you tell me you have such a rich family? This home is so gorgeous, and your mother is a beauty herself."

"Yes, she is, and outer wealth does not mean much to me. Wealth is what is inside, not what you see around," Nikos said while tapping his chest and moving his other arm around.

"I agree with you, my love, but it is good to be spoiled on occasion. Anyhow, I like your mother. She has such good taste in what she did—I mean with the villa—and she also delivered you, not to forget," Erika said happily.

"Come here and let me hug you, my beautiful angel."

They took a shower, unpacked, got dressed casually, and went downstairs. It was around one o'clock in the afternoon when they walked down the stairs to the lavish living room. The butler asked if they cared for a drink, and they settled for lemonade. Both Pavlo and his father were at work and would not be back before six or seven in the evening. The young sister was still at school. Irene suggested some light lunch, like a salad or sandwich. Then she asked them if they would like to accompany her as she still had some Christmas shopping to do. They both agreed to accompany her, and they went together to the nearby Klifada shopping center. Erika had not been in Greece before and was curious to go anywhere they suggested.

While they were shopping, Irene paid attention to Erika and talked to her while Nikos walked behind them. Irene told Erika she'd been to Stockholm a few times, and Erika talked about her parents. After a couple of hours, Nikos suggested they stop for coffee in a café, where they sat at a small table outside and watched people pass by.

Irene asked Nikos, "How could you hide this wonderful lady from us?"

"Mom, after I met her for a short while, she went back to Stockholm, and we've been together since she came back to NYU. Why don't you ask her?" Nikos said while Irene looked at Erika for a comment.

"It's true. Nikos and I did not hit it off well in the beginning. It was my fault. I turned my back on him because I was simply an idiot. I had issues with myself that needed work. After an argument we had, this wonderful son of yours advised me to seek professional help. And I did intense therapy for six months in Stockholm, until I was healed within. I loved Nikos so much, I could not see or be with another man. Again, I say I was stupid to have given him the cold shoulder before. I was too arrogant and stubborn to get what I wanted, which was not a healthy state of mind. I am back now after updating him on my condition by email, and I thank God now for having Nikos in my life. He's by far the nicest and smartest man I ever met—and I have met quite a few! So I am lucky he accepted me again."

"Wow! What a story, my dear. I'm so happy for you two. Why are you so quiet, Nikos? Aren't you happy too?"

"I'm more than happy, Mom. Erika is the only one I truly love. She knows about Tatiana, and she knows that it was not, um, the same relationship. Erika and I think alike and want the same happy future together. So now you have the whole story, and try not to broadcast it around Athens," Nikos said, smiling facetiously.

"Nikos, you don't talk to your mother like that. The story will now be known all over Greece, not just Athens. Happy now?" Irene said half-jokingly.

Nikos looked at Erika and said, "Don't get any wrong ideas. I love my mother. We're good friends, right, Mom?"

Erika smiled, admiring the relationship Nikos had with his mother. Then they left to join the rest of the family at home. They arrived around five thirty and excused themselves to go upstairs for some rest before dinnertime.

Pavlo arrived around six, eager to see his brother and the gorgeous Erika. Irene told him they were resting for a while and how great this Erika was. She described her as one of the most beautiful women she had ever seen and the nicest as well. He asked his mother if she was more beautiful than his girl, Helena.

His mother told him, "Helena *is* beautiful. Don't care about the others. Remain focused!"

Pavlo couldn't stand not seeing them already, and at 6:20 p.m., he hollered from the bottom of the stairs, "Hey, Nikos, you can sleep later at night. Come on down!"

Pavlo woke them up, and Erika asked Nikos, "Who is that?"

He told her, "It's my elder brother, Pavlo, whom I love dearly, though I feel like beating him right now."

Erika told Nikos, "It's OK. Go down, and I'll come down in ten minutes."

Nikos came down the stairs with his droopy eyes and hugged Pavlo without saying a word.

Pavlo then said, "I missed you, man. How is everything?"

"Fine, just fine. Tatiana and I broke up amicably three months ago, and now I am with Erika, whom I dearly love. Where's Helena?"

"She'll be here soon. Mom said that Erika is even more beautiful than Tatiana. Where do you find them, you lucky bas—I mean, shy brother?"

"Erika is different, and her beauty is first from the inside, and the outside completes her. You'll see," Nikos proudly said.

"Let's have a drink. What would you like? Whiskey?"

"I don't drink whiskey. I'll have a glass of red wine."

Pavlo called the butler and ordered the drinks. Irene was in the kitchen, supervising the dinner prepared by the chef. Nikos's sister, Nicky, came down from her room, and they hugged and spoke in

Greek for a couple of minutes. Then they heard Erika coming down. Nikos went to meet her at the bottom of the staircase, and curious Pavlo followed him.

*   *   *

When he saw her gracefully coming down, Pavlo kept saying silently, "Opa. Oh my god . . . Mamma Mia, what a knockout," and he poked Nikos in the back while saying it.

Nikos turned around and told him to stop. Then he said, "Darling! Let me introduce you to my crazy brother, Pavlo, and my adorable sister, Nicky."

"Hi, Pavlo. I've heard a lot about you—and you too, Nicky. I'm honored to meet you both." Erika smiled graciously.

Pavlo, the ex-womanizer, could not stay standing upright and held onto the railing to avoid falling. He was simply dumbfounded and could not say another word. Erika had one of her gorgeous dresses on with her low-heeled shoes and looked dazzling. The light-green dress held her body tightly and revealed the proportionate dimensions of her sculpted shape. Even Irene was wide-eyed when she saw her outside the kitchen on her way to the living room. The two brothers had their drinks and waited for a while in the hallway.

Pavlo took Nikos by his arm and told him, "Brother, you're my hero! What's your secret? I'm handsome too."

"Pavlo, grow up. Helena is gorgeous. Outer beauty is not enough. I am now with a different Erika than the one I first met and now fell in love with. She turned 180 degrees on the inside. She's an angel, and I adore her now. It's her inner beauty that I love. The same you feel toward Helena, no?"

"You're right. Have fun. But my lord! She's so . . . so beautiful too . . ."

"OK! Control yourself now. Get to know her, and you'll like her even more."

As soon as they walked into the living room to join the others, the main door opened, and Yanni, the father, walked in. He gave his briefcase to the butler.

They all stood up to greet him as a gesture of respect. He hugged Nikos and kissed him on both cheeks. He was introduced to Erika, who stood a bit taller than him, and he welcomed her to his home. He excused himself to go upstairs and freshen up before dinner. Irene joined him. As soon as the door to their master bedroom closed, Irene rushed to ask Yanni what he thought of Erika.

Yanni said, "I just met her. I don't know her yet."

"I know. I'm asking you about her beauty, Yanni."

"Oh, that. What do you expect from your son Nikos? He's always with beautiful girls since he moved to New York. I don't know how he can concentrate on his studies. Do you?"

"Nikos is brilliant, and you know that. He used to be so shy— and look at him now! They love his personality also. He's sweet, like you," Irene said.

"Wow, I get a compliment now. Thanks! She's very beautiful and tall, for Pete's sake! Why wasn't I born a couple of inches taller?"

Irene laughed and told him, "You are tall enough for me and great enough as well. Can we go downstairs now?"

"Go ahead. I need a few more minutes. I'll join you at the dining table. I'm hungry!"

They were all standing behind the dining-room chairs, waiting for Yanni to come down. He walked in a minute later and took his seat at the head of the table while asking everyone to please be seated.

Erika was taken by these respectful and traditional traditions. She sat comfortably in her chair next to Nikos and across from Irene, who sat on Yanni's right. Helena arrived late and joined them in the dining room before dinner was served. She was introduced to Erika and was happy to see Nikos again. She sat between Pavlo and Nicky. Helena kept looking at Erika, admiring her beauty too.

Wine was served, followed by the first appetizer. Yanni raised his glass, welcomed Nikos and Erika, and wished them a happy holiday together with the family. They all clinked their glasses, saying, "Yassas," which was Greek for "cheers."

Yanni then looked at Erika and said, "I understand you're from Sweden, a beautiful country with beautiful people. What brings you to New York?"

"My father is the ambassador to the United Nations. He's been there more than two years already," Erika gently replied.

"Are you by any chance related to the Swedish actress Ingrid Bergman? You remind me of her."

"No, sir, I am not. I was told I resemble Uma Thurman except that she is even three inches taller than me. What difference does it make? I am me," Erika answered.

"Where did you meet my Nikos?" Yanni asked.

"At NYU last year. We took a philosophy class together, and he taught me. Otherwise, I would not have understood it. Then I went back to Stockholm for almost a year, and I came back to NYU three months ago to continue my education and to be with

Nikos, whom I dearly love," Erika said courageously with a big smile gracing her face.

"I see. Nikos is a good boy, isn't he?"

"The very best, sir. I congratulate you and Irene for having brought such a unique man to this world. You too, Pavlo. Nikos is truly a blessed soul," Erika said proudly.

"Irene, you and I should not underestimate our son," Yanni said.

"Thanks, Dad, for underestimating me," Nikos jumped in.

"Don't misunderstand me, son. I meant you were shy, remember?"

"Oh. Then it's OK," Nikos said and laughed.

The second course was served, fresh fish from the oven. It was a big fish covered with salt and some vegetables and potatoes brought in on a wheel trolley to be cleaned and cut by the chef standing next to Yanni. It was big enough to serve seven people.

Pavlo had his second whiskey, looked at Erika, and asked her, "First, thank you for equaling me to Nikos. What's your major at NYU going to be?"

"I don't know yet, Pavlo. Actually, it's something I am now thinking about and wanted to ask Nikos's advice in this regard. He's a very good adviser, you know." She looked at Nikos and giggled.

"I agree with you, Erika. He's one of the best. If it were not for him, I wouldn't be with Helena, my adorable darling and future wife. I am so proud of him as my brother. I tell you did well by choosing to be with him—I mean a man like me!" Pavlo said proudly.

SAMEER ZAHR

"Are you kidding me? I am lucky he accepted to even see me again. I hurt his feelings deeply, yet he forgave me. How many men have the strength to do that? I told your mom how he helped me heal my inner wounds and, um, my discords until I rediscovered who I truly am. I've had my good share of going out with other men before, but I tell you, none—and I mean none—are like him." Erika spoke passionately and then turned in her chair and hugged Nikos.

Nikos looked in wonder and said, "I better leave you all to talk about me. Uh, I don't need to listen anymore. Call me when you finish," Nikos said sarcastically and pretended to be leaving.

Erika held him back, and his father said, "Son, we are all proud of you and admire your character. That's all. Please sit, and let's talk about how great your mother is," he said, smiling while reaching to hold her hand and squeeze it.

Everyone clapped and lifted their glasses in her honor.

Dessert was served along with a platter of cheese. Erika ate so well and told Nikos to prepare himself to accept a fat woman soon. He laughed. They all moved to the living room for coffee and after-dinner drinks. Erika joined Yanni and Pavlo with a glass of cognac. They asked her about her country and commented how helpful they were with the refugee problem.

Erika told them that the people were beginning to object the government's open-door policy. It had become a big burden financially and, more importantly, interfered with Swedish culture and social life. She said that the Swedish "spirit" was willing to help, but their "flesh" was getting weaker and weaker. The men agreed with her and admired the Swedish open-door policy, unlike the situation in Greece. Meanwhile, Nikos was chatting with his mother and sister, asking them when they would come to visit him in New York.

His sister said, "I will come if you promise me that Erika will be there."

"Wow, you love her more than me now? I am jealous. She'll be here for a few days. Why don't you spend some one-on-one time together?"

"Yeah, I would love to. She looks like an angel."

"That's nice of you to say, Nicky. I've heard that from other people too."

"OK, Nicky, go to bed please. It's time."

Nicky kissed them both and went straight to Erika and said good night.

Erika grabbed her arm and asked her, "Don't I get a good-night hug?"

Erika reached down a bit and hugged her. Nicky kissed her on both cheeks and said good night to everybody. An hour later, before midnight, they all said good night and went to their respective rooms. It was a beautiful day and night, and they all slept well.

CHAPTER 9

I T WAS JUST two days before Christmas. Yanni and Pavlo went to work as usual. Nikos decided to take Erika on a quick tour of Athens to show her the Acropolis and the new museum nearby. They went in the family car with the driver, as Irene did not need him that day. Nikos was excited to also show Erika the place on the hill where the great ancient philosophers conducted their teachings. He told her he could visualize them debating and arguing every time he visited the spot. They spent two hours walking around the old ruins, and Nikos knew the history so well, they did not need a tour guide.

After an hour at the new museum, they walked down toward the Plaka, old Athens, with its narrow streets, shops, and authentic Greek restaurants. He told Erika that it was one of his favorite places in Athens. They stopped at an outdoor restaurant he knew and ordered Greek dishes for Erika to try.

Everyone around was looking at beautiful Erika with their eyes wide open and their jaws dropped. She humbly smiled to everyone who looked. Nikos bought her a couple of small souvenirs to remember their time together. Around 4:00 p.m., they returned to rest for a while before another dinner at the house.

At home, Erika spent thirty minutes talking to Irene before she went upstairs to rest and join Nikos, who had gone straight up. They bonded together, and Erika was so thrilled to hear the stories about Nikos growing up. She was impressed with Irene's opinion of Nikos and how he had developed on his own to be such a gorgeous young man with great manners, an intelligent mind, and a straightforward personality. Erika felt truly honored to be with such a man and such a great family. She excused herself and went upstairs, gently opening the door. She took her clothes off and sneaked into the bed, softly hugging his back. They slept peacefully for an hour and then got up and took a shower together, got dressed, and were downstairs by six thirty.

*　*　*

Nikos found Pavlo and Nicky already home. They chatted for a while, and then Nikos asked Pavlo what he thought about taking an eight-hour tour on the boat if the weather was nice between Christmas and New Year's. Pavlo told him they had bought a bigger boat, a ninety-foot yacht that Yanni chose. It was very luxurious and had five staterooms. He told Nikos that Yanni intended to invite the family and some close friends to sail on Christmas Day in the nearby region. The climate control on the boat would regulate the inside temperature, and they should have no problem sailing unless it was very stormy. Pavlo suggested, for Erika's sake, to fly to Mykonos for three nights. Pavlo said he would take care of the flights and the hotel.

Nikos thought it was not a bad idea to leave on December 26 and return on December 30. Nikos told Erika what Pavlo had suggested, and she was so thrilled, she stood up and hugged Pavlo with thanks. The weather forecast was supposed to be sunny and moderate throughout the week.

Nikos told his mother that he would like to shop for Christmas gifts for the family, but she advised him not to because she had bought enough for everybody. He told her about the plan to go to Mykonos, and she said, "That sounds romantic. Do it." She whispered in his ear how much she liked Erika and to make sure he kept her.

Erika asked Nikos if she could use the phone to call her mother and wish her happy holidays. He told her to feel free to use the house phone and showed her Yanni's office for privacy. Erika proceeded to Yanni's lavish office and sat on the sofa and dialed her mother's number. They spoke for about ten minutes, and Erika expressed how happy she was and how great Nikos's family was. When she came back to the living room, she told Nikos that her parents would like to meet him, and he was invited for dinner at their home on January 6.

When Yanni came home from work, they all gathered around the dinner table and enjoyed a different meal that consisted of soup, lamb chops, roasted potatoes, and Greek salad. For dessert and coffee, they adjourned to the living room.

Yanni asked Erika, "How do you celebrate Christmas in Sweden?"

"Um, pretty much the same as anywhere else in the Western world. My family is not religious, and neither am I. As Nikos knows, I am a spiritual person who believes in God as the creator of the universe," Erika answered comfortably.

"So you don't go to church?" Yanni asked again.

"No, I don't, and hardly anyone does nowadays," Erika answered.

Nikos then stepped in to help out and said, "Dad, Erika and I believe that we don't have to go church to find God. He is within our consciousness, and we connect with him, um, by practicing meditation."

Yanni's eyes opened wide, and he said, "Meditation?"

"Yes, Dad. We meditate every morning. We are grateful for every new day, and we connect with our higher selves. That takes us to a universal field of infinite possibilities for about fifteen minutes. It's amazing. You should try it," Nikos gleefully said.

"Are you guys normal? Are you from this planet? Is this, um, what foreign education does to your brains?" Yanni wondered.

"Dad, listen to me, please. We are normal people who discovered the truth about who we are. We are not against religion. We just don't practice it ourselves. We've found that spirituality is always with us every minute of the day. That gives us great freedom, and we experience peace, love, and happiness in ways never enjoyed before. Am I right, Erika?" Nikos smartly directed the discussion to her again.

She added, "Well, I can only talk from my experience. As I mentioned earlier, I spent six months soul-searching within. I can firmly say they were the most important six months of my life. I found out who I am and what I want from life. That, to me, *is* spirituality. It is not adverse to religion but more personal and productive. I am now, thanks to the advice of my mentor here"—she pointed at Nikos—"taking a course in modern spirituality to understand its concepts better. I am now living a life without stress, without pain, and without confusion."

There was silence for a few seconds, with everyone looking at Yanni, wondering what he would say next.

Then Yanni soberly said, "I guess that we are all entitled to our own life choices. I admire your choices for your own lives." He pointed at both Erika and Nikos. "And as we say, 'to each to his own.' I admit that evidently, a new wave of spirituality is rapidly surfacing, and we traditionalists are wondering how to cope with its rise. So go ahead and live your life the way you see fit as long as you don't move to an ashram in the Himalayas," Yanni said with a big smile on his face.

Pavlo, who had been silent during the discussion, stepped in and asked Nikos, "Do you take courses to become spiritual?"

"No, you don't have to. Sometimes circumstances occur that lead you to become spiritual, as was the case with Erika. The key is awareness of what's going on in your life. Stop and ask yourself what you really want from your life, albeit with an open mind and heart, and the universe will answer you when it is least expected."

"Mom, Dad, we have a spiritual guru in the family, not just a philosopher! We're so lucky," Pavlo said sarcastically while laughing.

"You need professional help, Pavlo. I mean it!" Nikos bounced back at him.

"Stop it, you two. You're not kids anymore," Irene said affirmatively.

"OK, who wants an after-dinner drink?" Yanni asked to change the atmosphere.

Erika raised her hand and said she'd join him for a cognac. She cracked a joke to lighten the mood. "My psychoanalyst was quite a fat fellow. I used to call him Dr. Four-Chin Teller, and he would laugh his heart out. That always eased the pain. Life is a joke. Let us always laugh about it."

The rest of the evening was spent jovially, and several jokes were exchanged, including many from Pavlo.

They had an easygoing Christmas Eve gathering, including the visit of Yanni's brother, Stelios, and his family. Gifts were exchanged while they all listened to Christmas carols. Irene gave Erika a Loro Piana cashmere sweater and Nikos a soft red cashmere scarf from Hermes. The weather was moderate and sunny on Christmas Day, and Yanni announced the boat trip was on.

*   *   *

They all boarded the new yacht at 9:00 a.m. and sailed in the nearby azure Aegean Sea. The interior was superb, with tasteful decoration and great comfort. The tour was to hop from the island of Hydra to Poros to Aegina and back. A buffet lunch was served on board, and the boat returned by 5:00 p.m. It was a beautiful day enriched with fresh air and warm sun.

The following day, Nikos and Erika were driven to the airport in the morning to catch the short 11:00 a.m. flight to Mykonos. Pavlo had booked a deluxe room for them in the five-star Mykonos Grand Hotel and Resort. They had a nice room with a fabulous view of the sea. Erika was very excited to be there. They went for a walk on the premises and checked out the interesting places, such as the spa and the pool area.

Nikos suggested lunch to be at the hotel restaurant near the sea. Then they would take a quick tour of the island for an hour, come back, and relax a bit before they went to dinner at eight thirty to Limnios Tavern, which he knew well from previous visits. After dinner, he told Erika he would take her to Madon, a top nightclub in the old town, with great music to dance to, both Greek and foreign. He told her to dress casually; even flip-flops were OK.

While touring around in a hotel car, Erika told Nikos how excited she was to be visiting this great island with him. She added, "I pray that the seed of love we planted in our fertile soil will flourish and bear good fruit."

"You mean children?" Nikos said curiously.

"No, silly! Not yet. We are too young. I meant the fruit of love, peace, and happiness, my new motto, LPH. Children are not our priority now. You agree?"

"Oh. I am disappointed. I thought you meant children. I always dreamed to have four before I turn twenty-five," Nikos said with a poker face and looked to see her reaction.

She poked him in his side, and they both giggled with laughter. They had so much fun together and kept their relationship as light as possible.

The day was spent as planned. They rested for an hour and a half after lunch and before dinner. Erika enjoyed authentic Greek food for dinner with a glass of wine and then proceeded to the disco club Madon to dance. They ordered a bottle of champagne and danced their hearts out till 1:30 a.m. It was the first time Erika had seen Nikos dance and have so much fun. Erika was adorable on the dance floor along with dozens of enthusiasts like her with loose and flexible body moves.

The sun was shining the following day, and there were people hanging around the picturesque and heated pool. Erika asked Nikos if they could swim and sunbathe. They went to the store by the pool and bought their swimming suits and sat in the sun for a couple of hours. Erika, of course, looked smashing in her bikini. They had a light lunch in the pool restaurant. They stayed in the room the rest of the afternoon, made love, and took a short nap.

Before they prepared to go out again and while they were still in bathrobes, Erika looked at Nikos bashfully and said, "*Min kärlek*, I . . . I wanted to tell you this earlier, but I did not want to bother you. I think you should know anyhow."

"What is it, my love?"

"You remember I told you a long time ago about, um, a short relationship I had with an American guy before I met you? Well, he saw me recently walking to another class. I tried to avoid him, but he stopped me, asking where I'd been all this time. I told him that I was in a relationship now and to please leave me alone. He laughed and said, 'No way! I know you love me, and I want us back together again.' I said that was impossible and that I had no feelings for him and that I was in love with someone else, and I walked away. He tried to follow me, but luckily, I had already entered the classroom beforehand."

"Who is he, and what's his name?" Nikos asked calmly.

"His name is Tom Bowler, a tennis player on the varsity team. I was attracted to him during my stupid era, but now we have to find a way to stop him from harassing me. Do you think you should talk to him? I noticed him following me a few times, and I always run away. This cannot continue like that."

"I wouldn't mind getting involved, but it could turn out to be a nasty physical fight. I can handle it. Perhaps you can point him out to me or show me his picture, and I'll make sure he doesn't bother you again. I know he can be a pest, but he can't harm you," Nikos advised her firmly.

"Fine, let's report him to the dean when we go back. You would come with me, right? I just don't want anything to disturb our smooth relationship," Erika responded with care.

"I know. Let's get dressed and go out again and have some fun."

They had a nice dinner in a French restaurant, and they went for drinks and light music at the Skandinavian Bar in her honor. They had fun, and he promised to take her the next day, their last night, to dance at the Madon nightclub again.

The rest of the vacation went very well, and they both appreciated the island fun and were ready to go back to civilization on the mainland. On the flight back to Athens, Nikos asked Erika if that guy Tom knew where she lived.

She answered him, "I don't know. I never told him. He only has my cell-phone number, and perhaps I should get a new number. I don't know. He could be a stalker. You and I take the subway together in the morning and most of the evenings, so I don't know."

"We'll go talk to the dean, as I said. If he ever touches you, immediately contact the campus police and call me," Nikos said.

"Why do some people think they're entitled to get what they want from others when they have no idea what they really want for themselves? Anyhow, I am not going to say I am sorry I made a mistake. I have already forgiven myself, and this past history is behind me. I pray he will come to his senses and leave me alone." Erika showed some concern saying this.

"He will leave you alone one way or another, I assure you. I won't let anyone bother you or harass you as long as I live, you hear?" Nikos affirmed.

"Thank you so much, my love. I feel safe with you."

The family car picked them up at the airport and took them home. Irene was there to receive them and was happy they had a good time. Irene was eager to spend time with Erika to ask her more questions about spirituality. The two women sat together in the living room, while Nikos went upstairs to work on his pending courses.

Irene began, "I just want you to know how impressed I am with your story. And how you were able to transform to a more spiritual lifestyle. Was that easy to achieve?"

"Thank you for asking, and I am grateful to be a guest in your home. To answer your question, I wish it were an easy ride. I didn't realize how much mess I had in my system until your dear son Nikos shook me up. He refused to see me again after our short time together, and I really loved him. I suffered from a sex addiction, which made me believe that it was OK to enjoy it with, um, other men of my choice. Nikos found out and was angry, and he asked me to stay out of his life. Other men did not care if I turned my back on them once I was done with them or I had slept with others. Then Nikos nicely recommended that I take therapy sessions with a specialist. So I returned to Stockholm, and that was exactly what I did.

"It was truly a tough period of shoveling out all my dirt. I informed Nikos by email that I was doing therapy as he had suggested. He was happy to hear that and told me that he had a new relationship with Tatiana. I was jealous, but I was determined to improve and get rid of my addiction, which was purely a mental discord. After six months of thorough analysis, I succeeded. The therapist had a spiritual side to him and taught me meditation. I did it, and I loved it. I learned how to connect with my higher self and started feeling much better day by day.

"The email exchange with Nikos was increasingly positive at that time. He was thrilled to hear that I was healed and that I meditated to stay aligned with my newfound lifestyle. A month or so later, he told me he broke up amicably with Tatiana. That encouraged me to go back to New York. I wanted to regain my friendship with Nikos and to continue my education. And now as you can see, I love him very much. He saved my life, and he is the best person any woman could dream to be with. I am so grateful."

"Wow, Erika. This is such a touching story. You both are great together, and I wish you both a long journey ahead. My daughter, Nicky, said she would love to spend some one-on-one time with you when she comes back. Is that OK?" Irene asked.

"But of course! I would love that."

Shortly thereafter, Nicky walked in and kissed Erika on the cheek. Irene told her she could spend some time with Erika and walked out. The young teenager was nervous, but Erika succeeded to calm her down.

After some general talk about school and friends, Nicky asked her, "I'm so much impressed by you, not only by your amazing beauty but also by your wonderful personality. What is your secret?"

Erika smiled and looked at her warmly, saying, "That is sweet of you. You are a beautiful girl yourself. As I was telling your mom before you came, real beauty is in the heart and in the mind. What you think and how you feel determine how you live. A process of continued positive thinking and feeling all the time is bound to make you a very happy person. Anyone can do that, and it is not a secret. You will see that you will even look more beautiful inside and out."

"Do you think boys will find me more attractive then?" Nicky asked.

"Absolutely, and not only boys. Everybody, young and old, will notice the change within you, and it will reflect its beauty on your body as well. Then you need not look for them—I mean boys. They will come after you. Also, if there is one you like in particular, feel free to talk it over with your mother. She loves you very much, and it will help you trust her," Erika told Nicky with a big smile of encouragement. Nicky got off her seat and hugged her.

Later in the evening, Nikos told Erika, "What did you do to my mother and my sister? They adore you and appreciate what you discussed with them."

"Nothing special. I told them to love themselves, as I did."

*　　*　　*

The following evening, Pavlo and Helena invited them to go to a *bouzouki* club after dinner to listen and dance to Greek music. Erika was interested in dancing like the character in *Zorba the Greek*, which she loved from seeing the movie. Pavlo took her to the dance floor and showed her how. Everyone in the club was admiring her looks and her attempt to follow the dance. They all enjoyed dancing to the melodious Greek rhythms. Nikos also joined the group and moved well with the music to encourage her. They had a wonderful time. Erika bonded well with Helena, and they agreed to have a more quiet talk together before Erika returned to New York.

The next day, Helena came to see Erika before dinner. Nikos and Pavlo had their private conversation in Yanni's office, and the women sat in the living room to talk. Erika told her how happy she was to see Helena and Pavlo together.

Helena responded, "Our relationship is developing nicely given Pavlo's lack of experience in abiding by one relationship for more than a month. It's almost six months now, and it's getting better and better every day. Our love for each other is growing too."

"I fully understand Pavlo. I was like that before. I thought I was entitled to have any man I liked and felt free to give them the cold shoulder once the initial passion faded. I try not to think about it anymore. It was the stupidest thing I was addicted to. Totally shallow and meaningless! I thank God for Nikos, who shook me up and encouraged me to change. In a similar way, your personality and your inner and outer beauty shook Pavlo up and helped him settle down. Give yourself some credit! I am sure he has a great heart and he loves you dearly now. Thank goodness he was not addicted to uncontrolled sex as I was. He was strong enough to change without therapy, which I needed. Have faith. I see the two of you having a wonderful and healthy relationship as you move on," Erika said lovingly and truthfully.

"Wow! You are so humble and sweet, Erika. I appreciate your honest assessment of who you are now. Your love for Nikos is exemplary and true. He, like Pavlo, has a big heart as well, and may the two of you live a long happy life together," Helena happily commented.

"I am so glad to have met you, and I hope to see you with Pavlo in New York soon," Erika concluded, and then they were called for dinner.

During dinner, Pavlo told everybody that for the New Year's celebration, he booked a big table in the ballroom at the nearby Astir Hotel. It was the last day of the year, and the entire family wanted to make it a special celebration. They ate and danced, blew their horns, and threw confetti at one another. Yanni wore a paper king's crown on his head; Irene wore a queen's crown, while everybody else wore smaller crowns. The parents and Nicky left the party shortly after midnight. The two young couples did not leave before 2:30 a.m. of the first day of the New Year. They drank champagne and danced the past year away, feeling good.

The remaining time of their Greek vacation was spent relaxing. They packed and said goodbye with teary eyes and many hugs and kisses.

*　　*　　*

On the flight back to New York, Erika was extremely grateful to have come with Nikos on this trip. She loved his family, Athens, and the island of Mykonos. She said she felt at home and appreciated their great hospitality. Nikos was happy to hear that and reminded her that they all loved her too. The car dropped Erika at her family's home first, and she reminded him of the invitation on the sixth. Erika asked him to spend the evening with her parents. They kissed and agreed to see each other for lunch the next day at the university.

When Erika saw Nikos in the cafeteria waiting patiently for her, she looked nervous and rapidly said, "Tom saw me walking about an hour ago, and he insisted that I see him for dinner one evening. I said no, and he started to shout out loud and threaten me. I ignored him and went straight to the dean's office to file a complaint. He saw me going in that direction and tried to stop me. He grabbed me by the arm and begged me not to go in. I let go of his hand, which left a mark on my arm, and ran right into the office crying.

"The secretary asked me why I was crying, and I told her what happened. She went and spoke to the dean, who asked to see me right away. I repeated the story and gave him the full name of Tom. He looked him up on his computer and asked his secretary to find him and ask him to come to his office right away. The secretary found him still waiting for me outside the door.

"He came in and apologized to the dean. That wasn't enough. He was reprimanded and was suspended from the varsity tennis team. The dean told Tom he did not tolerate such behavior at all, and his record will be handed over to the police. The dean also told him if he were to harass me, talk to me, or touch me ever again, he would be expelled. We then walked out separately, and I came here running to see you. I am sorry I'm late."

"OK. Now relax. Drink some water. Here, Try to put this behind for now. We will make sure the police take note of what he did to you. I very much doubt this guy will do anything to bother you again. His record is blemished in school and with the police. Besides, he's off the tennis team. If he has any dignity, he should stop right there and chase other girls if that's his hobby," Nikos said to quiet her down.

"He threatened me and said if I don't go out with him again, I will have a big surprise—whatever he meant by that," Erika told Nikos after she cooled down a bit.

"Hey, try not to take it seriously. He's just trying to coerce you. You did well by quickly filing your complaint. He didn't expect that, and I think he'll behave better now. I promise you, I am ready to go to jail if I have to just to make sure he does not bother you anymore. Let's have something to eat, my love," Nikos said.

Erika then said, "I slept so well last night, dreaming about the trip and the fun we had. Thanks again. I love you, and I love your family."

*   *   *

On January 6, the first day of the new semester, Nikos dressed up in a nice suit and tie and walked up to his dinner invitation at the Sverenson home. Erika opened the door and said how handsome he looked in a suit. She introduced him to her mother, Mariya, and they walked inside to the living room, and she introduced him to her father, Sven. Nikos was offered a drink, and he settled for a glass of wine.

The atmosphere was somewhat tense until jovial Erika broke the ice and told her parents, "Finally, you meet the man I love!"

They nodded happily, and Sven toasted Nikos and said, "We're very happy to meet you. Erika speaks very highly of you."

Nikos answered, "You have a great daughter in Erika. She's loving, mindful, and keen to have a happy life. I am honored she accepted me as her boyfriend," Nikos responded.

Erika then jumped in and said, "Wait a minute, Nikos. My parents know my story and how much you helped me. I am honored that you accepted me back in your life."

Nikos was flattered, and his pinkish cheeks showed how bashful he became.

Sven was about six feet and two inches, with blond hair, fair skin, and a harmonious face. He was slim and very good-looking and in good shape for a man in his early fifties. Mariya was also a tall woman, about Erika's height. She looked very beautiful, and her facial features resembled those of Erika. Nikos realized by seeing her parents where Erika got her beauty.

Sven said, "Erika tells us you love philosophy and you intend to teach it one day."

"That's true. I love the logic it teaches me. I am now combining it with moral spirituality, and I find the combination fascinating," Nikos replied with dignity.

"I want to thank you for the good influence and advice you gave Erika when she needed it most," Mariya said.

"Erika did all the work herself. I just helped her be aware of the things happening in her life, and she did the right thing on her own. I admire her inner strength and willingness to live a good life. I guess you now can say we make a good team," Nikos humbly said.

"Yes, yes! A good team indeed," Erika added enthusiastically.

"Erika was very happy that you took her with you to Greece. She loved your family and the country. I remember Sven and I visited Athens and some islands before Erika was born. We had a lot of fun, right, Sven?" Mariya said.

Sven was put on the spot. He sat up straight in his seat and said, "Yes, we did, Mariya. It was a lot of fun. I remember when we arrived by boat to beautiful Santorini and how our luggage was taken to the hotel on a donkey. I thought that was very practical because of the steep uphill road."

"You must be hungry now. I prepared a traditional Swedish dinner for us tonight. I hope you will like it, Nikos."

"I'm sure I will," Nikos replied, and they all rose to sit at the dinner table.

Erika was so happy to see Nikos with her family. He was the first male friend invited to meet them. They continued with the wine while the first course was served, sautéed chanterelle mushrooms along with a small bowl of shredded red sugar beets on the side. It was followed by the second course, a typical Swedish dish, namely meatballs with pungent berry jam. The family was looking at Nikos, trying to decipher if he liked it.

He did and said, "Um, this is incredible! It is spicy and delicious. The jam adds a great balance to it too."

"Wow, *min kärlek*, you are a good food connoisseur also!"

"I see you taught him some Swedish words too," Mariya said, smiling.

Before the hard, sharp cheese was served with *akavit*, which is vodka with herbs, Nikos asked the ambassador about the relations between Sweden and the United States.

Sven answered, "Well, in general, the relationship has always been good. We hold each other in high esteem. A lot of the discussions we have nowadays with the secretary of state in Washington and the UN is how to figure out a solution for the overwhelming rise in refugees seeking a home in Europe and in Sweden in particular."

"Do you see any light at the end of the tunnel?" Nikos curiously asked.

"There's always hope. It is slow and not easy. Many countries are closing their borders except for Germany, which is now trying to cut back, and Scandinavian countries, who are also modifying their open-door policies."

"Would you agree, sir, that the root of the problem lies in the hand of the governments in the Middle East who mishandled their own destiny with the civil uprisings and wars in their own land and who succumbed to the pressure from opposing sources of influence, including countries like Russia, Iran, and Saudi Arabia?" Nikos asked attentively.

"Right you are. You summarized the situation beautifully," Sven said.

Erika jumped in and joyfully said, "Wow, Nikos! You're not only a brilliant student and a great boyfriend and a connoisseur of food but also politically savvy. What else are you going to surprise me with?"

"That should be enough for now, don't you think?" Nikos told Erika and smiled.

Then Sven continued, "Erika told us your father and brother run a shipping company in Greece. How come you didn't follow in their footsteps?"

"Oh no. It's not my calling. I would love to teach philosophy to university students. It's much more fun. I am grateful for their hard work, which has provided me with an abundant living."

Nikos thanked the family for a great dinner and said how happy he was to finally meet them. He said he would invite them soon to a dinner that Erika would cook. Everyone, including Erika, laughed when they heard that.

Then he corrected himself and said, "Oops, I meant a restaurant."

Erika thanked him for the correction and told her parents she would go with Nikos and spend the night at his place.

On the way over to his apartment, Erika asked Nikos if he would like her to take cooking lessons so that she could cook at home. He told her to forget about it for now and just focus on her studies. The rest of the evening was memorable. Erika went out of her way to please him, the kind of pleasure he had not experienced before. They hugged and slept very well all night.

*   *   *

The following months went smoothly and without any disturbance from Tom. The second semester was about to finish in the second half of May. Preparations for the final exams began in earnest. Nikos helped Erika understand some difficult chapters in spirituality and philosophy courses, and she managed to pass her exams with B grades. Nikos, as expected, averaged A on all his tests. He had completed all 120 credits to get his bachelor's degree.

Commencement day was on May 22, and his parents, Pavlo, and Helena flew in from Athens to attend the ceremony. Erika's parents attended as well. The two families met at the apartment and had dinner at Cipriani the day before graduation. James was invited to dinner as well. They all sat at a big table and hit it off well. Erika was thrilled to see them all having a good time together.

Yanni and Irene brought a gold Rolex watch as a gift to Nikos and a beautiful gold necklace studded with small diamonds to Erika, designed by a Greek artist/jeweler. The Bestidis family stayed for three nights before they returned to Athens. Irene, accompanied by Erika and Helena, made sure she had her shopping spree on Madison Avenue before she left. Nikos turned twenty-one two months ago, and Erika's birthday was coming up in three days.

CHAPTER 10

NIKOS AND ERIKA had decided to take certain summer courses. Nikos selected two courses as part of his postgraduate program, whereas Erika chose two electives for the start of her third year. Classes were scheduled to start on May 30, and they had five more days of vacation to celebrate Erika's twenty-first birthday. The time was too short to go to Greece. Nikos agreed with Erika to go for three nights to South Beach in Miami, Florida. The weather forecast was good and warm, around seventy-eight degrees, and Erika could sunbathe on the white sandy beaches during the day and dance at night.

He booked a nice room with a view of the Atlantic Ocean at the Ritz-Carlton Hotel. They flew South with very casual clothing and bathing suits, and a hotel car picked them up from the airport. They arrived early afternoon, and after checking in, they put on their bathing suits under their robes and went straight to the beach. Erika's birthday was the following day. It was the first time the two of them had been to Miami. The weather was wonderful and not too hot. They sat under the umbrella, took a quick dip in the ocean, and went back to enjoy some sun. The beach was crowded with tourists.

After a cold winter and spring in New York, the Miami weather was more than welcome. Erika found it heavenly. They had an early dinner at the main restaurant in the hotel and went to bed not late that night. The visits of the families and the graduation parties had taken a toll on them.

After they had a good night's rest, they woke up feeling refreshed, and Nikos wanted to take her shopping nearby at the Bal Harbor mall. His mother had recommended that he take Erika there and buy her a nice dress for her birthday when he informed her they were going to Miami. After breakfast, they took a car from the hotel to Bal Harbor, a vast open shopping mall with many restaurants. They checked the various boutiques, and Nikos insisted on buying a nice dress for her birthday dinner. Erika finally found a gorgeous suit at Chanel that she liked. She also bought a matching pair of shoes.

They had lunch at the O'Lima restaurant. It served fusion food with a Peruvian flavor. They liked the new taste and enjoyed being at this high-end shopping mall. They were back at the hotel at 3:00 p.m., and Erika insisted they go to the beach again for a couple of hours. They sunbathed and tanned nicely. They took a rest in their room from 5:00 to 6:30 p.m. They showered and got dressed to go to dinner. Nikos reserved a top cozy place at Tuyo, recommended by the concierge, on a high floor that looked out on the Miami skyline.

They were seated at a nice table with a good view at seven thirty. Nikos ordered a bottle of champagne. The food was light contemporary American cuisine, which they thoroughly enjoyed. Nikos had ordered a chocolate cake that came to the table with a candle in the middle, and three waiters sang happy birthday. Erika blew out the candle, and everyone around them clapped.

After eating the first bite of the delicious cake, Nikos moved to get closer to Erika, asked for her right hand, and knelt on one knee.

He looked straight into her eyes and opened the small velvet box in his right hand and said, "Erika, I met you two years ago, and I fell in love with you the moment we shook hands in the classroom. I continued to love you even when you had to go away. I love you so much more now, and I want to spend the rest of my life with you. Will you marry me?"

Erika was sobbing, with tears running down her cheeks, while listening to him propose. She looked at the amazing diamond ring in the box. As soon as he finished, she screamed out loud for the whole place to hear, "Yes, yes, and a million times yes!"

Nikos stood up and took out the ring and placed it on her finger. Then he kissed and hugged her, and the folks at the restaurant clapped and cheered them with words of congratulations. Erika took a deep breath and transformed her sobbing into big smiles of joy. They sat down and held hands across the table.

She asked, "How did you get this amazing ring, and when did you buy it?"

"I didn't buy it. Mother brought it with her from Athens. I had told her to order it more than a month ago when I planned this event in my head."

"Oh my god! I can't believe we are engaged and we are getting married! I am so, so happy. I love you, and I adore you. I am so lucky to have you. This is such a special birthday present. Thank you so much, my love." Erika happily expressed her passionate feelings to Nikos. She could not wait to tell her parents and to call Irene in the morning to thank her for this wonderful surprise.

* * *

The NYU summer courses began two days after their return from Miami. Nikos met with James and informed him that they got engaged, and he was very happy for them. Erika went to see her parents in the morning and showed them the ring. They embraced her with exceptional love and affection, which was normally more subdued among the Swedes. Sweet Nikos even sent a text message to Tatiana telling her that he had gotten engaged to Erika. She answered him back with warm congratulations and told him that Dmitri also proposed to marry her and they were discussing the plans for their marriage in Moscow soon. He wrote her back with his own message of congratulations and good wishes.

So all went well, and the summer courses were worthwhile and easily handled. Nikos's skills in ice-skating were improving, and they both continued jogging around the reservoir in Central Park. On many occasions, Erika could not keep up with his pace and frequently had to stop or simply just walk instead. She had repeated feelings of fatigue, and Nikos understood that it was due to her previous illness. Before the end of the summer courses in August, they registered for the new fall semester courses.

*   *   *

Nikos and Erika were invited to join the family on their new yacht for a week's vacation before the end of summer. The invitation was timely, and Erika looked forward to a jovial and restful time with Nikos's family, who overwhelmed them with their love.

The journey on the luxurious yacht was something to remember for a very long time. Yanni chose to sail from the Port of Piraeus in Athens to Nafplio, a romantic medieval town in the Peloponnese region, admired for its narrow cobblestone alleys in the old town. From there, the yacht sailed to Mykonos.

The next stop was the island of Patmos or the sacred island where St. John had written the Book of Revelation and the cave of the apocalypse stood. Thereafter, the yacht continued to the magical volcanic island of Santorini, known for its spectacular cliffs and the alleged hidden ruins of Atlantis. On the way back, Yanni planned a stop in Monemvasia, which resembled Gibraltar with a single thread of causeway that tied it to the mainland. It was also known for the Byzantine church of Hagia Sophia and the Venetian mansions in the old town.

It was truly a marvelous cruising adventure that brought the entire family more closely together. Erika was welcomed as a new member of the Bestidis clan. She was very grateful to Yanni as the cruise also allowed Erika and Nikos to spend private, separate one-on-one talks with the three ladies and the two other men.

*   *   *

They lived a quiet and fruitful life together in Nikos's apartment. They regularly visited their families and James, who became a very close friend of theirs. James had finished his master's degree and was continuing to study for his doctoral degree in eighteen months. Nikos had another year and a half to get his master's degree in philosophy around the same time Erika obtained her BA degree.

Nikos and Erika were twenty-three years old when they got their university degrees, his MA and her BA. The eighteen months since they got engaged had passed smoothly, and their love for each other had grown to a higher and more mature level. Classes were over, and graduations were behind them.

One evening, while they were discussing what to do next, Erika unexpectedly ran to the bathroom and vomited. Nikos ran after her and noticed questionable stains in her vomit. He wandered what they were. He took her right away to the emergency room of nearby Mount Sinai Hospital.

The doctor in charge that evening was a Dr. Romsakov, a young intern, Nikos thought. The doctor ordered a blood test, measured her blood pressure, and asked a few questions about what had happened. Nikos explained to him what he saw in the bathroom. He noticed that the doctor had a Russian accent. It crossed his mind that he could be the one that Tatiana had chosen to be with.

While waiting for the blood-test results, Nikos introduced himself and told him who he was. The doctor smiled when he was told that he was Tatiana's ex-boyfriend. He was polite and friendly toward Nikos and told him not to worry about Erika; he would take good care of her.

The blood-test results were given to Dr. Romsakov. He had a close look and did not seem to be satisfied with what he saw. He ordered an immediate X-ray of her abdomen and an MRI of her liver. Nikos was with Erika the entire time, holding her hand and telling her not to worry; these were routine tests. The time was close to 9:00 p.m. by the time the images of her abdomen and the MRI were handed to the doctor. He checked them and excused himself. He told Nikos he needed to consult with a senior doctor and would be back.

Erika was panicking already, and she was afraid that this time, it was more serious than the fatigue she was used to having from her past hepatitis C infections. Nikos tried his best to calm her down, kissing her hand while waiting for the doctor to return. After ten minutes, Dr. Romsakov was back and told Nikos that Erika must spend the night at the hospital for further examination and closer monitoring.

Nikos got nervous and asked him, "Why? What is it, Doctor? Please tell me."

"Her liver is inflamed because of some infections that may have reoccurred from previous chronic hepatitis C infections. We have to check her liver more thoroughly and do more tests. Please. She needs to stay here overnight."

Nikos looked desolate and tried to keep a smile when he informed Erika that they needed more tests tomorrow. He told her he'd stay with her as long as they would let him. She agreed, and they admitted her to a private room that Nikos had insisted upon. The doctor gave her some light sedatives to help her go to sleep. Nikos kept telling her to be strong and not to worry. By 11:00 p.m., Erika fell asleep, and Nikos left her to come back first thing in the morning.

At eight in the morning, Nikos was at the hospital and went straight to her room. He hugged and kissed her, trying to bring some color to her pale face. She was silent for a while and then asked him if he knew what was going on.

He told her, "They found an inflammation in the liver, perhaps caused by the hepatitis C infections you have had before. And they want to do more tests to figure out how to treat it."

"What if it is not treatable, my love?" Erika asked with concern.

"Oh, come on. Of course, they can treat it. I don't know how, but they will. Relax, sweet honeybun. You'll be OK."

After five minutes, a middle-aged doctor and a nurse walked in to the room. He introduced himself as Dr. Woodside and the nurse as Ms. Hedrick. The doctor checked her pulse while the nurse measured her blood pressure.

Then he said, "We need to take you downstairs to do some more tests and try to find out the extent of the possible damage this inflammation may have caused." He looked at Nikos, who introduced himself as her fiancé, and told him he could come down with them if he wanted.

The tests took more than an hour, and Nikos was patiently waiting outside the examination room. They later took Erika up to her room, and Nikos stayed with her all day. She slept for several hours and smiled when she woke up, seeing him on the chair next to her bed. All kinds of unwanted thoughts were racing in his mind while she was asleep. He had not yet told anyone that Erika was in the hospital.

Around 3:00 p.m., Dr. Woodside walked into the room and stood by the bed, held Erika's hand, and softly said, "Erika, it looks like you have some cancerous tumors that are damaging parts of your liver. We have a consortium of specialists meeting in one hour to discuss your case. It seems that the cancer is a hepatocellular type normally associated with previous hepatitis infections. Allow us some time to assess your condition and evaluate the required treatment. OK?"

"OK, Doctor. Thank you."

As soon as he walked out of the room, Erika started sobbing. She held Nikos's hand tightly and said, "Death does not scare me.

I just want us to be together for a while longer. The time we had together is too short. I pray to God for his mercy and to . . . to extend our relationship much longer . . ."

"Have no fear, my beautiful angel. All will be fine. Let us see what happens step by step. Let's not jump to conclusions yet," Nikos said lovingly and kissed her hand.

He asked her if they should notify the families, and she nodded. He asked her if she fancied anything special to eat. She said she had no appetite. He told her to rest for about an hour, and he would come back soon to hear the outcome of the specialists' meeting. He then ran to his apartment and broke down crying like a child as soon as he walked in. He felt devastated but could not show it front of her.

*   *   *

After a few minutes, he held himself together and called his mother, who refused to believe the news and then said she was coming to New York. He then called Mariya and told her the same story and gave her the room number. She said she'd be at the hospital right away. Before he returned to the hospital, he managed to find James and informed him as well. James said he'd come to see them in one hour.

Ten minutes after his return to her room, he was called to go see the doctors, who were still in session. He walked in and found four doctors sitting at a conference table; Dr. Woodside was among them.

They were introduced to Nikos by name, and the chief among them then said, "Unfortunately, we don't have very good news to share with you. Your fiancée has advanced liver cancer, stage three, and could possibly spread to stage four. We will do some more tests to see if the cancer has metastasized to the lymph nodes. We need to start her treatment right away. There are different treatments that Dr. Woodside will explain to you later in more detail. We highly recommend that she stay with us to begin her treatments, and we hope for the best. Dr. Woodside will answer any questions you may have. Please excuse us. We have to leave you now."

The three doctors left, and Nikos had Dr. Woodside to himself. Nikos asked several questions, which the doctor answered in detail, explaining the various stages of the disease, and the fact that stages three and four were the most advanced stages, and they had, with treatment, a low five-year survival rate, between 3 to 11 percent. He explained how vicious this type of cancer was and how it sneaked in without the patient feeling it until it was too late. He also added that surgery or a transplant was not an option as it was not in its early stage.

He added, "The remaining treatments include localized heating or freezing the cancer cells. Another treatment is a form of chemotherapy that targets the cells directly called chemoembolization. All that is to slow down the growth of tumors in the liver. Radiation therapy could also be used. We will determine the best course of action as we go along with the treatment."

Dr. Woodside told Nikos he would keep him updated, that the treatments should start tomorrow, and to feel free to ask him any other questions. Nikos parted with his head down and his mind racing with all kinds of worrying thoughts. His heart was overflowing with despair. He could not return to the room right

SAMEER ZAHR

away. He went down to the cafeteria for some coffee and sat in a corner for about ten minutes to regain his inner strength. Upon his return to the room, he found Mariya speaking with Erika in Swedish. She turned to greet him with a hug, and they continued in English.

Shortly thereafter, James came by, followed by Sven, her father. They came with bouquets of flowers to cheer Erika up. Nikos told them that Erika would be in the hospital for a while and told Mariya she might need more clothing. Nikos wouldn't and couldn't elaborate on the diagnostic conclusion of the consortium of doctors. He said that she needed further monitoring and tests. Erika's parents left after one hour, and Mariya said she'd return in the morning. James stayed with Nikos, and they left together when Erika fell asleep around ten at night.

*   *   *

James went up with Nikos to his apartment, and he heard the details of the meeting of specialists. Nikos could not control his tears and was sobbing while talking.

He asked James angrily, "But why, James, why? Why so soon? Are we being punished for doing something wrong now or in our past lives? Why her and not me? She is a transformed angel who deserves a long and healthy life. Can you tell me why?"

"Calm down, Nikos. The universe works in mysterious ways. I don't have an answer to many questions. The answer will soon be revealed. There has to be a lesson to learn from this experience. Take it easy now and wish her well. Did the doctors . . . tell you what caused it?"

"According to them, it is a hepatocellular type of cancer, developed from chronic hepatitis attacks that she suffered from during her earlier uncontrolled way of life. It started as a contagious virus transmitted from another person or from infected blood. I don't know what kind of intimate life she had before other than what she told me—that she'd been with many different guys, and I don't know if it is from something else. I cannot judge. It's in the past. But I thought now that she's emotionally and psychologically stable, it would be different. And I . . . I'm not so sure if I am strong enough to cope with this horrific situation. I am broken and dismayed."

"Come on, let us have a glass of wine. I'll stay with you tonight, and we'll see what tomorrow brings."

The two of them stayed up talking till midnight. James went to sleep in the guest room.

James woke up earlier the next morning and knocked on Nikos's door. He was still asleep at seven thirty when he woke him up. They had some coffee after Nikos showered. James told Nikos he had some work to do but would see him at the hospital around 5:00 p.m. Nikos was still feeling drowsy from sleeping poorly that night. He mustered enough energy and walked to the hospital a few blocks away.

He entered her room at 8:10 a.m., and she received him with open arms, telling him how much she had missed him. They hugged and kissed, and she told him she had slept well and felt no pain. A few minutes later, Mariya walked in with a small suitcase containing extra clothes.

Erika told them that they were coming to take her downstairs for some treatment before nine o'clock. She said she had no appetite to eat her breakfast and just had some tea with dry toast. Nikos tried his best to cheer her up and asked her to be strong. The nurse came with the orderly and took her on a gurney. Both Nikos and Mariya walked by her on each side.

She entered an imaging and special therapy room, and they waited outside. Nikos offered Mariya some coffee, and when they started to talk, he could not hold it in and started to cry again. Mariya held his hand and asked him to take it easy, but he couldn't for about three minutes. When he stopped crying, she asked him what it was that he had not told Erika yet.

Nikos, still sobbing, said, "Her liver cancer is advanced and may metastasize, spread to other organs. We should pray for a miracle."

"Are you saying her cancer is not at an early stage?" Mariya asked, shocked.

"That's correct. It is not at an early stage," Nikos replied with a sad face and then added, "The survival rate in her case is very low. She needs a lot of chemotherapy and a lot of love and care."

"We can only hope for the best. We have to stay strong around her. It is what it is, and we have to live with it," Mariya said.

While waiting in silence, Nikos received an email message from Tatiana.

> *Hi, Nikos. Dmitri told me he had met you in the hospital, and I'm sorry to hear about Erika. I wish her a quick recovery, and stay strong. Please let me know if there is anything I can do to help.*
>
> *Hugs,*
> *Tatiana*

*   *   *

Nikos appreciated her concern but did not feel like answering her. He had intended to continue his studies toward his doctorate degree, but now everything was on hold. His mind was simply focused on Erika's condition. He had gotten used to having her in his daily life. The thought of her being treated in the hospital with no definite guarantee of regaining her full health was a new challenge to his inner being. He prayed that she would have the spiritual insight to believe that she could be healed by the power of her own inner strength and determination to rise above the physical and scientific work of physicians.

Mariya interrupted his deep thoughts and said, "Nikos, my dear, I . . . I feel the troubling thoughts you're going through. We know how much you love Erika, and we are with you in this ordeal. Please don't exclude Sven and me from participating in the emotional and psychological struggle you're facing now. She's our only child, and like you, we love her very much. Please accept our help and don't feel you are alone in this regard."

Nikos looked at her with great compassion and said, "I appreciate that, Mariya. Erika is a very strong person. Her spiritual strength will heal her beyond any doctor's treatment. I . . . I just don't want her to experience any physical pain. She suffered enough in the past, and it's time for her to live a happy and healthy life now with us. I can't describe to you how much she means to me. Her transformation to become the angel she is today has been the greatest blessing and gift to me. She inspires me to develop my own strength and to change my outlook on life for the better every day. I thank you anyhow for your love and support."

"By the way, you need not worry about the hospital and treatment costs. Sven has an excellent health-insurance policy for the three of us from the government because of his service as an ambassador," Mariya added.

"Mariya, I appreciate you saying that, and I am the least concerned about the money part. I would beg on the street and sell everything I have if you or my family were not able to help. We all love Erika and will do whatever we can to get her out of this dilemma. Nevertheless, she is the only one who can heal herself, with her strong belief that the universe will answer all her prayers in due course. All she has to do is to repeat with perseverance her desire to live longer, and I am certain her wish will be fulfilled," Nikos said affirmatively.

"I am so proud of the faith the two of you have, and may all your prayers come true," Mariya concluded.

All of a sudden, the double doors flung open, and Erika was brought out on the gurney. Mariya and Nikos jumped up to join her on her way back to her room.

She smiled at them and held their hands from both sides of the mobile bed and fearlessly said, "I don't know exactly what they did, but I didn't feel any pain at all."

"Good, good!" Nikos responded.

Once in the room, Erika talked to her mother. The nurse told Nikos that Dr. Woodside would like to see him in his office. She showed him where, and he walked briskly to see him. He knocked and was told to come in. Nikos greeted him and sat down on a chair across from his desk.

Dr. Woodside said, "The good news is that her cancer did not metastasize outside her liver. The challenge now is to get rid of three small tumors and a larger one with a host of treatment options, including chemotherapy and radiation. We will do this as quickly as we can. Technology today permits us to use accurate targeting to attack those tumors, first to halt their growth and then to kill the bad cells. This is a fairly long process that takes several months, during which Erika has to be treated in the hospital for two days every month. The rest of the time, she can rest at home and have a pretty normal life. I want you to know that I am a believer in holistic treatment as well. Your love and care and the family's, plus her own personal desire to be healed play a big role in the process of complete healing. I saw that happen several times before. For now, she'll stay with us for three more days before she can go home. Any questions?"

"Thank you, Dr. Woodside, for the news that the cancer has not spread and could be treated within her liver. I appreciate very much your belief in alternative holistic treatment. Both Erika and I are spiritual beings, and we know how to connect with our higher selves via the process of meditation and visualization. We do that daily, and we practice the power of imagination and visualization that all is OK within us and with our bodies. So I am glad we have greater hope now. Can she eat normally, and should I stop our physical union in bed?" Nikos asked with a funny smile.

"First, it is good to hear about your spiritual practices. That will definitely help. Miracles do happen, you know. Yes, she can eat whatever she has appetite for, which is not always easy especially after treatment. And yes. You can have safe sex as this will make her feel loved and empowered. Anything else?"

"That's good for now, thank you."

"Oh, one more thing. There are forms that the nurse will bring to the room to be filled and signed," Dr. Woodside said.

"But of course. Thanks again."

Nikos walked back to Erika's room, feeling better. He entered the room with a smile on his face. Erika took his hand and asked him what he was smiling about.

He winked at her and said, "I just met with Dr. Woodside, who said that the bad cells in your liver can be treated and there is no evidence that the cancer has spread. It can now can be contained and removed with both medical treatment and and—guess what?—your spiritual inner desire to heal. How about that, huh?"

"What else did he say, *min kärlek*?" Erika asked and smiled while she looked at Mariya.

"He said to make sure I continue to love you and to let the love our families have for you be added as an extra bonus over mine," Nikos gleefully said.

"Come on, be serious for a second. What else?"

"He said you will go home in three days. Then they will continue with the treatment once a month for two days in the hospital each month and for a few months only. Meanwhile, you and I can continue to have a normal life. We can hug and kiss all the time, and you can eat whatever your sweet heart desires. How about that? Huh?" Nikos did his best to cheer up and to reignite her faith in her strong inner self.

"Lean over and kiss me. I love you!" Erika responded happily.

"Come on, Mariya, give your lovely daughter a hug!" Nikos demanded, and her mother acted accordingly.

It was close to noon, and Mariya said she needed to go, but she'd be back that evening with Sven. As soon as she left, Irene called him from Athens and told him she would arrive the next day at 3:00 p.m. and that she was looking forward to seeing Erika. He told his mother he'd be at the airport to receive her and asked her to speak with Erika. He passed the phone, and Erika spoke with her for a few minutes, repeating how happy she was to see her again tomorrow.

When Nikos was alone with Erika, he waited till she woke up from an hour's rest before he elaborated further on the talk he had had with Dr. Woodside and emphasized the valuable contribution of her inner strength to the healing process. He reassured her that he'd be by her side all the time.

He explained, "We have no other choice but to bring the future into the present and imagine or visualize our situation is completely back to normal. You can do it by continuing your meditation and visualization of how well you are already, and then *boom!* It happens when it is least expected. Ask, and you shall receive. As Neville Goddard said, 'We have to see the process from the end.' Just focus on that imagination, and all that you wish from the inside will be actualized in the body. Think that you are healed already."

"I am grateful to have you with me. We will go through this ordeal swiftly, and we will celebrate soon," Erika said.

"I also wanted to tell you that Dr. Woodside believes in spiritual healing, and he has seen it before. He said it's a miracle, and more scientists now believe in the power of mind over body."

"Any idea when the tumors will be gone?" Erika asked.

"It depends on the combination of the treatment they use and the extent of your perseverance and inner persuasion that the healing is already done. It's just a matter of some time," Nikos explained with conviction.

"What an experience, my love. We will, and I mean it. We will be much stronger in and out once it is over," Erika said confidently.

"That's my girl. That's the attitude to remember always," Nikos proudly said.

James showed up around 6:00 p.m. He kissed Erika on the cheek and told her she looked better. The three of them talked about the power of mind over body and had a wonderful positive discussion for about an hour. At 7:00 p.m., Sven and Mariya walked in with a nice bouquet of flowers. Erika was happy to see them and told them not to worry and that she'd be OK soon. Sven then took Nikos to the side, showed him an insurance card, and told him to use the detailed information when he filled out the hospital forms. Nikos thanked him, and they filled out the forms together on the spot. An hour later, they all left except for Nikos, who insisted on staying with Erika till she fell asleep.

The next day, Nikos was there at 8:00 a.m. with some fresh croissants that he begged Erika to try and eat. She had a bite before they came to take her down for continued therapy. An hour later, she was back in her room, slightly sedated, and the nurse told Nikos she needed some sleep to shake out the dose of radiation she took. He let her sleep and went down to get some coffee and eat his croissant that he had forgotten about. Erika had a long sleep and woke up around 1:00 p.m. They brought her some lunch and juice, but she could not eat. The nurse said it was OK; she would start eating by tomorrow at the latest.

* * *

Nikos then excused himself to go get his mother from JFK Airport. He hired a car and a driver to take him. The plane arrived on time, and Irene was out at 3:45 p.m. with the luggage, which she handed over to the driver. Nikos hugged and kissed his mother, and she was eager to hear Erika's news. Nikos briefed her on the details, including the latest hopeful conversation he had had with her doctor. She was silent for a while and then all of a sudden started sobbing. Nikos told her everything was OK and not to worry.

She said, "I love Erika. She is like my own daughter, and I cannot imagine her going through all this pain and discomfort. She doesn't deserve this!"

"I know, Mother. It is what it is, but I am sure that she will pull through with her inner strength and determination. She has an amazing positive attitude, and you'll see that for yourself."

"How are you holding up, son?" Irene asked.

"I was scared the first thirty-six hours, and I broke down in tears privately. I am feeling much better now after the news from the doctor this morning. I have faith and strong hope that she will be healed soon."

"How soon?"

"I don't know exactly. We put our wish out there, and we leave it to the universe to decide. It is a universal law."

"How about the cost of hospitalization and doctors? Can we help out?"

"Sven took care of that. He and the family have excellent insurance coverage gratis from the government. Thanks anyhow, Mom. I don't remember if I mentioned to you that in two days, she'll be discharged. There will be follow-up visits to check on her progress for two days once a month. The rest of the time, she will rest at home with me. Her mother lives near us and can see her anytime she wants."

Irene stopped at the building and left the luggage with the doorman and continued with Nikos to go see Erika.

She entered the room around 4:45 p.m., and Erika was awake, reading a book that Nikos had given her. She was thrilled to see Irene, and they enjoyed a long hug and kisses on both cheeks. Irene held herself quite well and was smiling without showing Erika any concern. Erika asked about everybody, and Irene told her that Pavlo and Helena were planning to get married soon.

"This is great news!" Erika said.

"Now they are wondering if they should postpone it until you get better. You know how much they love you and wish you quick recovery," Irene said.

"Oh no! No, don't let them do that. I insist! I will talk to them and tell them not, I repeat, not to change their plans. I'll be there in spirit, and they can come to New York for their honeymoon. Do you agree with me, my love?" Erika insisted emphatically.

"Well, it's up to them, no? If I were in their shoes, I would not change my plans. I will talk to Pavlo about it too."

"But then how about you, Nikos? Your brother wants you to be the best man," Irene asked.

"Mother, you know I can't leave Erika alone," Nikos answered.

"No and no again, my dearest. You'll go for a few days! I will stay with my mother, and that's an order! *Please*," Erika demanded gently.

Nikos thought for a while before he asked his mother, "When were they planning to get married?"

His mother answered, "In about three months."

"OK, let me think about it," Nikos said.

"You need to answer quickly before they cancel their plans."

"OK, OK, I will let him know at the latest tomorrow morning."

Mariya came in and saw Irene, and the two of them hugged and talked after greeting Erika and Nikos.

Around 7:30 p.m., Nikos asked Erika if it was OK to take Irene home and offer her dinner as she might need to rest early after her long trip. Mariya said she'd stay an extra hour because Sven had dinner plans elsewhere. They kissed Erika and left, promising to see her in the morning. Nikos and Irene agreed to have a bite at Cipriani before they went to the apartment.

They had a pleasant dinner, and Nikos told his mother how difficult it would be to live without Erika. He wanted to take good care of her and nourish her well as she would definitely get much thinner from all the treatment she'd be receiving. He added they both believed in miracles and that something good would come out of this discomfort. Irene said her plan was to stay about one week in New York. She was happy to hear that Erika would be coming home the next day.

The next day, Erika had another small chemotherapy session, and Dr. Woodside said she could go home now, to be back in thirty days for a checkup. Erika got dressed and was happy to be on her way home with Nikos and Irene. Her mother said she'd come to visit in the afternoon.

CHAPTER 11

NIKOS CALLED PAVLO and told him not to cancel the wedding and that he would come for three to four days by himself. He added that Erika would be feeling much better soon. Erika and Irene were happy with his decision.

Meanwhile, Irene was keen to spoil her with love and care at home. That lifted a big burden off Nikos's shoulders, and he was very grateful for that. Irene cooked and cleaned and sat next to her, reminiscing over her youthful upbringing and when she had met Yanni as a penniless young man. Nikos went to the big bookstore on Fifth Avenue and bought several autobiographies by many people who had succeeded to heal themselves. He pointed to two books in particular: *Wishes Fulfilled*, by Dr. Wayne Dyer, and one by Anita Moorjani called *Dying to Be Me*. They explained how to draw on one's own reservoir of inner power to heal.

To keep himself occupied, Nikos discussed with his professors at NYU how he could prepare for his doctorate in philosophy online. It was easier than he had thought, and they informed him what books he should study and what exams to take while he worked on his thesis. He was told that it could take about eighteen months without interruption. He registered and started a week later, which coincided with the return of his mother to Athens.

During a normal day, they would both be immersed in reading, Erika reading the books Nikos gave her while he sat on a chair next to her, reading the books for his doctorate degree.

James came to visit at least twice a week in the afternoon, and they would discuss his studies together. Nikos told James he was contemplating to write his thesis about spiritual philosophy. James advised him to modify the topic as "philosophical spirituality." He said it was much stronger as it emphasized the logic behind pursuing spirituality. Erika was amused, hearing them talk, and she learned from them silently. James mentioned he was less than six months away from getting his doctorate in divinity at the age of twenty-six.

"What do you intend to do after graduation?" Erika asked him.

"I'm not sure yet. I don't think I want to be ordained as a priest."

"Why?" Erika asked James.

"I'm not a traditionalist anymore. It would be in conflict with my current spiritual preferences. I may become a scholar and write books that teach religious people how to be more spiritual in their daily lives," James answered.

"But isn't this what priests should do to their congregations as well?" Erika responded.

"My dear Erika, books can be accessed by a much larger number of people than a smaller church congregation. Besides, I would be free, without having to report to the hierarchy of the church," James said defensively.

"You may have a point there. Nikos, why are you silent about the subject? Say something," Erika demanded from Nikos.

"Oh. Because I enjoy listening to you talk. You succeeded in asking James key questions about his future life. Marvelous! He's also hinting that he might want to be married and not be subjected to the Catholic Church rules. Right, James?"

"Come on, Nikos, what do you know?"

"I know the secrets of your heart, buddy. Stop hiding the truth!" Nikos replied with a facetious smile.

"OK, that's it. You're not my friend anymore," James responded with a wicked look on his face.

A few seconds later, they both started laughing. Erika understood their game and joined them in the laughter. That exchange lightened her mood, and they both intended to entertain her. She loved this act and told them they should write comedy skits together.

Around 5:00 p.m., the doorbell rang. It was Mariya. She came to see her daughter and spend two hours with her before Sven came home. They were left alone to speak Swedish while Nikos and James continued talking in the living room.

*　　*　　*

After a few weeks, a new routine was established: two days of therapy in the hospital and the rest of the month resting at home, with regular short walks in the park and occasional attempts to eat some pasta at Cipriani. Erika lost more than twenty pounds in three months. She kept her spirits high nevertheless. She started feeling better before the end of the third month, and the doctors said that the three smaller tumors were practically gone. The remaining challenge was to get rid of the larger one, which was slightly reduced but stubbornly still around. Erika focused all her inner energy and imagination on getting rid of it.

She set her mind on the thought that it was already gone and kept repeating that same visualization day after day. She was relentless in her strong inner belief that it had already disappeared, even if it took a miracle. Her subconscious mind was fully aligned with her conscious awareness during that period. The books she read helped her a lot, along with the daily meditations and visualization sessions. She read *Wishes Fulfilled* again and again, realizing that her prayers were already answered and her wish to be healed was already fulfilled.

She always told Nikos, "It's only a matter of time. You'll see!"

One night, close to the end of the third month, she had a dream that had caused her to jump and sit up in bed. Nikos was jolted awake, and he woke up and saw her gazing at the ceiling, sobbing softly.

He hugged her, and after a few moments of silence, he asked her, "What is it, my love?"

"I . . . I dreamed that a giant rose from within my abdomen, jumped out, and ran away like thunder. Then suddenly, I saw angels hovering over my head peacefully. I felt relieved for some reason, um . . . I mean, I was not scared at all. What could this be, my love?" Erika spoke calmly and with a smile.

Nikos saw her face lighten up despite the dim light in the room. He was astounded by the contrast of images she had described. He held her tight and asked her, "Do you think it was a strange dream, a good dream, or a nightmare?"

"No, no, not a nightmare. The first scene of the giant that jumped out of me was instantly replaced with the scene of angels. No, it was not a scary dream. I felt it was a transformation of sorts from one troubling condition to another peaceful condition," Erika said confidently.

"Interesting. There is a message for you in that dream. Let's try to go back to sleep. In a few hours, we have to go to the hospital for a checkup. You need to rest now. I will hug you until you fall asleep."

The next morning, he helped her get dressed to go. The doorman found him a taxi right away. They arrived at the hospital on time for the imaging room before the therapy. Erika felt good and refused to go in the wheelchair and preferred to walk. Nikos wondered why and noticed her new determined attitude. He waited outside the imaging department while the technicians were taking an MRI image of her liver tumors. The plan was to do that before they would give her chemotherapy.

Once the MRI was completed, he saw Dr. Woodside rushing to go inside. The technician had called him; he saw a completely different image than the one taken a month ago. Dr. Woodside studied the images carefully and couldn't believe what he saw. He checked again and again to make sure that what he saw was correct. He then walked out and asked Nikos to join him inside.

He put the images on a light screen and told him, "Look here at this one taken last month, and look here at this same one just taken. Do you see any difference?"

Nikos looked and told him, "This new image is missing a part here. Why is that?" Nikos pointed at the missing part.

Dr. Woodside looked at him and smiled before he said, "The larger tumor is gone. It's a miracle! I've seen it happen before but not in such a short span of time. Congratulations! Erika is cancer free."

Nikos could not believe what he had just heard and asked if he could see Erika. The doctor took him to the other room and had the images with him. They both walked in with big smiles and told Erika that she was cancer free, and Dr. Woodside showed her the images to prove it. He repeated that the entire liver was clean now, and no damage or residue of the tumors could be found. Erika hugged Nikos and the doctor and started crying from joy. She told Dr. Woodside she knew this would happen, and she told him about the dream she had seen. Naturally, the giant that had jumped out of her abdomen was the disappearance of the tumors, and the appearance of the angels was the confirmation that she was healed.

Erika did not require any more chemotherapy, and the doctor told her to check with him again in three months. He concluded by saying, "I am so happy for you both. You can start living a normal life again, Erika. You need to start eating to regain the weight you lost. You promise?"

"I promise, and all of a sudden, I feel hungry."

*　　*　　*

They left the hospital feeling very elated and uplifted now that the past ordeal was behind them. Before they took a taxi back home, Erika told Nikos to take her to the French bakery around the corner to have a good almond croissant and a cup of coffee. While having their delicious breakfast, Nikos called both mothers and told them the good news.

Nikos's twenty-third birthday was coming up in a few weeks before the marriage of Pavlo and Helena. Erika's health was improving daily. She was eating better and gained seven pounds in the first two weeks after her release. She arranged with her family to celebrate Nikos's birthday at their home and to invite James as well. Nikos did not care for a big party, which was suggested by his family in Athens. The celebration was subdued, and he succeeded to turn it around as a celebration in honor of Erika's good health.

Nikos checked with Dr. Woodside if Erika could travel long distance to Athens for a week. The answer was positive and to let her live a full normal life. He told Erika, and she was very happy indeed. He notified his parents, and they were elated to hear the news of her joining Nikos to attend Pavlo's wedding.

In fact, planning the trip lifted her up, and she felt much stronger. She ate well during that week before their departure. She gained two more pounds and looked quite healthy already. They wanted to arrive one day before the rehearsal dinner. The wedding was planned for the next day at a big Orthodox church in Athens.

The flight to Athens was comfortable, and Nikos booked two first-class tickets to maximize the level of comfort for Erika. He encouraged her to sleep most of the flight, which she did after eating a nice meal. She arrived feeling good, and the car picked them up at the Athens Airport on time. The entire family and other relatives were at the villa when they had arrived, and they all cheered Erika when they had seen her coming out of the car. Nikos and Irene let her spend a few minutes downstairs before they took her up to their room to rest.

Erika wanted to go downstairs and join the crowd in the afternoon. Nikos did not mind if she stayed with the family for a couple of hours. Pavlo and Helena were quite happy to see her, and they found her to be looking quite healthy. Nicky, the younger sister, was thrilled to see Erika again and sat next to her all evening. Erika truly felt very much loved by the entire family. Yanni gave her a big hug when he saw her. She was very glad she could join Nikos for this special event. Her spirits were high, and she felt completely normal.

Erika also participated in the rehearsal dinner the next day at a fancy seafood restaurant by the beach. There was good food and good music, and the party lasted till 11:00 p.m. Nikos did not hang around with Pavlo and the other men and instead was always next to Erika.

*   *   *

For the wedding ceremony, Erika did not go to the church service. The church was about fifty minutes' drive by car, and she preferred to stay at home and rest. The reception in the late afternoon was held in the ballroom of the nearby Astir Hotel. Close to three hundred people were expected to be there. Erika and Nikos participated and enjoyed the cocktail celebration in the open air near the sea.

They later went inside to a seated dinner in the ballroom. Dinner was served late, after nine o'clock, and at around ten, Nikos took Erika back to the villa as he did not want to expose her too much to the deafening buzzing and noise inside. Erika did not mind sitting and watching people having fun, but Nikos put a limit as to how much she should take. The bride and groom came over to talk to her at their table, and they sat with Erika for ten minutes, telling her how grateful they were that she could be with them.

Back at the villa, they both enjoyed the temporary quiet surroundings and went to their room to rest and go to sleep before the house got crowded again. Nikos was so happy to see Erika in such a normal condition and was grateful to the miraculous healing that took place. His faith in God became much stronger, and he admired Erika's continued practice of meditation and connection with the source of all energy that had brought her back to life.

SAMEER ZAHR

To her, the experience she had was a pure manifestation of the alignment of her inner being, her spirit, with the outer being, her body. She realized and actualized her mental wishes into newly created physical realities.

After resting for one day at the hotel, Pavlo and Helena went to Tahiti for their honeymoon.

*   *   *

Irene spent a lot of her time with Erika during the day, which gave Erika the chance to explain to her the power of spiritual exercises and benefits of meditation. She told Irene that was the reason why the miracle that saved her life had happened. She told Nikos and his mother one morning when they were alone that the experience she had gone through plus the healing books she read inspired her to do something special.

She told them, "I want to write a book and share my story with the rest of the world. Will you help me with this project, my love?"

"Sweet angel, it's a great idea. Do it. I will find you the best professional editor to help you write it, publish it, and make it a best-selling book. You have a great story to share with the world," Nikos said enthusiastically.

"Wow . . . wow! I admire your courage, Erika. You have no qualms about sharing your private life with the world. What a transformation! You suffered and now want to help others heal. That is the Christ in you. Oh my god, you are truly an angel, as Nikos keeps saying," said Irene.

"Thank you, Irene. I am not worthy to be associated with such a high honor, but I will humbly do whatever I can to help others. I owe it to those who can benefit from my life story. It's the law of dharma. I found my life purpose, which is to help others."

"Nikos, my son, God loves you so much to have brought this angel into your life. Enjoy every moment with her."

"Thank you, Mother, and yes, I am blessed."

"How about you? I heard you started working on your doctorate degree. What is your book going to be about? A philosophical topic?" Irene asked.

"Yes, I started, and by virtue of the spiritual awareness that I have been experiencing since Erika and I got back together, I am thinking of the title 'Philosophical Spirituality' for my thesis. There are several spiritual philosophies out there but not the other way around. I would like to prove that it is logical to be spiritual," Nikos explained.

"That's interesting, my son. I've noticed the evolution of your thoughts, both of you, and that's what makes relationships grow and last a long time. Congratulations to the new writers and philosophers of the family. I love you both."

"We love you too," Nikos and Erika said simultaneously.

The family dinner the night after the wedding did not include Pavlo and Helena. Yanni was more relaxed now that the preoccupation with the wedding and the large number of guests was behind him. He wanted to focus on Nikos and Erika.

In his own loving way, feeling very happy that Erika was healed and present with them, he asked her, "How do you feel now, my dear? Tell me what you went through, please."

"Thank you for asking. I feel much, much better, thank god! To tell you the truth, I was afraid in the beginning. I also had a lot of pain, which I tried to hide from Nikos and my mother. The painkillers they gave me were not enough to ease the terrible pain that the illness caused. It became a true battle for me. But I decided to fight that horrible disease. Slowly but surely, supported with the continued love of Nikos, Irene, and my family, I was determined to win this battle. I developed a stronger inner power within me on a daily basis during the terrible first two and a half months. I followed the practice of regular meditation and visualization, convinced that I was healed already and had won the battle. It was truly a miracle, and I dreamed about it before it happened."

Erika explained what she had gone through, and Yanni could not hold himself back. He rose from his chair and walked over to kiss her head, repeating three times, "Thank you, God," in Greek. He sat down and took a deep breath and asked Nikos, "How did you cope with this ordeal, my son?"

"What can I say, Dad? It's an experience I will never forget. It started very painful and ended very joyful. I witnessed good conquer evil, and I discovered what a true angel this amazing woman is in fighting this awful disease. I suffered too. I felt her pain and carried the cross with her. I prayed, and I meditated, but it was her firm belief that the divine power would save her. And she won the battle. She healed herself, and this alleviated the sympathetic pain I suffered from during the process. I am a lucky man. I did not lose her. That's all I can say," Nikos said gleefully.

"I want you both to know that your spiritual strength and faith in the divine power has influenced us all in this family and is definitely transforming us to become stronger believers in the power of Christ, the author of all miracles. What a story to remember. We love you dearly," Yanni said affirmatively.

Both Erika and Nikos got up from their chairs at the same time and went around to kiss and hug Yanni with great love and gratitude. Before they left the table, Irene told Yanni and Nicky that Erika decided to write a book about her miraculous story, to share it with the world. They were thrilled to hear that.

After a very enjoyable and loving dinner, Erika and Nikos went to the room to rest. Erika assured Nicky that they would spend private time together around 10:00 a.m. as there were no classes that day.

Nicky was eagerly waiting to meet with Erika alone and share with her the latest developments in her school life. After a warm hug, they sat close together in the living room, and Erika asked her for an update on her relationships with friends. Nicky had recently turned sixteen, and being in love with someone was to be expected as a major happening at her tender age. Nicky confided in Erika and told her things that were not necessarily shared with her own mother.

Erika said, "The last time we met, we talked about inner beauty, right? Have you had a chance to experience that since?"

"In a way, yes. I built up enough courage to present myself confidently in the company of my friends, and they asked me what has changed about me. I told them that outer beauty was not enough, so jokingly, they started calling me Ms. Inner Beauty, and I did not mind. The rumor caught the attention of the boys and one in particular whom I liked, Alex. After class, he asked me why the girls called me that, and I told him what inner beauty meant to me. He admired me for saying it, and since then, we have become good friends. I want to thank you for teaching me that several months ago," Nicky explained.

SAMEER ZAHR

"This is good news, Nicky. What do you do when you spend time together?" Erika asked.

"We talk about classwork, and we laugh. Other classmates think we are a couple now, and I don't care because I like him a lot," Nicky said.

"Does your mother know about him?" Erika asked.

"Yes, I told her. I took your advice. She thanked me and said she trusts me."

"Is he nice to you? Does he respect you?"

"Yes, he does, and he has no intention to have sex with me. He respects me. We kiss sometimes in hiding, but that's about it. We both know it is too early," Nicky said gleefully.

"That's excellent, Nicky. You are both responsible and respectful of each other. I congratulate you. I wish I was that careful when I was your age. I am very proud of you. There is a time for everything. Don't rush," Erika told her.

"I want you to know how happy I am to see you in good health. I was so scared when I heard what had happened. You are an angel, and I want you around forever so I can learn more from you. I love you," Nicky said and turned to hug Erika.

Irene walked in at that moment and brought some tea and cookies for them to enjoy. Nikos was still upstairs, preparing to pack for their return to New York the next day. Erika told Irene what a wonderful daughter she had and complimented Nicky as an aware young lady who knew right from wrong already. Nikos joined them a few minutes later, and they all sat around, enjoying a nice family gathering with tea and cookies.

When Nicky went upstairs to her room, Irene was eager to discuss the project of Erika writing a book about her life story.

Nikos said, "I'm already searching for a seasoned editor online."

Then Erika said, "This would be a perfect time for me to work on the book as I have no classes to attend. I'm certain that dedicating a few hours a day would be sufficient, even if it takes a few months to finish it. I have the message clearly in my head, and all that is required is to put it down on paper."

"I will also be around to help if she needs me. I am working on my degree mostly online," Nikos added.

"That will further encourage me to work knowing you are near me. I would even be more inspired, my dear," Erika said, enthused.

"When do you intend to start writing, Erika, and what will your message be?" Irene asked.

Erika thought for a few seconds and confidently replied, "As soon as we settle down after we return home. It will be basically a message emphasizing the power of divine true love, its effect on our bodies, and the practice of imagination and visualization to help us connect with our higher selves. I simply want to affirm the belief that we truly are spiritual beings having a physical experience."

*   *   *

Overall, the visit was definitely worthwhile. It brought the family closer to Erika, and the wedding of Pavlo and Helena was an event to remember. The flight back home was comfortable, and Erika managed to rest most of the trip. Her parents came to visit her the same evening they had arrived and were happy that she was feeling good and living a normal life.

Nikos got in touch with James, who said he'd be coming the next day to see them. Erika took the time to put down her thoughts about the book on a sheet of paper. Nikos lined up three different candidates for the writing and editing job, who were all living in Manhattan. He scheduled meetings with them at the apartment the following week, and Erika was looking forward to the interviews.

Nikos started to work on his doctoral dissertation in earnest. He was excited about the theme that would incorporate his philosophical approach to the realm of spirituality and its application to everyday life. When James came to see them, Erika excused herself after thirty minutes of general talk to take a rest. The two men stayed in the living room and started a question-and-answer session.

James asked, "So where are you on your dissertation?"

"I haven't really started yet. I am still working on the outline of my paper. The theme is 'philosophical spirituality,' as I mentioned before." Nikos answered.

"Good. You decided to choose this title then?"

"My own love of philosophy and Erika's recent miracle inspired me. You see, the ancient Greek philosophers who loved wisdom believed that philosophy was not a dry analytical discourse. It was a way to find harmony in life and to live it well. They taught how not to get angry or hate others but to reason out how to act and how to find a place in the vast universe they believed in," Nikos answered thoughtfully.

"Do you find a link between philosophy and spirituality?" James asked.

"There could be a link as long as we understand the distinct difference between the two realms," Nikos answered.

"What do you mean?" James responded.

"Um . . . let me try and explain. Philosophy alone cannot change the reason why we want to grow spiritually. It is a bunch of ideas that can be changed as we like. It teaches us what is real and how to think logically. And philosophy alone is mere speculation. No matter how deep we ask the question 'What if?' it cannot go deep enough beyond our five senses. Spirituality, however, goes beyond speculation. It slowly creates energy frequencies in the body to connect with higher frequencies to a higher level of an infinite source. Normally, it is achieved via the practice of silence and meditation. It transforms what we think and what we want to achieve as our reality via the increased awareness beyond the five senses," Nikos eloquently explained.

"How is philosophy different now from the ancient days?" James continued his questioning.

"The ancient philosophy was geared to applied *living*. Today though, it is a very noble work of education. It is basically a mere academic subject. Hence, in my opinion, a philosopher should be someone who does more than just think and talk but also lives a thoughtful, principled, and consistent life," Nikos replied reflectively.

"Then what is the difference between philosophy and philosophical spirituality? Can you explain it to me in simple words?" James asked.

"First, let me remind you—and as we studied—spirituality is when we live by our spiritual *intentions*. That is when we desire to have a life with a good purpose, to be compassionate and loving. Philosophical spirituality, on the other hand, is when we understand the basis or the foundation of these spiritual *intentions*," Nikos explained.

"Is this why stoicism and Buddhism are considered philosophies as well as religious and spiritual paths?" James asked again.

"In a way, yes, you could say that because these philosophies were, in fact, personal practices in daily life, and that is essential to living a spiritual life. So yes, Buddhism could be considered a spiritual practice founded on philosophical principles," Nikos articulated.

"So forgive me if I ask you—what then will you be adding to what Buddhism did thousands of years ago?" James smartly asked.

"You hit the nail on the head. That is my challenge. I would like to come up with modern practical ways that would explain how to apply the logic of our true philosophical principles in our everyday spiritual lives. You can also help me with that, James, to discuss it as we're doing now," Nikos concluded.

Nikos and Erika had their first interview with one literary candidate named George, a middle-aged man. He was the shy type, but his résumé revealed his high education and vast experience, writing biographies of many celebrities and high-level politicians. They spent an hour talking, during which he was sympathetic to Erika's story. Nevertheless, he admitted he had no prior experience in the realm of spirituality or miraculous healing. As an atheist, he did not believe he was the right person for the job, so he politely passed.

The second candidate was a man in his thirties who also had decent experience writing and editing. His main work mainly involved corporate clients and official textbooks. That did not jibe well with Nikos and Erika.

The third candidate was a British woman in her late fifties who had been living in Manhattan for more than fifteen years.

Her name was Agnes, and she had an astute and jovial demeanor with a beautiful British accent that Erika liked. Her résumé also showed that she used to be a member of a spiritual organization that had worked closely with hospitals in London.

Agnes Woodward had written more than ten books, mostly self-help, since she came to the United States. She showed them a couple of copies she had with her. One of the books was on the New York Times Best Sellers list. She also worked as a ghostwriter for many other authors. She spent about an hour with them and expressed her keen interest to help Erika out. They told her they would let her know their decision within twenty-four hours.

As soon as Agnes left, Nikos and Erika looked and smiled at each other, practically agreeing that she was the one. Erika felt very comfortable with her.

She told Nikos, "I really like her. Not only does she seem qualified, but she also has this loving, motherly air around her. If it's OK with you, love, I want her."

"Perfect. I liked her too. I'll call her tomorrow, and I will engage her services officially. Good luck!" Nikos responded.

"Thanks. Perhaps she can start soon and spend about three hours a day with me. What do you think?" Erika asked.

"That sounds about right, I will check it out."

"Oh! I'm so happy. Thank you so much, my love."

The following morning was a Tuesday. Nikos called Agnes and told her she got the job. She was happy and agreed to start next Monday from 10:00 a.m. to 1:00 p.m. They discussed the terms of the agreement, and Agnes said she would bring a typed copy with her when she came to work.

CHAPTER 12

DURING THE FIRST session with Agnes, Erika shared her life story, starting with her place of birth, school education, social life, travels, and the events that had occurred after the move to New York with her family. Agnes insisted that she should not hide any important details and reassured her that she could be trusted. They conducted their recorded conversation in the master bedroom, leaving Nikos to have full privacy for his own work in the living-room area. Once Agnes got the general picture, she said she would ask questions for more elaborate explanations when needed.

Agnes asked Erika, "Please tell me in your own words why you want to write this book and what message you want to send out to the public."

"I owe it to the public to know that one should not live a careless life as I did. One should not become arrogant or aloof if blessed with outer beauty as I had. People should look within and discover their own identity. I'd like to help them view life from the inside out, not the other way around. People should be aware that they are spiritual beings first, having a human experience second. I want to tell them how to see their desires fulfilled 'from the end,' as Neville Goddard said. To develop a practice for a daily spiritual life that would help them overcome hardships and discords. I would like to tell them to have deep inner belief that physical illness can be healed with the inner power of the mind, to believe in miracles, not to live in fear, and to believe in love and helping others as the ultimate purpose for their life. Along these lines, OK?"

Agnes listened carefully to what Erika had said in her simple words and took notes in addition to the recorded material. She told Erika not be concerned about the title of the book yet; it would come in due course. It had to be a unique and powerful title.

Nikos received an email message from Tatiana.

Hi, Nikos.

I heard from Dmitri that Erika did not require further treatment at the hospital and that she was miraculously healed. I am very happy to hear that, and I sincerely wish her well. I heard she is a wonderful woman and wish you both the happiest life. To amuse you, I will tell you an interesting story.

Oleg sneaked into the country, crossing the Canadian border by car. He knocked on my door and did not find me. The next day, he came to my old company, Valentino, and asked to see me. They told him I work at Saks. He came to Saks and asked for me. I did not know it was he. I thought it was a client. Then I saw him. I did not want to create a scene, though I could have simply called the police. The stupid guy knew he was on the wanted list, yet he did not care. I decided to confront him. I told him that I am engaged to a Russian man, and it is best if he leaves. He laughed and thought I was joking.

I called Dmitri on the cell phone and told him that Oleg was in the store and that he did not believe that we were engaged. I passed the phone to Oleg, and they spoke in Russian, of course. A few seconds later, Oleg threw the phone back at me and ran down the stairs like a scared dog. I never saw him again. Dmitri told me later that he pretended he was a Russian secret-service officer and told Oleg that he had better run for his life or else he was on his way over. We both laughed.

Isn't Oleg an obsessed coward? Anyhow, I hope all is well and wanted you to know that Dmitri and I are getting married in Moscow in thirty days. I will always hold you in great esteem. You are a great man.

Tatiana

Nikos was turning twenty-four years old soon, and so was Erika shortly thereafter. The news of Pavlo and Helena now married and the announcement that Tatiana and Dmitri were getting married lit a bulb in his head that told him, *Why not us?* He thought about it for a while and decided to plan a wedding soon. He figured that Erika was strong enough to handle a celebration of this sort.

He thought, *She is the love of my life, and sooner or later, we're going to get married anyhow, so why not sooner? I am certain that this would enhance her inner happiness and improve her health even further. The question is when. Do I wait till she's finished with the book in about three months or sooner? Should I wait till*

I graduate with my doctoral degree in about a year? Should I discuss it with Erika first? He finally decided to sleep on it.

Nikos woke up to a bright sunny day and felt excited about the idea of his marriage to Erika. He preferred to have it in New York without a lavish reception. The question was whether the wedding would be a religious ceremony or just a civil one. He decided to discuss it with Erika.

The two of them were having coffee and toast, sitting around the kitchen table. Nikos held her hand and abruptly said, "Let's get married, my love!"

Erika almost choked on her coffee, put down the cup, and looked at Nikos with wide-open eyes and said, "You're kidding, aren't you?"

"I'm serious. I love you and want to seal our relationship with this act. Are you OK with this?" Nikos responded affirmatively.

"But I'm not 100 percent back in shape yet. When are you thinking to perform this sacred task?" Erika asked gleefully.

"Whenever Your Highness is ready. You decide."

"Wow! This is exciting. I didn't expect you to suggest this so soon. How about in four months? I would be finished with the book by then and put on a few more pounds to impress you. What do you think?" Erika said.

"This sounds perfect for me too," Nikos replied and gave her a kiss.

Erika noticed he had a folded sheet of paper on the table and asked Nikos what it was. He tried to hide it, but she insisted on seeing it. He told her it was just a small poem he was writing about her, and it was not finished. She took the paper, and it read,

At last, I found the precious catch
Who saw in me the right match
I treat her well with no demand
She helps me always to understand
We walk the twilight and sip our wine
We thank the heavens for our dime
The sunset fades but not her smile
My love for her grows a long while
I dare not make another wrong
And learn the tune of this song
It comes only once, and is aware
A moment like this, you do not spare
No more errors and no more search
I shut the door to all my fears
I move forward with her to flourish
And now I have a new soul to nourish

"Wow! This is so sweet of you, my love. You are truly multitalented, and I thank you for enjoying being with me. I wish I could write a poem about you one day. I love you."

*   *   *

Agnes showed her a few pages typed already. Erika read them and loved her smooth style and clear use of words and sentences. They worked together for three hours, and as soon as Agnes left, Erika got on the phone to share the good news about the marriage with her mother. Nikos had already informed his mother by phone while Erika was busy with Agnes.

The Bestidis family wanted a big wedding, preferably in Greece. Nikos and Erika thought of a small civil ceremony with two witnesses and a small reception party at Cipriani. The families argued differently, and it was left for the young couple to decide. They did not believe that big weddings and receptions would be more meaningful to them. It became a question of whether they would want to please their parents.

In the middle of discussing the issue, Pavlo called. First, he expressed his excitement about the news but also told them he had a good idea. He asked Nikos to put the phone on the speaker so Erika could hear him too.

He said, "Listen, I know what you like, and please trust me for what I'm about to suggest. Imagine a sandy beach as a venue for your wedding. We'll find a licensed official if you don't want a priest to perform the ceremony. The reception party will be held right after the ceremony. It can be as small or big as you like at the same venue on a higher level from the beach for maximum one hundred people. The place is not far from where we live, and it is very romantic. So what do you think? I can send you photos of the place!"

Erika and Nikos were smiling while listening to the excited Pavlo. Nikos thanked him for the idea and told him, "We'll think about it and will let you know, big brother. Thanks."

"Please agree. The first half of September will be perfect."

"OK, I will call you back in a couple of hours. Thanks again."

After they hung up with Pavlo, they looked at each other, and then Erika said, "Honestly, my dear, I always dreamed of a wedding on a sandy beach."

SAMEER ZAHR

"Then that's it. Consider it done. We'll invite your parents to be there for sure, and my family will take care of all the details. We'll be there as guests of honor," Nikos explained.

"Can I wear a colorful sarong, a white top, and a jasmine flower crown on my head? And can we get married, um . . . barefoot?" Erika was enthused to ask.

"Whatever your heart desires. It's your wedding, my love. I will also wear white shorts with a Hawaiian shirt and be barefoot too. How about that?"

The two of them laughed happily as they imagined other scenes of most people formally dressed while the two of them would surprise them all with their beach attire.

Irene called while they were still talking. She told them how happy she was to hear about the beach plan and how eager Pavlo was to hear their final decision. Nikos told her that they would go ahead with the beach idea, and he'd notify them with dates and such soon. They thought the ideal date would be the first weekend in September. Pavlo called them back, saying he had heard from his mother that they had agreed to the beach idea, and he was very excited.

He told them, "Don't worry about anything. I'll make sure everything is to your liking. I'll tell my parents to limit their invitations to maximum eighty people. You tell me how many you'll invite. I'll have a live band and a great selection of summer food. I'll do everything, and I am so happy. I love you both," Pavlo said, full of excitement.

Mariya invited Erika and Nikos to dinner that evening at their home. Erika and Nikos described the wedding plans with her parents, and they both booked the date. Erika asked if they wanted to invite other relatives from Sweden. Mariya said she would like to invite her mother, whom Erika called Grannie. Sven said he'd ask if his brother could come with his wife and two children.

*   *   *

James came over the next day to see them and to have another discussion with Nikos about his dissertation. Nikos told him about the wedding plans, and he was thrilled to hear the news and said he'd be there, come what may. They spent an hour discussing the dissertation in the living room while Erika was resting in bed.

James expressed his remarks about the paper, telling Nikos, "It sounds somewhat controversial, which is OK as long as you don't have religious professors on the review panel when you sit with them. They will grill you right and left. I have to go through this in a couple of weeks too."

"Is your paper controversial too?"

"But of course! There will be priests or professors on my panel, and they might challenge me to rewrite it." James disclosed.

"Why?"

"What do you mean, why? Don't forget. I am suggesting spiritual practices to complement the traditional Catholic rituals and rules. They can easily turn me down. They hold those old traditions dear. Who knows? But I'm not going to budge. I'll be prepared to persuade them with the validity of my dissertation," James explained.

"Well, I doubt if any of my panelists care. They are secular, and all are philosophy professors. They might appreciate that I intend to underline the role of philosophy to enhance the individual's spirituality. We'll see. I am still far from finishing it. Anyhow, I'll

SAMEER ZAHR

ask you to review it for me before I hand it over. By then, you'll be eligible, Dr. James Cordwell."

Erika walked out of the bedroom and asked them if they wanted any coffee, and they both shouted, "Yes! Thank you."

After drinking his coffee, James left and promised to be back soon. Nikos and Erika sat calmly on the sofa, holding hands and feeling great love and appreciation for each other. Nikos started a conversation with her.

"You know, sweet angel, I love our life together. We went through two tough periods since we had met. The first was when you were still trying to figure out what you wanted from life, which caused a brief distance between us, and, recently, the second one, your unwanted illness, which magically brought us closer together. We moved from distance to closeness, from outer to inner, from confusion to clarity. Isn't that romantic?"

"My love, you are a romantic philosopher. I love the way you describe situations and how you turn them into poetic philosophies. Why are you so smart? Huh? Am I smart enough for you, or do I disappoint you?" Erika wanted to know.

"You are so smart that you chose to be with me. How much smarter can you get? No, joking aside, you are very smart. Just look how you turned around two serious issues in your life. The first taught you who you truly are and transformed you into a loving and beautiful being, in and out, and the second was your relentless belief that you were already inwardly convinced that you *were* 'healed' before the healing was physically manifested and the miracle did happen. To me, that is very smart indeed for a child of the universe. To learn how to be confident and how to become spiritual in such a short period *is* a high level of awareness and intelligence. Am I not right?" Nikos expressed his opinion.

"What a brilliant diplomat! Are you sure you don't want to be a diplomat like my father?" Erika said teasingly.

"Sorry, that's not me."

"Now tell me, Professor, I don't mean to interrupt you, but are you excited about our forthcoming marriage?" Erika asked. Then she continued, "Oh, wait, before I forget, I have a small joke about a smart husband and his loving wife. A woman said, 'I haven't spoken to my husband in eighteen months.' Her friend asked, 'Why?' and the woman said, 'I don't want to interrupt him.' So tell me—and I will not interrupt you again—are you excited about our marriage?"

"Before I answer that, tell me, am I the kind that talks nonstop? I also have a joke. A son once asked his father, 'Dad, what is the difference between love and marriage?' The father said, 'Son, love is blind. Marriage is an eye-opener.' So wait till you're married. Your eyes will see *us* more clearly. Yes, to answer your question, I am very excited. For me to introduce you as 'my wife' is a dream come true. We shall forever be the inseparable couple," Nikos said romantically.

"Wow, you're on a roll today! It looks like marriage will definitely suit you and transform you into a new being," Erika commented. "What's also exciting is that we are both writers now, you and your dissertation, me and my life story."

"That's so true, but your story will be much more meaningful and will touch many people's lives. My book will be hidden in the university library stacks for no one to read," Nikos corrected her to emphasize the importance of her book.

SAMEER ZAHR

"You're wrong, my love. Your controversial dissertation will become a textbook that all—and I mean *all*—philosophy and seminary students will study. You'll see," Erika returned the compliment.

"How do you know?" Nikos asked.

"I know that I know that I know."

Nikos leaned over, held her closely in his arms, and kissed her passionately.

The sessions with Agnes continued, and the process of narrating the story helped Erika see more clearly how she'd been guided to evolve and transform into a spiritual being. She realized that everything had truly happened for a reason. She understood why the divine power had meant for her to meet Nikos and appreciate the difference between him and other men. She realized that she was meant to go through the difficult experiences in her life so she could learn about forgiveness and true love. Her intense journey, still at such a young age, was an early awakening to learn the true values of life and how to forgive herself for not knowing any better before.

*   *   *

After Agnes had written the first forty pages, Erika realized she appreciated her style and ability to express Erika's true thoughts in such a simple manner. Those pages covered her story until age nineteen, when she had had her first encounters and misunderstandings with Nikos. Agnes told Erika that the book would be no less than two hundred pages, hence the need for two more months of work. That news suited Erika well as the book would be ready and self-published around the time of her marriage.

Erika told Agnes that she would like the title of the book to be *Erika and Me*. Agnes responded favorably and suggested to change it to *Erika and the Real Me*. She explained that this would explain how the dual characters transformed and merged to become one. Erika liked the idea, and they agreed to look into it again soon.

Nikos wanted to expedite his work on his dissertation because of his impending marriage. He worked extra hours during the day and in many evenings. Two months before the wedding, he had about half of his work done. He had two other discussions with James as a sounding board, which helped.

The dissertation, which would be practically a book of about 180 pages, tested his knowledge in both philosophy and spirituality. He was more comfortable with the philosophy part, but he needed more reading and research on the spiritual side. He wanted to make sure he was not duplicating what others might have already written on the same subject. In his perfectionist style, he wanted to send out a unique practical message. He was not concerned about the other courses he took online to supplement his dissertation. He was certain he'd finish those on time.

After three months, Erika went for her checkup in the hospital. Both Nikos and Erika were at the hospital at 9:00 a.m. as scheduled, and they spent twenty minutes with Dr. Woodside, briefing him on how the last three months were spent, including their trip to Athens, and their plan to get married in about two months. They also told him about the book Erika was writing. He asked to be guaranteed a copy once it was published. The doctor was happy to see Erika looking much better and noticed the fifteen pounds of weight she had put on.

Then they went downstairs to take another MRI image of her liver, and everything looked clean and healthy. They were happy with the evaluation and went back home to return for a follow-up visit after only six months.

They walked back home through Central Park, enjoying the warm summer breeze and celebrating Erika's continued good health. Erika had been walking with Nikos regularly after her discharge from the hospital. Nikos remained faithful to his routine of jogging around the reservoir in the park. He asked Erika to have lunch with him at Cipriani since Agnes was excused from work that day. They went upstairs to change their clothes and went down again around noon for lunch and to celebrate Erika's good health.

*　　*　　*

Reservations were made to fly to Athens on August 20, about two weeks before the wedding. This allowed them ample time to get updated on the details of the event from the wedding planner whom Pavlo had hired. The interviews with Agnes were completed by then, and she said the manuscript would be ready upon Erika's return for her to review. James said he'd fly out two days before the wedding and stay for three days after. Erika's parents would also arrive three days in advance. Her uncle also agreed to fly from Stockholm with his wife and with Erika's grandmother two days earlier.

Pavlo chose a very fine beach spot for the wedding and reception at a private beach part of the Grand Resort Lagonissi, about twenty minutes' drive from the villa in Vouliagmeni. Nikos was about 70 percent done with his dissertation, and he would finish when he returned from Athens.

They had a very warm welcome by Irene when they arrived at the villa around noon on August 21. The house was not crowded, and they had a chance to relax for a couple of hours after a quick lunch with Irene, which was served upon their arrival. The entire family gathered in the evening, and the house started buzzing with discussions about the wedding details. Pavlo told them he would like to drive them to see the venue the next day.

Nikos and Erika were very grateful for his help. A meeting was arranged with the wedding planner to show all the details and decorations. Erika chose Helena as her maid of honor, and Nikos asked Pavlo to be the best man.

Nikos took Pavlo on the side before dinner and explained to him, "Erika would like to have the ceremony on the beach barefoot and wearing a sarong. And I will wear white shorts and a Hawaiian shirt. What will you and Helena wear?"

"No problem. It can be arranged, and we will dress similarly. Let Erika live her dream. We can always change after the short ceremony on the beach and before the reception to be held on the higher level. It will be outdoors if the weather is nice, otherwise in the ballroom. You will see it all tomorrow," Pavlo said.

"How about the official? Who will marry us? We prefer not to have a priest. Neither one of us is religious."

"Um . . . that is still an ongoing discussion with our parents. They recommend a priest in lay clothes as a compromise."

"That won't work. He will be using the scriptures and prayers and so on. It will take forever. That is why we wanted a licensed layperson to make it short and be done in ten or fifteen minutes," Nikos complained.

"Then, Nikos, you need to talk to our parents yourself. Anyhow, we have time to resolve this small issue." Pavlo did not want to dwell on this subject any further.

"You have to support me there, Pavlo. You see, this is why we wanted a small wedding in New York."

"OK, OK, we'll talk to them together later. Let us go eat now."

At the dinner table, Yanni told Erika that she looked very beautiful, just as when he had first met her. Erika was happy to hear that and said she was back at almost the same weight as before.

Yanni continued, "Irene and I are so happy you decided to marry now and to celebrate with us here, not in New York."

Nikos answered, "We're happy too, Dad and Mom. We need to decide together who will officiate the ceremony. We prefer not to have a religious person, only a licensed official."

Yanni looked at Irene and smiled before he said, "Please, you two. We are in Greece, and we have certain traditions we'd like to uphold. Please accept, for our sake."

Nikos looked at Erika and whispered something in her ear. Then he broke the silence and said, "Fine, provided he would not be dressed as a priest. He could be in black clothes with a cross around his neck only. He would not give a sermon, and he would be finished in maximum fifteen minutes."

"OK, I understand, and Pavlo will instruct him accordingly," Yanni said, seeing it as a fair compromise.

"Thank you, Dad and Mom. We really appreciate your understanding. Otherwise, we are absolutely delighted to celebrate this important occasion with you. Erika's parents will be here together with her grandmother, her uncle, and his wife. Perhaps they can stay at the Lagonissi resort as our guests and . . . oops, I almost forgot. My friend James—Dr. James, I should say—is coming too. They are the only foreigners invited on our part."

"They are welcome with great pleasure! Perhaps you need to find time to go with your brother to buy or rent a tuxedo, unless you brought one with you from New York," Yanni said.

"Well, neither one of us brought fancy wedding clothes with us. We will be dressed casually during the ceremony. I have a suit, and Erika has an evening gown to wear for the reception. I hope that's OK with you," Nikos explained.

"That sounds good. It's your choice, so feel free to wear what you like," Yanni said with a gracious smile.

The next day, Nikos and Erika went to see the venue. It was amazing. The resort was built on a small hill facing the sea, and the property stretched all the way down to the beach, with bungalows along the sides. The sandy beach would be the place where the ceremony would take place. Then the guests would walk up to a vast main area where the reception would continue. The rooms were well appointed and the food rumored to be top notch. The lovely couple accepted the whole arrangement very happily.

They later met with the wedding planner, and they selected the flower centerpieces for the tables, the decoration of the tables and chairs, and the cake. The following day, they went to a special shop with Pavlo and Helena to choose their beach outfits and ordered the floral crowns for the women. They laughed a lot while shopping together, which set the mood for how original this would be for the occasion.

Time flew fast, and the guests from New York and Stockholm arrived one day before the rehearsal dinner at the same venue.

The setting on the beach was already done, with a pergola for the priest, bride, and groom in front of rows of chairs for the guests on the sand as well. The weather was great, and the small gathering dined outdoors, enjoying the fresh breeze from the sea.

The Swedish guests and James were truly grateful for the invitation to attend, and they were thrilled to participate in this special event. Toasts and small speeches were made, and everyone had fun awaiting the main event the next day.

*   *   *

Nikos and Erika woke up and stayed in bed for ten minutes, holding hands and looking at each other with the happiest smiles anyone could imagine. It was the *big day* for them. They slowly sat up and meditated for another ten minutes, connecting with their higher selves in gratitude for what was coming ahead.

They went downstairs to have coffee and toast with the parents and Nicky. Pavlo and Helena were still at their new home nearby, which they moved into after their return from their honeymoon several months ago. Yanni and Irene were excited about the event. For them, the miracle was to see beautiful Erika, alive and in good health, getting married to their son, the man she loved so much.

The plan was for them to be at the venue around 1:00 p.m. to check into their suite and prepare for the ceremony at the beach at 4:00 p.m. The reception party and music would start around 6:00 p.m., followed by the dinner party at 8:00 p.m. The weather was great and sunny, so the event would be held outdoors.

The guests were gathered at the beach-designated area a few minutes before the ceremony began. The dark-suited priest, the bridegroom, and the best man were standing barefoot on the sand under the pergola. Hawaiian music was playing in the background, accentuating the Pacific Legend tropical shirts Nikos and Pavlo had on, along with their identical white shorts. They had flower leis around their necks. The guests were amused to watch this unusual scene in contrast to their suits and evening gowns.

The music stopped for ten seconds, and then a Hawaiian wedding march played. Everyone looked around and saw the bride walk in slowly, holding the arm of her father, who was in an all-white suit. Erika looked dazzling in a turquoise-and-blue orchid-patterned sarong and a matching top, barefoot as well.

Her eyes were focused on Nikos, with a huge smile gracing her beautiful face and the fresh jasmine crown on her head and the lei around her neck. Sven, the father, proudly passed on her hand to Nikos to receive. The music stopped, and the priest began, following the instructions given to him by Pavlo.

When it was time for their personal vows, Nikos smiled and said, "Erika, I loved you from the first moment I set my eyes on you. I vow that I will always love you. I dedicate my heart to you no matter what circumstances we go through. You have given me the greatest gift in my life. I open my eyes in the morning, and I see the beautiful face of an angel who radiates peace and joy, and that makes me love you even more. I am so fortunate to have you as my wife. I love you."

Erika was touched by his spontaneous words, and her response was equally spontaneous. "Nikos, you are the apple of my eye. You are the rock I rely on. You are my best friend ever. You stood by me when I was down, and you cheered me up when I needed it the most. You believed in me when others did not, and you lifted me up from my deepest valleys. You helped me become a better person, and you are truly my best friend. I will honor you, respect you, and make you laugh, and I'm so proud to be your wife. I love you more."

Pavlo handed them the rings, and they placed them on each other's fingers. The officiating priest pronounced them "husband and wife," and they kissed. Everyone clapped while standing to watch the newlyweds when they turned and walked back slowly, hand in hand. The whole ceremony took twelve minutes, and that pleased them.

At 6:00 p.m., the reception party started with drinks, canapés, and live music. Small tables were spread out in the reception area, adjacent to the big dining room.

*   *   *

The newlywed couple came out from their suite, smiling and greeting everyone they saw from the ninety-plus invited guests. Nikos looked handsome in a dark-blue suit over a white shirt and no tie. Erika looked dazzling dressed in a long off-white gown designed by Gucci. It was a crystal-embellished wrap-effect georgette gown with elegant long sleeves. She wore matching two-inch-heeled sandals in off pink made by Aquazzura. She truly resembled a very beautiful Greek goddess. The guests adored her look and her amazing beauty.

During dinner, the couple sat at the head table together with their immediate families. Speeches began, and Pavlo was the first to speak.

He said, "I only have one brother, Nikos, and thank god. I am so grateful for that. Imagine if there was another one like him. That would be too much love for me to handle at once. I used to be his big brother and advised him how to live. I was wrong. He turned out to be the younger brother whose wisdom and good heart turned him into my adviser, and I am so proud of him. I always asked him as a teenager, 'Why are you so shy, and why don't you have a girlfriend?' He always answered, 'I haven't met the right one yet.' Now I know why. He had his eye on Erika before he had even met her. He told me it was a true love at first sight."

They all clapped and cheered for him. The guests clinked their glasses loudly, asking to hear a word from the bride.

Erika controlled her shyness, stood up with a glass of champagne in her hand, and said, "I thank you all for sharing this happy occasion with Nikos and me. I thank my grandmother and my parents for their love and care but mostly for trusting me to choose what I wanted to do in my life without judging me. They figured if I made mistakes, I would eventually learn my lessons the hard way on my own. I thank my new parents, Yanni and Irene, for their incredible generosity and love and mostly for bringing my most wonderful husband, Nikos, into this world and you too, Pavlo, my new brother, and Nicky, my young sister.

"To my Nikos, my only true love and life partner, I don't know in what mess I would have been today if it were not for you. You guided me, you helped me, you stood by me in my darkest hours, and you comforted me during my unbearable pain. You were sent to me by a divine power, and I am eternally grateful for your love."

Nikos leaned over and kissed her. He held his glass and said, "Thank you all for coming, and we hope you are having a good time. I thank my parents for their love and support and for their dedication to make sure their children are always happy. I thank Pavlo and Nicky for understanding my absence from home the

SAMEER ZAHR

last five years to search for my own life and future. Pavlo, you did a great job organizing this great event for us, and we are very grateful indeed.

"To you, my love, there are no words that can describe what you mean to me. I was socially naive, and you made me smart. I was fearful, and you made me brave. I was doubtful, and you made me believe. I was bashful, and you made smile. I witnessed your perseverance and your strong will to change, I witnessed your inner strength to overcome the impossible, and I witnessed your relentless inner faith, which created miracles. I am honored you accepted me to be your husband, and I promise to always be there for you."

All the guests stood up and applauded them both for having expressed such a strong romantic love for each other. The cake was cut, and the DJ played the special song chosen by Nikos and Erika for their first dance: "All for Love," sung by three big stars, Bryan Adams, Sting, and Rod Stewart. Nikos sang softly with the line "I will be there when you need me" in Erika's ear. The dance floor was later filled up with people dancing and having fun. It was truly a celebration to remember.

CHAPTER 13

THE NEWLYWEDS FLEW back to New York three days after their wedding and were eager to continue with the work they had started. Nikos focused on finishing his dissertation, and Erika was anxious to read a PDF copy of the book for her review before it got published.

Agnes succeeded in presenting Erika's character as an individual who ironed out her controversial adversities in a subtle and realistic manner. She did not exaggerate Erika's dramatic scenes or dwell on her earlier flamboyant and unrealistic episodes. She presented her as someone who was believable and genuine. Erika, as such, would appeal to normal people who went through similar experiences. The book's theme exemplified the consistent focus on inner beauty, the only kind that grows and lasts forever. Outer appearances could be deceptive and misleading.

The book emphasized the power of mind over body with passages such as these: "Whatever thoughts and wishes one feeds the mind with are bound to be manifested in the body. It is a universal law. If you believe you are healed, then you are already healed. Just imagine it and visualize it relentlessly, and your wish is fulfilled. The timing is not in human hands, only in the hands of the universe. Just believe and surrender. A miracle defies science and anoints you to recover from a fatal ailment." The book went on to describe the dream Erika had as a spiritual surgery. Erika was determined to move beyond the physical form of reality and succeeded to be aligned by a coherent harmony of body soul and mind.

Agnes recommended the use of photos of Erika before, during, and after the treatments. She also asked for the images of her liver when they had tumors and when they were clean. She also suggested that a testimonial by the doctor who had treated her would be required to confirm the sequence of events. Erika was not so sure she needed to incorporate these charts and photos, but Agnes and Nikos persuaded her to agree as readers would find her story more convincing.

Nikos went to the hospital the next day and met with Dr. Woodward and asked him for the evidence required for Erika's book and his permission to write a review of her situation. The doctor said he'd be glad to help if Erika would sign a sheet of paper he handed over to Nikos. He told Nikos to come the next day with the signed document, and he would give him the required material in return. Nikos did that while Erika was lucky to find some photos showing her weight loss during the treatments.

Erika's message in the book was intended to simplify the process of healing both spiritually and physically. She explained how one could be completely healed without solely being dependent on medical treatment. "You only need to rely on your own personal belief from the bottom of your heart that your body is naturally healed with the power of your own mind and faith." The story of Erika's life was weaved to experience the rise and fall of her self-esteem and self-love, only to conclude that "inner peace is the key to good feelings, and good feelings are the key to getting healed."

Erika had a discussion with Agnes after the first reading and said, "Agnes, you did a great job, and I appreciate your description of my character as someone who focused on her faith and inner beauty. You explained well how outer beauty alone caused me emotional and social issues and how that eventually led to my physical illness. My only remark is about the limited reference to my romantic relationship with Nikos. You must have a good reason for that. Can you tell me why?"

"I understand what you're saying, and I agree that the focus was on your transformation into a spiritual being and your inner power to heal yourself. I did not dwell much on the romantic part of your life partly because of the harm it had caused you before you met Nikos," Agnes said defensively.

"But, Agnes, if it were not for Nikos, I wouldn't have become spiritual, which eventually led me to be healed from my physical illness. He's the one who guided me to follow the right path and to correct my mistakes. That's what I mean by 'romantic.' It is the power of his true love that also helped me heal. I am not only talking, um, about hugging and kissing or bed talk. The other relationships I had with men before Nikos were totally meaningless and the least romantic. Mentioning them in the book is totally irrelevant. Romance and true love can be very positive to the health of the individual and should not be looked upon from its physical aspect only," Erika explained convincingly.

"Um . . . I see your point. I will modify the editing of my work, though as you may agree, not everyone who has a fatal illness has a person in their life to support them like Nikos did," Agnes responded.

"Yes, but they most probably have family members who truly love them and support them. They don't have to have a love partner

SAMEER ZAHR

as I did. True love can be provided from many different sources. Do you agree?" Erika insisted.

"I hear you. I will emphasize the additional power of true love from other loved ones in helping patients heal and miracles happen. Having said that, I'm sure you still agree that the essential work is derived primarily from the patient's own beliefs and desires to heal," Agnes suggested.

"I appreciate your understanding, and I will ask Nikos to read it for his opinion too and in case he has other remarks. Is that OK?"

"Fine with me, Erika. Once I have the green light from you to go ahead, I will do a final edit and show it to you again. We may need about two months to allow the printers to finish their work before the book can be published."

"Great! Thank you for the work done already," Erika said.

Erika took a copy of the manuscript to ask Nikos for his comments. She would notify Agnes as soon as Nikos was finished reading it. Agnes said she would meanwhile modify the text to include the points discussed.

*   *   *

Nikos finished writing his dissertation three weeks after his return from Athens. He had it professionally printed as a book and made several copies to hand to the members of the verbal examination committee. He asked James to read it before his meeting with the panel. James read it and gave him a thumbs-up. The dissertation was somewhat controversial in the sense that it presented new original ideas. Nikos hoped the professors during the interview would be open-minded enough to accept his new ideas.

Nikos was self-confident when he appeared in front of the committee of professors to discuss his dissertation. The panel consisted of Professor Adams, the head of the department, and two others, Professor Johnson and Professor Winger. Professor Adams was a shrewd old-school person in his mid-sixties. He was known for his conniving and tactical questions, which made doctoral candidates nervous. One could fall in his trap unless one demonstrated real confidence in his or her persuasive arguments. The other two panelists were more direct in their questions, and Professor Johnson always tried to put students at ease with his smiles and open-mindedness.

They all had read the dissertation submitted by Nikos in advance of the session. Professor Adams sat in the middle of a long table across from Nikos, who was seated on a chair facing them.

Professor Adams spoke first and said, "You are a philosophy student. Why do you want to connect it to spiritual matters?"

"The very meaning of philosophy, as we all know, is 'love of wisdom,' which is a very spiritual expression in and of itself. Unfortunately, we have somehow restricted the meaning of philosophy to the realm of logic. It has become an academic form of teaching, which is fine, but I experienced its influence and value in my own life. That is the reason why I appreciate its implementation in my spiritual life and my social behavior. And that is the reason why I wanted my dissertation to reflect these new ideas," Nikos replied calmly and passionately.

"But aren't the spiritual practices derived from religious teachings? What has this to do with philosophy?" Professor Adams asked.

"Yes, religious influences cannot be denied. However, the varied religious teachings did not always succeed to enhance spiritual living. They succeeded to create rituals for people to follow blindly, without incorporating the role of spirit in such rituals. As you may agree, one can be spiritual without necessarily being religious. You also know that during the hedonistic era of Socrates, Plato, and Aristotle, their teachings were highly respected and considered to be the source of learning how humans could live and interact with one another. That by itself was a spiritual approach to human life. There were no religious teachers that could outclass them. I consider the ancient Greek great philosophers as great spiritual teachers also," Nikos answered confidently.

The three professors looked at one another silently with wondering eyes. Professor Winger seized the moment and broke the silence to ask Nikos, "Tell me, please, how would the ancient Greek philosophies apply to the modern times we live in now?"

"Perhaps you would agree that ancient Greek philosophy started a new way of thinking that provided the basis for the Western intellectual traditions that are still alive nowadays. In the spiritual realm, Socrates inquired into ethical matters and described how the best life for human beings should be like. Plato elaborated further and wrote dialogues about ethics and metaphysics that are still of interest today. His student Aristotle similarly followed in his footsteps and argued that moral virtues are part of the ultimate purpose of human life. I can go on and on with other ancient philosophers, as I explained in my dissertation, who contributed many practical ideas to what we refer to today as spirituality. So yes, the old Greek philosophies still apply to our modern way of life," Nikos explained in his convincing style.

Professor Johnson asked Nikos, "Are you then saying that philosophical theories can further clarify or enhance the level of spirituality?"

"Absolutely, sir. Philosophy explains more clearly the reasoning behind human spirituality," Nikos agreed.

The grueling questioning kept on going for a couple of hours. Nikos remained calm and confident and answered all questions with conviction. He supported his answers with references from material he had studied. He was then asked what he intended to do if he passed his exams and got his doctorate. Nikos simply answered that his wish was to teach philosophy, hopefully at NYU. Professor Adams thanked him for his time and told him they would reply with their decision in one week. Nikos went home after the marathon interview with the professors and told Erika that he was confident the committee would approve his work.

*   *   *

He then started reading the book that Erika and Agnes had worked on. A few days later, he told Erika that he thought that it was a masterpiece. Agnes had modified the text of the manuscript to reflect the power of true love, as discussed with Erika. She did it in such a manner that truly elevated the importance and power of love in the ultimate message of the book.

Agnes had a meeting with Erika and Nikos to discuss the printing and publishing task. She said, "I know a good literary agent whom you might like to query, but traditional publishers require a long time before they go to print. It can be a painful process of several rounds of editing, reviewing, and waiting.

Perhaps it would be best to find a good self-publishing house that normally finishes the work in much less time. What do you think?"

Nikos and Erika looked at each other, and Nikos commented, "We are new in this business. You know better, Agnes, and we would follow your suggestions. Don't you agree, Erika?"

"Yes, I do."

Hiring Agnes as an editor/writer proved to be the right decision. Not only did she do a magnificent job with the book, but also, she found the right method to go about the publishing. A quick review by the self-publishers convinced them that the book would be a big hit, and they agreed to copyedit it and finish the printing within seventy-five days.

As the book was to be self-published, Erika had all the rights reserved in her name as the author. The title of the book was *Erika and the Real Me.* The subtitle was *Healed by Faith and the Power of Love.* It was the subtitle that attracted the attention of the literary and marketing services. There were several other books written about healing miracles and such, but almost none dealt with the effect of unconditional human love from partners and family members. The story of Erika and her relentless belief that she had considered herself already healed was the underlying force that had generated her miracle.

A week later, Nikos was notified by Professor Adams that he had passed the examination report and that his book could be used as a textbook to be taught at the university if he gave the right to publish it. Nikos was beside himself, feeling extremely happy that he had finally gotten his doctoral degree with flying colors. The recommendation he had received from the panel encouraged him to apply for a teaching job at the university. He could not wait to share the good news with Erika and James. They both met him for lunch to celebrate the event.

Erika held her glass of champagne and said, "What else did you expect, my love? I called you 'my professor' the first day I met you. Remember when you explained to me the different types of love and the great ancient Greek philosophers? You were a genius then, and you are a greater genius now. Congratulations!"

Then James added, "You beat me by one year, and I am so proud of you. You'll be an associate professor at the age of twenty-five. That is incredible, my friend, and my heartfelt congrats too!"

Nikos was flattered and told them, "I thank you both. Your love and support certainly helped me achieve these results. It is a dream come true for me. The combination of both my love for philosophy and my spiritual experiences motivate me to be a good teacher. And you, my love, have been the biggest inspiration for the continued faith in my true self. James, your friendship has meant a lot to me and helped me delve deeper into the spiritual realm. Thank you both for being with me all along."

Erika responded, "Hey, wait a minute, don't thank me. I thank you! Do you think I would be here today, alive and well, without your true love and support? I don't think so. Give yourself some credit for your great achievements and your great unconditional love."

*　　*　　*

Nikos was grateful for the compliments he had received and asked James about his future plans.

James said, "I decided not to be ordained as a priest. I want to serve humankind with my scholarly capabilities and write many books that will enhance their religious beliefs by adopting spiritual approaches first. Another thing. You remember, Nikos, the girl I told you I once loved in my teenage years? Well, guess what? I contacted her after I came back from your wedding in Athens, and she's still available." James smiled bashfully and looked at them, noticing the change in their facial expressions.

Nikos jumped in and said, "What? Am I hearing church bells ringing now? This is good news, my man! Tell me more. I want to be your best man. That's my only condition."

"Easy, easy, tiger! I saw her twice last week and discovered that the flame of love we had ignited many years ago has not been fully extinguished. We are in the process of reigniting that flame, and we are both looking forward to a happy long-term relationship in the future. So!" James said joyfully.

Erika asked, "When are we going to meet her? I need a sister around here!"

"You'll meet her soon. I wanted to tell you first. She's a quiet and intellectual young lady with a master's degree in humanities. She's about twenty-five years old, a brunette with brown eyes. She has a slim figure and is about five feet and six inches, which is quite good for my height. Her main attraction is her endless smile and belief in enjoying the present moment. I am intrigued by her warm personality, and I hope you will agree with me when you meet her. Her name is Alice, and she teaches at the local high school in Midtown Manhattan." James spoke with delight.

"So, James, let's get together, the four of us, for dinner soon. Any special request where you would like to dine and when?" Nikos asked.

"Let me check with Alice, and I'll get back to you," James replied.

Nikos informed his family that he had passed his doctoral review board and invited them to attend the commencement that would take place in two weeks. Erika informed her parents and invited them to attend as well. They all congratulated him and referred to him as Dr. Nikos Bestidis.

James told Nikos that Saturday evening would be convenient for a get-together. They agreed to come over to the apartment and have a drink first and then go to a restaurant nearby.

James and Alice showed up at 6:30 p.m., and they were warmly received. Erika managed to make Alice feel at home. They had an enjoyable conversation while Nikos and James were chatting at the other end of the living room. Alice liked Erika from the moment she had met her. She told her she was eager to read her forthcoming book. She asked Erika to feel free to call her whenever she needed any help for anything. Alice knew the ins and outs of the city she grew up in pretty well. Erika was very grateful for her good gestures.

The dinner party went well, with renewed congratulations to Nikos as a doctor of philosophy, to James as a doctor of divinity, and to the new author/writer Erika. Good wishes were expressed to James and Alice, with the promise of more frequent visits in the future. Erika told Nikos after they got back home how much she had enjoyed meeting Alice and how much she looked forward to developing a close friendship with her.

*　　*　　*

The commencement event was to be held in three days, and Nikos expected his family to arrive two days in advance. Pavlo, Helena, and Nicky were coming, along with the parents. Sven and Mariya promised to attend the celebration too. Young Nicky chose to stay with Nikos and Erika, while the others decided to stay at the Pierre Hotel nearby. They all dined together at Cipriani the evening of their arrival. Yanni was so proud of his son and kept calling him Dr. Bestidis all night.

Nikos reminded them that the focus should be on Erika, whose book was supposed to be a much bigger success. He said it should attract huge attention from many future fans. Pavlo was eager to read a copy of the manuscript, and Erika told him she had one copy to give him to read. The published book wouldn't be in the market for another two months. Nikos seized this opportunity to thank his parents for letting him use the apartment and trusting him to make good use of his time in New York. Yanni answered that the apartment had been one of his best investments because of its availability to provide a good home to Nikos for the past six and a half years.

They all found Erika in great health and a happy mood. They reiterated how pleased they were to have her as their new daughter. Nicky was particularly thrilled to spend more time with her during the five days' visit. To Nicky, Erika was her role model, and she cherished the valuable moments they had together. Nicky had ample time to update Erika on her social and emotional life. She told her how proud she was of herself to be eighteen years old and still a virgin. She repeated to Erika that her inner beauty led her to be so strong and determined to resist luring attempts by boys in school. Erika encouraged her to stay the course and not to make the mistakes that she had done when she was Nicky's age.

They all agreed to have dinner together at the Oak Room of the Plaza Hotel the next day, and they invited Sven and Mariya to join them. Nikos invited James and Alice to dinner the following night after the graduation ceremony.

Pavlo shared with Nikos a secret—Helena was almost three months pregnant. He told his brother they planned to name the child after either one of the parents. Pavlo said they intended to inform the parents once they had the final confirmation from the doctor that all was OK in about one week. Pavlo showed true excitement about becoming a father soon. He hoped it would be a son; it would make his father happy to have an heir to the throne after Pavlo. Nikos smiled but understood the old tradition that discriminated the gender of the newly born.

The commencement ceremony started on time, and the graduates' names were called to go on stage to receive their certificates. When Nikos Bestidis's name was called, Dr. Adams added the term "with high honors" before he handed him his doctoral certificate. Many of his classmates applauded him, and the family and friends clapped, cheering for him loudly. Erika could not stop sobbing during the presentation, and she turned to Irene sitting next to her and told her how proud she was of Nikos.

Photos were taken of Nikos with the family while he was still dressed in his cap and gown. Nikos thanked and hugged everyone who had come to participate in this important event of his life. Yanni invited everyone to celebrate the event at Perrine, the new French restaurant at the Pierre Hotel. He reserved a table for eleven people, including James and Alice, along with Sven and Mariya.

They all had a fantastic time and gave congratulation speeches honoring Nikos and wishing him a successful career ahead.

Nikos seized this opportunity to say something new to everyone. He stood up and said, "I thank you all for honoring me with your presence. I thank you, Mom and Dad, for supporting me to get this high education and to provide me with a comfortable home to live in, and I thank you, Erika, for being in my life and giving me the space to focus on my studies. I thank you, James, for being a good sounding board that helped me center my spiritual thoughts in the right direction.

I would like to add that yesterday, um, the dean of the Arts and Science School at NYU called me. He offered me a position in the philosophy department as an associate professor to teach a new course the university will have for the first time in their history. The course is called Philosophical Spirituality, based on the material I wrote. I feel truly honored, and I am going to accept this offer."

They all clapped and cheered him with more words of congratulations. Erika turned and kissed him. Irene had tears coming down, and Yanni was full of pride for his son's success. The champagne was poured, and dinner was served to the full satisfaction of everyone. Nikos was very grateful for this occasion. He thanked his father again before they dispersed in different directions.

Yanni called Nikos the next morning and told him they would like to come over to have coffee with him and Erika. Pavlo and Helena came along as well.

They were all seated in the living room, and Yanni said, "I would like to tell you, your mother and I talked about what I am going to say to you, Nikos and Erika. Since you will be living in New York for a while longer now as a professor and no more a student, we decided to turn over the title of this apartment in your names. I will instruct the lawyer to do the work. It is our humble gift to you two, and we love you both very much."

Nikos and Erika looked at each other with joyous wonder and misty eyes. They jumped from their seats and kissed Yanni and Irene, expressing their gratitude.

Nikos asked his father, "How about Pavlo and Nicky, Dad? They should be on the deed as well. Please do that as this place belongs to the whole family."

"That's very sweet of you, and we know that your doors will always be open for us here. Pavlo, Helena, and Nicky still have plenty of other property to share that we've been blessed with. You will continue to have your share in the ships as well. We are all one big family now, and we are sharing our abundant love and blessings," Yanni explained with a big smile gracing his face.

"Again, thank you, Dad and Mom, for your generous gift, and we want you to always remember this is your home too," Nikos said while holding Erika's hand, feeling elated and grateful.

Then they all decided to walk in the park and do some shopping on Madison Avenue. Nicky asked Erika if she could help her choose some clothes. Everyone was happy in the company of the newly expanded family.

The following day, the family returned to Athens. Nikos and Erika promised to come and visit during the summer break before the start of the new school year. The newlyweds were so grateful for the abundant love they had received from the family's visit and the generous gift of the apartment.

EPILOGUE

NEW YORK CITY continued to be the home for Nikos and Erika for the ensuing years. Nikos rapidly climbed the ladder and became a full professor after three years. He was highly respected by both the students and the faculty. The students appreciated his thorough explanation of the courses that he taught and liked his good sense of humor too. Many of his students adopted his philosophy to enhance their spiritual lives as well.

*   *   *

Erika's book got published. It was marketed professionally, and it stayed on the New York Times Best Sellers list for eight consecutive weeks. Erika made sure Agnes Woodward was acknowledged on the book cover as the cowriter. About seven hundred thousand copies were sold during the first year, and the book was translated into several languages, including Swedish, German, Spanish, and French.

Erika agreed to share her story in a video documentary made by a Hollywood filmmaker. The book's success continued to grow and sold about two million copies in three years. Erika became an admired celebrity, and her beauty contributed to the attraction of many fans and admirers. She was also a keynote speaker in a few conferences organized by holistic groups.

Erika and Nikos shared a very happy and busy life together, and they gave birth to one child before the end of the third year of their marriage. Nikos insisted on calling him Eric to honor his mother, Erika. They visited the family in Greece twice a year, and the baby was the source of joy to many, especially his grandfather, Yanni. Mariya was with Erika during her pregnancy and the birth of the baby. Sven's term as an ambassador ended three months later, and Erika's parents had to move back to Stockholm. Nikos promised that they would visit them on their way back from Athens.

* * *

Pavlo and Helena had two children in the first three years of their marriage, a girl named Irene and a boy named Yanni. James and Alice got married six months after they had resumed their relationship, and Nikos was James's best man. His friendship with James continued to grow. Erika and Alice became best friends. James had written his first book two years after his graduation, and it was well received by the Catholic community all over the country.

* * *

The young bashful Nikos who had arrived in the Big Apple seven years ago became a highly respected professor, helping students understand the value of philosophy in living a better life based on true love. Erika, who was a confused teenager when she had come to New York University and who had later suffered from a near-fatal illness, got healed miraculously and became a famous celebrity whose life story and belief in the power of true love touched and transformed the lives of many.

ABOUT THE AUTHOR

SAMEER ZAHR is a retired businessman currently living in Florida. He is a dedicated author/writer now. His vast career gave him deeper knowledge of both the Greek and the Scandinavian cultures. His close personal relationships in both cultures inspired him to write this romantic novel as part of his seven-book series based on the theme of "love is all there is." This book is number six in addition to the other stories he has written and published.

Printed and bound by PG in the USA